Readers Love Am. Lane

Fish Out of Water

"This book is gritty and urban. It's suspenseful and I found myself gasping more than a few times…I'm looking forward to see where this series goes from here."

—Diverse Reader

The Mastermind

"*The Mastermind* is the kind of book that can be re-read multiple times to absorb every nuance between Felix and Danny…(a)bove all, it's the characters that make the novel worthy of your reading time."

—Love Bytes Reviews

Shades of Henry

"If you want emotions, character drama without it translating into a third-rate show and a romance that makes you feel tingly, go ahead with *Shades of Henry.*"

—Leer sin Limites

The Rising Tide

"If you're looking for a well-written urban fantasy with hot sex, this one will do it. Nicely."

—Sparkling Book Reviews

Weirdos

"The 80 pages is just as sweet as you think and pulls on your heart strings…It did mine."

—Paranormal Romance Guild

By Amy Lane

An Amy Lane Christmas
Behind the Curtain
Bewitched by Bella's Brother
Bolt-hole
Christmas Kitsch
Christmas with Danny Fit
Clear Water
Do-over
Food for Thought
Freckles
Gambling Men
Going Up
Hammer & Air
Homebird
If I Must
Immortal
It's Not Shakespeare
Late for Christmas
Left on St. Truth-be-Well
The Locker Room
Mourning Heaven
Phonebook
Puppy, Car, and Snow
Racing for the Sun
Hiding the Moon
Raising the Stakes
Regret Me Not
Shiny!
Shirt
Sidecar

Slow Pitch
String Boys
A Solid Core of Alpha
Swipe Left, Power Down, Look Up
Three Fates
Truth in the Dark
Turkey in the Snow
The Twelve Kittens of Christmas
Under the Rushes
Weirdos
Wishing on a Blue Star

BENEATH THE STAIN
Beneath the Stain
Paint It Black

BONFIRES
Bonfires
Crocus
Sunset

CANDY MAN
Candy Man
Bitter Taffy
Lollipop
Tart and Sweet

COVERT
Under Cover

Published by DREAMSPINNER PRESS
www.dreamspinnerpress.com

By Amy Lane (cont'd)

Published by DREAMSPINNER PRESS
www.dreamspinnerpress.com

By Amy Lane (cont'd)

Published by DSP Publications

ALL THAT HEAVEN
WILL ALLOW
All the Rules of Heaven

LONG CON ADVENTURES
The Mastermind
The Muscle
The Driver
The Suit
The Tech
The Face Man

GREEN'S HILL
The Green's Hill Novellas

LITTLE GODDESS
Vulnerable
Wounded, Vol. 1
Wounded, Vol. 2
Bound, Vol. 1
Bound, Vol. 2
Rampant, Vol. 1
Rampant, Vol. 2
Quickening, Vol. 1
Quickening, Vol. 2
Green's Hill Werewolves, Vol. 1
Green's Hill Werewolves, Vol. 2

LUCK MECHANICS
The Rising Tide
A Salt Bitter Sea

TALKER
Talker
Talker's Redemption
Talker's Graduation
The Talker Collection Anthology

WINTER BALL
Winter Ball
Summer Lessons
Fall Through Spring

Published by Harmony Ink Press

BITTER MOON SAGA
Triane's Son Rising
Triane's Son Learning
Triane's Son Fighting
Triane's Son Reigning

Published by DREAMSPINNER PRESS
www.dreamspinnerpress.com

ONLY FISH

Amy Lane

REAMSPINNER PRESS

Published by
DREAMSPINNER PRESS

8219 Woodville Hwy #1245
Woodville, FL 32362 USA
www.dreamspinnerpress.com

Only Fish
© 2024 Amy Lane

Cover Art
© 2024 L.C. Chase
http://www.lcchase.com
Cover content is for illustrative purposes only and any person depicted on the cover is a model.

Trade Paperback ISBN: 978-1-64108-772-8
Digital ISBN: 978-1-64108-771-1
Trade Paperback published July 2019
v. 1.0

Mate knows all the guys in the Fishiverse, and Mary reads every story, so this is for them. It's also to EVERYBODY who goes online and asks me questions about, "Hey, has Ernie ever met the inlaws?" or "Wow, there's a storm in the desert—I wonder how Sonny's doing?" or even, "Wow, I loved this character Jackson and Ellery met—I wonder how the gang in Victoriana would like him!" These novellas and shorts—this entire book—is a product of people who love this world wanting to know how their characters are doing. Thanks for asking, guys—they're doing fine. Keep reading and see!

Author's Note

Just for the record, vigilante justice is really only okay if you're Batman or a Fish in the desert. In real life I don't actually approve, but fiction is for fantasies, right?

Heart's Fortress

This story was originally published in Loving Hearts, an anthology about a love precisely like Burton and Ernie's—although the part about being a government assassin and a psychic was purely their own situation. The anthology went out of print, but people loved the story and wanted to see it somewhere else.

LEE BURTON was an assassin—a certified badass. He'd spent the last ten years of his life becoming a killing machine, learning how to orchestrate events using deadly weapons and target vulnerabilities to put bad guys in the ground. He was *fantastic* at it. Intelligent, invisible, tough, and ruthless when needed. He'd worked very hard to be a deadly weapon.

But that didn't help him with his panicky boyfriend, and he was starting to panic himself.

"Ernie," he said, keeping his voice patient. "Baby. You need to calm down."

"Crullers, I can't. I can't meet them. Why did you say yes? We're happy here. Please don't make me go see them. Lie. Tell them I'm sick. Tell them I'm dead. Please, please. I just can't. I can't see… I can't see…."

Ernie Caulfield had been a lot of things—baker, club boy, psychic, illegal military test subject, orphan—but he was usually *not* the panicky mess curled in a corner of his beloved kitchen in their spacious house out in the middle of the desert.

His curly black hair was hanging in his indigo eyes, and his pale skin was blotchy with tears and panic, and as Burton crouched in front of him, he felt his own flash of panic. He'd never—*never*—seen Ernie like this. Ernie was dreamy and unflappable. Ernie gazed up at the stars and saw the future, and it never bothered him, never fazed him, just sort of swept through him and left him to pass on the impressions he'd gotten from some sort of big psychic wind that had blown through his slender body.

Ernie didn't cry, not even when confronted with danger. He didn't panic, not even when fighting off bad guys or "guys with bugs in their brain," as he called the assassins who had come after him when Burton had. Ernie simply didn't *do* this.

Ever.

But one call—that's all it had taken. One call from Burton's parents, his brother, and his old fiancé, saying, "Hey, we're going to be out San Diego way, and we were wondering if we could meet for lunch. Does that work for you?" and Burton's dreamy, self-contained lover was a puddle of inconsolable angst and self-doubt in the corner of their vast white-tiled kitchen.

Burton swallowed and fought the urge to tell him it was fine, he could stay here, Burton would go meet his parents alone. That would work for the short term. Crisis avoided, right? But Burton needed to know why there was a crisis in the first place or Ernie would forever be a shadowy figure, not real to his parents, a figurative and not an absolute.

So much in Burton's life happened in the shadow world. His job in covert ops, the side work he did with his friend Ace that may not have been legal but definitely kept their little corner of the world safer. Hell, even his house with Ernie, all of it was off the books. Even *Ernie* was off book; he was supposed to have *died*, according to all the available records, in the same car accident that had claimed his parents. Originally his paperwork had been scrubbed to protect the government agency that had wanted to exploit Ernie's strong psychic gift, but once Ernie and Burton had hooked up, they realized that keeping Ernie in the wind completely made him less available for *anybody* to exploit.

So Burton did a job that didn't exist, lived in a house that had been built and supplied with water and power through shadowy government means, and was in love with a man whose official paperwork said he was dead.

It mattered, dammit, if Burton's parents knew Ernie existed. Burton may not have been able to tell his parents everything about his life—or even much at all—but they could at least know the person who meant the most to him, and know he was a good guy, a guy who wanted to take care of Burton the best way he could.

But that couldn't happen if Ernie was sobbing in the corner of the kitchen floor.

"Ernie, baby," Burton murmured, cupping Ernie's blotchy cheeks between his callused palms. The contrast between Burton's aged-whiskey brown skin and Ernie's barely-tanned cream color usually fascinated him, but now it just served to set them apart. "Ernie, c'mon. Tell me why this is such a big deal."

"I'm too everything," Ernie sobbed. "Too white, too weird, too male. It's all the wrong things, Crullers, and they'll hate me, and I already know I'm not what they wanted for you, and you should have all the good things, and you've got the crazy, witchy donut maker who has all the cats and—"

And Ernie couldn't breathe anymore, and Burton was forced to calm him down until he stopped sobbing in Burton's arms and fell asleep in a limp pile of long limbs and pajama pants on the cool white tile.

Well, it was September in Death Valley. Wasn't a *bad* idea.

Burton grabbed a cushion from the couch for under his head, and a cotton throw, because the AC had teeth in the morning, and went to take a shower and then to call his friend Ace, who might have some idea of what had just happened to his life.

ACE, IT seemed, was not at all surprised.

"You wanted him to meet your folks," he clarified, his uneducated country-boy voice obscuring one of the shrewdest brains Burton had ever encountered. Ace and his partner, Sonny, had taken their pay from their military deployment and turned it into a thriving business out in the middle of fucking nowhere. Every now and then, someone would pull into their garage, and either Ernie—who worked there when Burton was out on assignment—or Ace himself would notice something "off" about them. They could be criminals or they could be in danger *from* criminals, but either way, Ace, his employee Jai, Sonny, Ernie, and sometimes Burton himself would be on the case.

Nobody knew what happened to some of the bad men who crossed their desert, but the five of them didn't really feel bad about that.

Ace's certain… moral ambiguity and his sharp mind made him about the best friend Burton had ever had.

"Yes, Ace. Is that so hard?"

Ace's cleared throat over the phone was not reassuring. "It shouldn't be," Ace said like he was considering. "But, you know, there's folks and there's folks."

Burton scowled. "What's that supposed to mean?"

Ace let out a hard breath through his nose. "That means you wouldn't bring me home to your mama either, Lee. And you shouldn't. I'm a fucking criminal."

"Ace, the only thing separating you and me is—"

"Race, income, education, and military rank," Ace filled in ruthlessly. "I am enlisted white trash, and who wants that at their table?"

Ace's folks were working class. Burton *knew* that, but until this moment it had never really hit him that his friend might see himself as inferior in any particular way.

"But you're my brother," Burton muttered miserably.

"Yeah. You're mine too," Ace said, like he was trying to pat Burton on the back. "But sometimes people only see the differences, and it sucks when you're on the wrong side of those. There's nothing you can do about it, do you understand? I can't go out and buy an education at Rite Aid, and Sonny can't get a better childhood at the grocery store. Ernie can't go to the cleaners and not be psychic. You think Ernie's a basket case? You should've seen Sonny when I took him to meet *my* folks. He was gonna open the car door and throw himself on the pavement, and I couldn't've been goin' slower than eighty."

Burton's eyes opened wide. Ace didn't drive slower than eighty when he was backing out of the garage. Apparently seeing Ace's folks was scary enough to make Sonny Daye become a grease spot on the side of a rough road.

"How'd you get him past that?" Burton asked, glancing over his shoulder to where Ernie still slept. Ernie tended to keep vampire's hours anyway—a leftover from when he lived in a city and was trying to shelter his sensitive psychic ability from the many minds there—and Burton had gotten the call from his parents about an hour before Ernie would have gone to nap.

The emotional meltdown just sort of hurried everything along.

"Maybe you should have Ernie ask Sonny," Ace said diplomatically, which was sort of Ace code for "I have no idea what makes my psychotic boyfriend tick, but hey, you're welcome to find out."

Burton swallowed. Oh, he hated to ask Sonny to do that. Sonny Daye's rabbit-jumping brain and single-minded fixation on Ace were not healthy, but Burton had known from the moment he'd met the guy, years ago in another desert, that if it wasn't for Ace, Sonny would have been a much more dangerous creature.

"Would he?" Burton asked, casting another look at Ernie's limp form. He'd taken the blanket and pulled it over his head as if protecting himself from all the hard, dangerous things in the air that his poor sensitive brain was subjected to without consent. His favorite three cats had curled up, on, and around his body like furry sentinels.

"'Course. Sonny loves Ernie, you know that. They've bonded over small four-legged critters that crap half their body weight."

In Ernie's case it was every unattached cat for miles. In Sonny's case it was an eight-pound Chihuahua named Duke.

Burton gave a weak smile. "My folks are going to be in San Diego tomorrow, Ace. I've already cleared the time away with Jason, and Cotton's going to be here this weekend to take care of the cats. It would be great if Sonny could come by tonight, after Ernie wakes up from his nap. I'd be so grateful." Burton's CO had moved out to this half-finished housing tract in the desert too, and his boyfriend split his time between the desert and nursing school near San Diego. The other occupied house belonged to Ace's employee, Jai, and his boyfriend, George. The almost desolate neighborhood was a covert little corner of unregistered gay, and sometimes Burton wished Ace and Sonny would buy one of the three other houses that had power and water hookups. But Ace and Sonny owned the house attached to their gas station, and they'd bought that and made it thrive with nobody's help and a lot of illegal street racing. Burton didn't want to take that away from two men who had so blessedly little in their lives as it was.

That didn't stop him from inviting them over a lot for the air-conditioning and the pool and to let Sonny pet the cats.

"So," Burton said, "do you think maybe after you close down the garage, you and Sonny might want to come over for dinner?"

Ace made a sound, and then there was another sound, as though Ace was moving somewhere—perhaps somewhere Sonny couldn't hear.

"Well, about that...."

Uh-oh.

"See," Ace continued, "you know George is working the midnight shift and such, right?"

"Yeah, I do." George worked as a nurse in Victoriana's very small hospital, and while he was the most law-abiding citizen their little group knew, he was also very aware his boyfriend's people in the desert were very much... off the books.

"Well, he says there's a new meth supplier working out of the suburbs. Family who lives next door came in last night with respiratory distress, sweats, and such. The hospital called the po-po, but they say it's going to take sixty days to get those folks off the property."

"Oh Lord," Burton breathed. In sixty days a neighbor could go bankrupt or die of poisoning or, hey, blow up with the house. "Are the people still in the hospital?"

"Yes, they are. All of them," Ace said. "And the folks on the other side have gone to Arizona until Christmas, and the place backs up against an unfinished housing tract that's mostly desert."

Burton sucked in a breath. This was tricky, especially because collateral damage was not particularly acceptable here. It's what they were trying to avoid.

"I'll ask Ernie when he wakes up," Burton said. "And either way, you all come over for dinner. If Ernie says we can do this clean, you, me, and Jai can go party after dinner."

"Is 'you all' Jai and George?" Ace asked, making sure, perhaps, because Ace had stiff-necked pride like that.

"'Course. Cotton and Jason are coming in tomorrow, or they'd be welcome too."

Ace grunted. "You really think your boss wants a piece of this?"

Burton had to smile to himself. His CO was a brilliant, organized strategist, a first-rate commander, and a really good friend who wasn't above breaking a few rules for the greater good.

"I think Jason's *dying* to blow something up, but you're right. This can't wait, and if the houses on either side are vacant, this really *is* a good time to go in. You done any recon?"

Ace grunted negative. "But I worry. Sometimes these douchebags in the meth houses have kids and girls and shit. I feel like we're gonna need some surveillance and some listening and shit to make sure the place is clear."

Burton grunted affirmative on that. "All right. Like I said, I'll ask Ernie when he gets up." Ernie's psychic abilities had proved invaluable for these capers in the past. Asking Ernie about the situation was a prerequisite to Burton's every deployment. "Dinner at seven," Burton continued, "but, uhm, he's sort of napping on the kitchen tile right now, so if everyone can be quiet when they come in...?"

There was an unimpressed silence on the other end of the line. "You can bench press three hundred pounds, asshole. Pick that buck-twenty kid up and put him to bed."

Burton looked over his shoulder again at the three reproachful sets of feline eyes regarding him from Ernie's huddled form. Wow, he must have been rattled not to have thought of that.

"Sure, Ace. See you in a bit."

"Can do." And then he rang off.

ERNIE WOKE up to find Sonny Daye sitting on the side of his bed, staring at him.

Sonny had a scrawny jackrabbit build with a pointed chin and cheekbones, enormous gray eyes, and an expression of almost perpetual irritation. Ernie had figured out a long time ago that his expression was like one of those nonpoisonous snakes that had markings like the venomous ones. Sonny knew damned well he was smaller than the other guys, so if he scowled, maybe predators would leave him the hell alone.

It worked a good deal of the time—and any other time, Sonny had some sort of weapon in his hand and people weren't looking at his face.

"You awake?" Sonny asked, cuddling his tiny brown dog next to his chest. "Ace said not to wake you, but they're plotting something, and I thought I'd come see."

Ernie frowned. "I thought you were here to talk me into visiting Burton's family."

Sonny brightened. "Yeah, really? I thought that was an excuse, but if that's a real thing, they might not be planning to go out and be heroes and shit tonight."

Ernie grunted as his "gift" gave him a teeny tap in the noggin. "Both," he said. "It's both."

Sonny sighed. "Well, at least I'm good for somethin'. I know they don't like to talk about hero shit in front of me."

"You worry," Ernie said kindly.

"Yeah. Speaking of which...."

Ernie didn't need to push it; from what he understood, his gift just sort of happened. Waking, sleeping, stoned, sober—the only difference was that being stoned kind of lessened the intensity. He didn't miss doing party drugs or lots of weed. It was one of the reasons he loved the loneliness of the desert.

"There's kids in the house," Ernie said, as naturally as breathing. "They need to get the kids out. And they should leave before dinner's done, 'cause it's going up tonight. Boom. Everyone's dead, and the neighborhood goes with it. They leave in an hour and they can ventilate the house and get the kids out."

Sonny stood up quickly. "Oh shit. Okay—you finish waking up, and I'll go tell 'em they need to go. Kids. That's bad. I'll be back."

Ernie used the time to go wash his face and brush his teeth and—oh God, was he really in his underwear? Wait, what had he been wearing when he'd…?

He'd fallen asleep on the tile floor. He remembered now. And like the impending danger to Burton hadn't, the memory of his emotional meltdown swept through him, leaving him exhausted and sad.

Burton would live, mostly uninjured. (Somebody was getting singed, he knew. First- or second-degree burns, some burn cream at most. He'd tell them all, but he knew they wouldn't change their course for a bandage and some lidocaine.) But Burton wanted his family to meet Ernie, and Ernie….

He clutched his heart. Not a good idea.

Sonny came in as Ernie pulled on a clean shirt. He had a cold soda with him, and Ernie smiled gratefully. Just the thing to help him perk up a little and to replenish his system after going to sleep on a good cry.

He cracked the soda and sat down on the bed right when George slipped into the room.

Not much surprised Ernie, but George's presence did.

"Sorry," George said, his smile sweet and gentle. George was midsized and perfectly average, with sandy hair and blue eyes. He worked as a nurse, and how he and Jai—who stood a zillion feet tall and looked like death if death shaved his head and smiled with all his teeth—had hooked up was a mystery to everybody in their friend group. It didn't matter. George may not have been a killer, and he'd never held a gun, but he'd proved himself loyal and useful and brave on more than one occasion.

He also had the same loose association with the rules that the rest of them had, and that helped cement him in their affections forever and ever, amen.

"No worries," Ernie said, trying to get a grip on the emotions in the room. "Are they leaving?"

"Riding out in ten," George said, and he scowled. "I offered to come wait in the car in case anybody needed me, but Jai told me to stay here and he'd take the first aid kit instead. I mean, I get that this isn't my wheelhouse—"

Ernie shook his head definitively, not sure how he knew but knowing he knew. "Don't go," he said. "You're fine. They'll be fine. Why are you all in my room?"

George's eyes got really big at Ernie's words, so Sonny was the one who spoke, while Ernie polished off his soda.

"See, Ace wanted me to tell you about the first time we went to visit his folks."

Ernie almost gleeked soda all over himself, and he was so busy managing his own tongue that Sonny took his silence as permission to keep talking.

"Yeah, see, he sort of sprang it on me. We were going to a race, and I… well, I hate him racing. I know you all know that, which is why he only goes when we're short on money. But I saw him wreck, right? In that one race where he swerved to miss the little girl? Anyway, a ways after that he had to race again. I was all wound up and shit, and we get in the car to head out to a race, and he sort of springs it on me that we're making a stop on the way there." He shook his head. "I almost dropped out of the damned car is what I did."

Ernie stared at him. "This? This is supposed to help me?"

Sonny grimaced and made one of his rabbit-shifting moves as he sat on the foot of the bed. Duke the Chihuahua twitched in his arms and fell back asleep.

"Story gets better," Sonny defended. "I mean, I didn't think it would. Thought they'd hate me. 'Cause, you know, his older brother committed suicide 'cause he didn't get to be with *his* boyfriend, and I wasn't much better, but—" He paused a moment and took in Ernie's and George's enormous eyes. "You knew that, right?"

"Not so much," Ernie said as George shook his head no. "Ace seems very… self-contained."

"Well, yeah, but you're a *witch*," Sonny protested, his voice full of reproach. "If you didn't know *that*, how you gonna know they'll all be back okay tonight?"

"I don't know how I know or don't know, Sonny," Ernie retorted. "I just know when I know."

George's face assumed the perfectly neutral expression of somebody who'd heard total gibberish and was humoring the idiot who said it, but Sonny nodded sagely, as though this made complete sense to him.

"All right, I get that," he said, and George's eyes got wider, but Ernie felt vindicated. "So anyway, Ace's family sitch was complicated, but then, I was freaking out about racing. All Ace wanted was for me to not feel like I'd be all alone if he crashed the damned SHO and didn't walk away."

George opened his mouth to protest, Ernie thought, but then Sonny glanced over his shoulder at him and said, "This was way before we started being a secret little fortress out in the middle of the desert. I mean, we had Jai and Alba, but we still didn't know they were family, and we hadn't met Ernie yet and shit. We were all on our own, and Ace wanted us not to be that way, so, you know, he took me to meet his mom."

"How'd it go?" Ernie asked hesitantly.

"Not bad. I didn't say much. Ace talked to his sisters. Said some secret stuff to his mom, I guess, that made her not feel so bad about him bein' gay. Wasn't my favorite, but we've visited a few more times after that. Not the worst thing in the world. I mean—" He let out a humorless laugh. "—I got no family. My mom's boyfriend sold me for a brick of meth when I was a kid. The fuck did I know about sitting in a nice woman's kitchen? But it was good Ace brought me there, 'cause I got to see that sitting at his mom's kitchen table was the same as sitting at ours."

Ernie had to blink because his eyes were drying out. He'd *suspected* something awful in Sonny's past since he'd met the man, but this was the first time he'd ever talked about it, even obliquely. And it hit Ernie if this was the part Sonny felt comfortable telling, how bad was the stuff he didn't mention?

But Sonny wasn't done yet.

"See, I figure the thing is, they know we're not suddenly going to be their parents' baby boys. We could even be girls and we still wouldn't be good enough. But our guys want their people to see that they've got their own people now. They want a blessing so they know that however they make their way in the world with us, they know they've been seen."

And then Ernie *really* got it.

"Wow," George said, sounding dazed. "Sonny Daye, that's really wise."

Sonny scowled. "There ain't no cause to make fun," he muttered.

"No!" George and Ernie both said in conjunction.

"That's really smart," Ernie said, and George piggybacked on that with, "That was some good insight."

Sonny glared at them both like he was pretty sure they were jerking his chain, and Ernie was wondering how to convince him that he'd really managed to say something important about the whole affair, when Burton called them all out into the living room.

As they entered the living room, Ace, Jai, and Burton all stood, weight on their toes, every atom vibrating to go out into the world and wreak some powerful chaos even while they were all leaning against the kitchen counter, or in Jai's case, because he was so tall, the divider between the kitchen and the living room.

All casual, nothing to see here, just a bunch of guys ready to go stop some crime.

Ernie narrowed his eyes, but Sonny spoke first. "Y'all are foolin' nobody. Don't give me any bullshit 'bout running down to the corner store for ice cream, 'cause if you do that, I'm gonna want some fuckin' ice cream, and I'd rather just have ya back not hurt."

They all gave a relieved chuckle and straightened their spines.

Burton drew close to Ernie and kissed his temple. "See you soon, Club Boy."

"Be careful, Crullers," Ernie whispered. "I've only got the one you."

The others were saying similar things—although in Sonny's case it involved a lot more cussing out and a lot less tenderness, because irritation was Sonny's love language—and then the warriors were gone.

Ernie suppressed a sigh, knowing they'd all be nervous and spacey until the heroes got back and also knowing that in situations like this, sometimes the gift came along and tumbled him like a rogue wave.

Still, there were practicalities.

"Fried chicken for dinner?" he asked.

"I'll make salad," George guaranteed.

"I can peel a spud," Sonny offered, and soon they were all busy, cranking out dinner.

Ernie had just put the first batch of chicken in the fryer when a psychic wave hit him like a concussive blast.

Cruller!

He was staring sightlessly at the fryer lid, as though he'd never used the device before when it was his favorite kitchen appliance, when George said, "Did you hear that?"

Ernie frowned. "You heard it too?" he asked, dazed.

But not so dazed he didn't feel the glance George and Sonny exchanged behind his back.

When Sonny spoke, the absolute constraint he'd placed on his emotions made Ernie proud.

"Uhm, Ernie? Are… are they all okay?"

Ernie took a deep breath and closed his eyes and trusted in his gift, trusted in the bond he'd formed with the men—not only Burton, his own lover, but with Jai, his friend, and Ace, the big brother to everybody in their little group.

He felt a searing pain along his arm, superficial but agonizing, at the thought of Ace, and another, sharp and pointy, in the back of the thigh when he thought of Jai.

Crullers had scrapes on his hands and knees—road rash—that would probably need some cleaning, Ernie thought, but nothing that would require George's services, although Ace and Jai might need them.

"Some cuts and scrapes," he said, taking a breath in relief. "Jai's going to need some wound irrigation, but I don't think it'll even slow him down. Ace is going to need some burn cream."

He heard the slow, steady release of breath from the two of them, and after a moment of relieved quiet, the work in the kitchen resumed. Sonny gave a muttered, "Spuds don't peel themselves," and they were suddenly back in the groove, and Ernie remembered how to put the lid on the fryer again.

Ernie turned and sagged back against the sink, and George came over to him quietly.

"Ernie?" he said, keeping his voice below Sonny's irritated muttering.

"Yeah?"

"Does your gift… I mean, it's pretty powerful sometimes. And it's pretty specific. Did it tell you anything about, you know, meeting Burton's family?"

Ernie felt his eyes burn and resolved he would absolutely positively not become the mess he'd been earlier that day.

"Yeah," he whispered, and apparently his voice said it all.

"Oh, Ernie. I'm so sorry."

He shrugged. "Sonny said it best. Nobody's going to be good enough for their baby boy." Least of all a dreamy, spacey, *unsuitable* ex party boy, and he wasn't sure if the emphasis would be on the party or the boy, but he was pretty sure it was all bad.

George snorted. "My folks are just so glad I've got a steady boyfriend who doesn't seem to be hitting every liquor store in town, I think they'd probably shake Jai's hand and say, 'So, you worked for the Russian mob. Do they have stock options?'"

Ernie couldn't help it. He snickered so hard he snorked. "No," he managed between gulps of laughter.

"I'm serious!" George said, pitching his voice loud so Sonny could hear. "I partied so hard in college, my folks almost enrolled me in rehab my senior year."

Ernie smiled a little, knowing that George's problem had been a little bit of aimlessness and a little bit of wanting to make everybody he knew happy. Some people really *were* too sweet for their own good.

"What changed their minds?" he asked.

George sighed. "It's really what changed mine. I didn't do the hard stuff—not my thing—but I had some friends who did. One of them OD'd one night from sheer boredom, and the paramedics came and gave him Narcan and then took him to the hospital, and I heard the nurses talking. I know. First responders, hospital staff, they're only human, and they're so overworked. But they also cared. I guess we were lucky because the woman who helped my friend wasn't judgy, but she *was* exasperated. I'm not sure if it was in her job description to tell Ansel to 'grow the fuck up' but she did, and *he* did, and then I realized that… that here was a thing I could do with my education. I had to go back and retake a bunch of stuff, and my folks were out of money, so I had to get loans, but, you know. It's been worth it."

Ernie gave him a respectful nod. "You… you're like all of us," he said in wonder. "You're a second chance. A fix-the-world person. You're…."

"You're like Clark Kent," Sonny said, making Ernie smile. "'Cause you look super quiet and all, but Jesus, George, you're totally Superman."

The smile George gave Sonny was both moved and kind. George got it that coming from Sonny Daye, it was high praise indeed. And he valued that praise because he valued Sonny as a human being.

"I left my tights at the house," George said. "I'll have to get them on my way to work."

Burton, Ace, and Jai arrived about ten minutes after that. Dinner was on the table, and after some washing up, some doctoring up, and some swearing—because apparently Ace's burn really *did* hurt like a motherfucker and the puncture in the back of Jai's leg was a bitch to irrigate—they all sat down to eat.

They didn't say prayers or anything; none of them were that kind of religious. But as Ace, Jai, and Burton started to give what Ernie suspected was a highly edited account of how Ace and Jai had hustled three kids off mattresses on the floor and out the window of their bedroom before the house went up in a ball of fire, Ernie thought that the lot of them probably gave more sincere thanks to the powers that be than an entire congregation.

THAT NIGHT, as Burton and Ernie lay in bed, Burton ran an absent caress from Ernie's shoulder blades down to the rise of his lean bottom and back. Ernie probably still had another hour to go before he fell asleep, but Burton was beat. They tended to have sex whenever the mood struck them—which was often—so bedtime was bedtime for Burton, and Ernie would lie down with him for a little while before getting up to bake or walk under the desert sky or pet the cats. Burton appreciated that Ernie needed that quiet time to cushion his specialized gray matter from peopling, and Ernie appreciated that when Burton wasn't deployed, he enjoyed the regular hours of working, either from home or at the nearby secret military base, when his CO put him on the schedule.

But tonight Ernie's usual quiet was fretful, and while Burton was tired, he didn't want to leave Ernie like this when he was upset. His unusual brain tended to get overactive if it was left to fret. He'd once predicted three mass shootings and a government takeover in a small African country after their one and only argument, which was over whether Burton should tell his family about Ernie in the first place.

Ernie had said no.

Burton was still not sure if Ernie expected Burton to go visit his family over holidays and pretend he was dating a woman or was just super focused on his "career" in the military at the moment. Ernie may have been dead to the US government, but did he really expect Burton not to mention him in any personal context whatsoever? Hell, Burton should at least mention his "friend" Ernie. He mentioned his CO or his other colleagues on occasion.

And Ernie was *so* much more important than Burton's work friends, many of whom didn't know Ernie existed.

Burton was an assassin and a covert operator. If it was a choice between keeping Ernie a secret and not keeping Ernie at all, there was no choice. Ernie was his. Burton wasn't sure how he had maintained his humanity in the time before Ernie, but Ernie was so necessary to his being a real person now that living without him was unthinkable.

But his parents…. He would like the people who'd raised him, who still loved him, who sent him charming Christmas cards and prayed for him on Sundays—*those* people—to know just a little bit who he was. And Ernie was the best part of that.

He wanted them to meet so they could exist in the same world the way they lived in his heart.

"Please," he said into the darkness, surprising himself with his own voice.

"Okay," Ernie whispered back.

"C'mere, Club Boy. I need to hold you." He was not often that raw about needing Ernie in his arms, but tonight was different.

Ernie came pliantly, which was funny because Ernie often seemed pliant, but he had the surprising strength of tree roots and long serrated grasses. He could bend or twist when need dictated, but he always remained essentially himself.

Tonight, though, he seemed as needy as Burton felt, and Burton kissed him, long and hard, the kiss growing urgent and greedy as it went on. They kicked off his boxers and Ernie's briefs and kept kissing, the lovemaking so necessary that the work that went into penetration was a needless encumbrance. The grasped each other in hard fists, stroking, moaning into each other's mouths, their only goal the bright climax that would put an end to this frantic itch to slide seamlessly into the other's soul.

It happened, their spend hot and animal in each other's fists, and that should have been the end of it, but they were both shaking, cold in the aftermath, until Burton wrapped his arms around Ernie's shoulders and held him still, waiting until their shudders stopped, their bodies caught up with their hearts, finding solace in the sudden quiet.

Finally their breathing evened out, and Ernie spoke against his chest. "I see you," he said quietly. "I see all of you, Cruller. You're a son and a friend and a soldier and my lover—all the things. Don't worry, I see you."

Burton's next breath was shaky. "I see you too, Club Boy. You're brave and dreamy, a baker and a seer and my boy. All the things. Thank you for letting them see *us*. Thank you."

That's all they needed to say for a while, but when Burton normally would have felt sleep closing in, he was beset by an unusual urge to talk.

"Did you see everything in your vision, or do I need to tell you how Ace saved mine and Jai's lives tonight?"

Ernie gave a rusty chuckle. "I saw none of it. I'm dying to know."

Burton told him in unedited detail about how they'd approached the house to discover the police were there first, having a standoff on the front lawn. Armed with Ernie's urgency, they had crept around back, and Ace had been the one to break into the back-porch room to urge the three half-starved, ragged children out the window. Jai had boosted them over the fence and into the next-door neighbor's yard, telling them to go around to the far side and wait until the excitement was over.

"So the kids were running around the house next door," Burton said, "and Jai and I were going in on the side. We were going to take out the meth dealers because whatever the police were doing out front, it was going to end badly. Those dealers were *loading up*. I've never seen an arsenal like that, not even in the military when we were *deployed*. And we were all heading for our positions when Ace smelled something. He said it was like cotton candy and drain cleaner—swore it almost made him puke."

"What'd he do?" Ernie asked, and Burton gazed at him besottedly, loving that Ernie was okay with the details as long as Burton came home to him.

"Well, he knew we were heading to the east side of the house. He was supposed to be going around the west. Instead he got that smell and jumped *into* the house through the back window and tore-ass through it.

As he was going, he clocked one of the bad guys on the head, and I saw him through my side window. He didn't even miss a step, but Jai and I did because he was screaming, 'She's gonna fucking blow!' So Jai and I are hesitating, staring at each other, as Ace is diving for the kitchen window. Jai and I *just* get it open when a fireball rips through the place and Ace is, like, on the concussive edge. That's why his arm was singed—the one he threw behind him as he jumped got caught by the flame. He landed on Jai, who tumbled to the ground, and they were both scrambling up and running away when a smaller explosion hit and got Jai with debris. We all vaulted over the fence toward the little kids. The kids were staring at us from the far side of the house, but we didn't have time to chat. We'd parked around the block, right? Where the unfinished part of the housing tract backed up against the desert. So we had to scramble over the fence in the back—which was how we got there in the first place—and then come out on the side of the other house to get to the car."

They'd taken Burton's black SUV, which was a lot less visible than Ace's tricked-out SHO, faster than Jai's current POS, and could fit three grown men better than anything anybody else had been driving.

"Do you think the kids are okay?" Ernie asked.

Burton nodded. "I called Jason and had him drop a word to local po-po. They should be okay."

"Good." Ernie spent a moment running his fingertips up and down Burton's chest. "Burton?"

"Yeah?"

"You'll... you'll still keep me if they don't like me, won't you?"

Burton's breath caught, and suddenly that terrible, terrible panic of earlier that day made sense. "I'll keep you forever, Club Boy," he rasped before kissing Ernie on the temple. "This, you and me, we're not up for negotiation or exchange, you hear me?"

"Yeah. Love you too, Cruller."

Burton's pulse was still thundering in his ears. "C'mere," he said, and for the second time that night, Ernie did.

ERNIE AND Burton rarely went out in public, and Ernie had forgotten the subtle, shimmering pleasure of a nice well-lit restaurant with the sparkling ocean view in the beyond. He had vague memories of his parents taking him to places like this when he'd been young, before his gift had started to manifest itself, making him fragile and unpredictable.

Burton had made their meeting around two, when everything was quiet and before Ernie positively had to nap. Burton had asked if he could spin a story about Ernie doing contracting computer work to explain his odd hours, and Ernie said that would be fine as long as he didn't have to answer any questions about what he did, because he didn't have the slightest idea as to what that was. His abortive college experience, before his parents had passed, had been mostly humanities with a few glimmers of high math, because sometimes when he was caught in the throes of his visions, that sort of thing made perfect sense.

Burton said his parents couldn't program a remote control, and they'd probably just nod and smile and ask what they liked to do together.

Bake, swim, and take long walks under the stars. That answer was easy. Also brush and discuss the cats—Burton had been surprised to find he enjoyed their company as much as Ernie did, and frequently made stops on the way from the base to bring home special toys or beds or brushes or even a couple of self-cleaning cat boxes—to indulge Ernie in his passion for all the furry bodies in their house and garage.

Without exchanging a word, they both agreed not to mention that they also enjoyed having sex on every surface of the house, including the kitchen floor. That seemed rude. Or their little side ventures with their friends in Victoriana, because what parent wanted to know about that, right?

As they walked into the restaurant, Ernie feeling odd wearing a button-down shirt and jeans and thinking Burton looked very handsome in his, caught sight of the family at one of the oceanfront tables.

Mother, father, brother, and former daughter-in-law hopeful all swung their heads toward the entrance of the restaurant like one being, and Ernie let out a little squeak without meaning to.

He could feel their enmity from where he stood. No, these people were *not* okay with the white, the male, the new, or the strange. All of it hit him in the stomach, and he had to struggle to breathe.

Unbidden, Burton wrapped his hand around Ernie's, clasping their fingers together, and then brought Ernie's knuckles to his lips, where he placed a tender, meaningful kiss.

Ernie took a deep breath and gazed up into Burton's face, where he saw a kindness that very few people in the world knew existed.

It was like a fortress erected itself around Ernie's heart, his soul, his sensitive brain—he was surrounded on all sides by Lee Burton, his friend and lover, his knight in shining armor who would kill to protect him.

He was safe.

"Ready, Club Boy?" Burton asked softly.

"Ready, Cruller."

"We'll leave in time for your nap, I promise."

"Love you."

"Love you too."

And then they started toward the table.

Impossible Storms
An Ace and Sonny Story

I did not expect this story to go where it did.

A rare, once in a lifetime hurricane was hitting the San Diego and Death Valley area of Southern California, and one of my FB group members said, "Hey, Amy—I hope the Victoriana gang is okay—a giant thunderstorm in the desert could be a lot of fun!"

And I thought, "It would be interesting to see what happened..."

And then, as I was writing, I realized that for people like Sonny and Ernie, an impossible storm in the desert was no fun at all. And everybody else was lucky to survive.

"ERNIE?" BURTON'S voice sounded very windblown, and Ernie had a vision of him down south somewhere, doing something Ernie wasn't supposed to know about.

"Yeah, Crullers?" He looked around, trying to get oriented. He was... standing in his living room? His feet were numb and sore from... standing in his living room? How long had he been there? He didn't even remember answering the phone.

"You watching the news about the storm?"

"No." Ernie wasn't great with news or social media. Usually his brain was a pretty big receptor for the forces of the universe, and that freaked him out enough. "Why?" There was something big and oppressive on top of him. Over his head. A miles-high blanket of warm water vapor pushing him into the floor. He'd been out in that, right? His brain, free-sailing, whipped savage by the wind, by the rain. He'd fallen through a hole and into a fetid whirlwind that wasn't his, stinking of sex and blood and death and... oh God, the wind!

Why was he standing in his living room? When had Burton left?

"There is a helluva storm headed your way—a hurricane, with strong winds and flash floods. Are you *sure* you haven't heard anything about it?"

Ernie blinked, and suddenly he was *in it*, with Burton, his body being thrown around like a leaf, flotsam on the floodwaters, surrounded by driving rain that sounded like machine-gun fire, sense-shocking rattles of angry water, drilling its way through shingles, roofs, and walls.

He sucked in a breath, hearing Burton's frantic screams in his ear. "Ernie? *Ernie!*"

"Here, Lee," he croaked. God, it was all around him, it was filling his nose, his throat, his lungs—

"Club Boy, are you fucking *with me*?" Burton demanded, and Ernie took another breath, and another.

And realized he *could* take breaths. He was standing in his living room, shivering, because the AC was still on full and unseasonable clouds had blocked the August sun.

"Here," he gasped again. "Really here. Sorry. Good thing you called. It's gonna be a gully washer."

Across the line, he heard Burton take an easier breath. "That's what they say. I'm hoping our people are gonna be fine. It's making landfall here in an hour, and it's no joke. Could you, uhm—"

"Check on folks," Ernie said, even though as he said it, he already knew what he would find. "I need to call George," he said abruptly.

"Wait!" Burton's panic forestalled him. "Ernie, baby, could you be careful?"

"Yeah," Ernie said, thinking about his cats and how he had to make sure they were all in the house. Not the garage, the house. "I'll be careful. Gotta call." Suddenly he was right there in the moment, needing to move so his feet could wake up, painful pins and needles flooding from his knees down. "Be careful, Crullers. Stay away from the giant cow. He's bad."

There was a startled silence that told him whatever he'd just said wasn't exactly expected.

"Giant cow?" Burton muttered. "Okay, baby. I'll do that."

"I gotta call George," Ernie said again. "Ace is gonna need reinforcements."

"Ace?"

Oh no, Burton was panicking again, and Ernie didn't have time for this.

"The giant fucking cow will kill you if you're not careful!" Ernie screamed at him and then went tearing out of the living room to shoo the cats in from the garage while he called George and scared the shit out of him.

"I NEED TO what?" George said into his phone, distracted and busy. "No! Do not put in that central line until the doctor orders it! Dammit, this was a car crash, and we don't know his status yet!"

George kept Ernie on a special ringtone, because Ernie would only call him when it was important. George was in the middle of triaging a mess of people who'd thought they could run away from the rain in the middle of a desert highway that was about to see more rain in two days than it normally saw in a year, so it had damned well better be important.

"You need to sedate Sonny," Ernie said seriously. "Now. Like, run medication to him and inject him *now*."

George had to dodge out of the way of the EMTs following the gurney as they ministered to a child. "I'm sorry, Ernie, we have to—"

"I don't know if Ace can hold him," Ernie said, his voice breaking. "I can't get the cats to come in and Crullers is in Mexico and I don't know if Ace can hold Sonny and the sky's about to open and—"

George's brain went even deeper into triage mode.

"Cotton is home. Get him to help with the cats. I'll call Jai—he can get the sedative." George had no idea how to do that. Jai would be at the garage, helping Ace and Sonny batten down the hatches for the storm, right? But at least he'd have warning, and sending Ernie out into the rain wasn't going to help any of them.

"Cotton's home?" Ernie asked, sounding small. "I don't know what happened, George. It's like I lost six hours after Crullers left, staring into space, surrounded by fuzz, and suddenly a storm *exploded* in my brain!"

"Yeah, honey," George said, comforting Ernie in a way that was probably appropriate for his age but that Ernie seldom seemed to need. Maybe the storm—and all of the fear and pain and chaos—had threatened to burn out Ernie's receptors, and he'd simply gone blank. Six hours was a lot of time to lose, and Ernie sounded *really* panicked. "Cotton's at Jason's this weekend. Jason texted all of us to watch out for him while Jason went and did whatever."

"Call Cotton," Ernie said, and it sounded like he was gulping air… and begging for guidance.

"Do that. Call me back."

George was up to his eyeballs in people who needed him *right now*—but that included Ernie, apparently, so that was what he needed to do.

"George!" Amal called urgently. "We need you down the hall!"

"One minute!" George called back desperately. "I've got an emergency here!"

With that he started sprinting to the room Amal indicated while speed-dialing Jai.

"SEDATIVE?" JAI asked, nonplussed. He and Ace and Sonny had spent the morning securing everything in the auto bay as the weather whipped the wind around their heads and rattled the tools on their hangers. Sonny had been snarly and jumpy, the rain and wind obviously getting to him as the bare edge of the storm touched their skies. But a sedative?

Jai had never thought of such a thing.

"Ernie said he needs it," George burst out. "So I'm trusting you. I gotta go." The phone clicked off, leaving Jai to gape.

"Sedative?" Ace asked, running by Jai with his arms full of air-compressor hose that he was going to store in a box. "For who?"

"Sonny," Jai replied, and to his consternation, Ace didn't laugh and didn't ask why. Didn't argue.

"Fuck us all," he said grimly. "How do we get that?"

"I don't know," Jai replied, panicking a little from Ace's seriousness. "The kid at the station across the street?"

Ace stopped in his tracks. "The kid who sells the homemade pot gummies?" he asked, surprised.

"Da?" Jai hadn't tried them. In his mob days, if he'd wanted drugs, he'd bought *real* drugs, but he'd known that for the trap it was and hadn't done it often. Those days were long gone now, and he had no idea what kind of drugs were out there or where. He didn't want to give Sonny fentanyl, for God's sake. He didn't even know how that shit was dosed!

"Okay, then," Ace said. "Careful crossing the highway. We'll be in the house."

Jai glanced around, thinking the garage was bigger, sturdier, and more secure than the house. The storm would be fully upon them in an hour. The house?

At that moment a clap of thunder rolled over them, rattling the metal doors of the bay and shaking the windows as the rain began to pound.

Sonny let out a sound then, a child's cry, terrified and young, and everything clicked into place. The flurry around the garage, the need to move to the house, and the need for a sedative for Sonny.

Sonny and Ace had fought in battle. Jai had been in firefights before, and for that matter, so had Ace, but Jai had never been somewhere with artillery, ordnance, explosions.

Ace and Sonny had.

Ace was the type of man to walk away from that with bad memories and bad moments.

Sonny was the type who left a part of himself in those situations, and when something happened, something that could pull him back at a moment's notice, he was suddenly whisked away from the here and now into the nightmare world of loud noises and screams that were totally out of his control.

Sonny needed the sedatives so Ace could hold him in the here and now.

"I'll be back," Jai said, wondering how much cash he had.

"Me and Sonny'll be in the front room," Ace said. "Bring ice cream."

Jai didn't question that either. As the hurricane moved up to make landfall in San Diego and pound into the desert, he thought they might all need ice cream when this was over.

"ACE, WHAT was that?"

Sonny's voice shook, and Ace tried not to let his own shake in return.

Goddammit. God*dammit*, he should have been more prepared. *Now* George called with the suggestion of sedatives? The time to drug Sonny would have been *hours* ago. They could have had him sitting on the couch in his underwear, smiling like an idiot, for this entire fucking weather event. Ace and Jai might have been losing their minds hoping the windows didn't shatter and the cars and house didn't wash away, but Sonny, for the sake of the holy mother of fucks, would be *fine*.

But instead, Ace had been seduced by Sonny's cleverness and quick thinking as they'd run around and locked up the garage. He'd had so many good ideas: where he thought the washes might run, where to put the cars so they wouldn't float away. Ace had treated him like an equal, like a partner, because goddammit all, most of the time that's what Sonny *was*.

But with that last hit of thunder right over their heads, with the shaking of the ground beneath their feet, Sonny had let out that *sound*, and Ace had remembered Sonny had broken places, and it was Ace's job to shore those up when things got sketchy, same as he, Sonny, and Jai had been shoring up the thin places in the garage.

"That was thunder, Sonny," Ace said, grabbing his hand and hauling him out the side door. Jai followed, shutting the door before he sprinted toward the gas station/fast food restaurant on the other side of the highway. Visibility was shit—Ace spent a moment to pray Jai didn't get skewered by a car doing 110 while an entire ocean threatened to open up on their heads.

The wind was blowing hard enough to make running a gamble, but Ace kept working it, because next to him, the wind, the rain, and the thunder were all taking their toll on Sonny. He started tugging against Ace's hand halfway to the house, and by the time they reached the door, their clothing soaked and dragging against their skin, he was actively trying to get away.

"You gotta let me go, Ace," he shouted as they got to the door. "I gotta—I gotta get my gun!"

Oh fuck.

"We don't need a gun!" Ace shouted, hauling the front door open and dragging Sonny through. "Sonny, this ain't a battle. This is weather!"

"I gotta get my gun, Ace! It'll keep us safe. You gotta let me get my gun!"

Ace saw it so clearly: Sonny getting the gun from the safe under their bed, shooting at the noise, at the wind, at the sky… at Ace, at the dog, at the mirror….

At himself, to stop the explosions and the chaos that had been loosed inside his fragile, scrambled head.

"No!" Ace yelled, desperate to be heard over the thunder of the rain as it pounded on their slightly sloped roof. God, would their roof hold? Would part of it be ripped off? Ace and Burton had refurbished it last year, with those super-pricy insulated tiles. Had they done a good job? The house was so small, and Ace had worked to make it snug, to keep the cool air in and the hot air out, but none of that work had kept this moment in mind, when the house shook in the roar of a monster that generally lived three thousand miles away on another coast.

"Ace!" Sonny turned a face contorted by fear toward him, tears seeping from the corners of his eyes. "I gotta! I gotta get my gun! I gotta make the noise stop. Please, I fuckin' gotta."

"No," Ace said, hoping this moment would calm him down. "Sonny, no. No gun. No—"

He was not prepared for Sonny to throw his head forward against Ace's nose, screaming, "I fuckin' gotta!" before lunging for the door to their bedroom.

Ace tackled him before he got there.

Sonny was small, but he was wiry and strong from days of fighting with car engines and equipment that were exponentially bigger than he was. He fought like a dervish, like a wolverine or a shrew. Ace caught an elbow in the face, then one in the kidneys, felt Sonny's teeth in his hand, and still dug in and hung on, knowing he outweighed Sonny by maybe sixty pounds of his own muscle and was organized and rational to boot.

The wind gusted outside, and something roared, broken, but it wasn't the fuckin' roof, and it wasn't the fuckin' windows or the door. The dog whimpered in his crate, and Ace wanted so badly to hold him, to comfort him, to keep him safe in his arms, and do it sweetly. But Sonny was fighting him, and Ace had to win. He couldn't afford to lose, because the consequences were terrifying, and Ace couldn't go out that way, couldn't let Sonny go out that way, he *motherfuckit absolutely must hang on*!

Another loud roar and the rain *really* opened up. Sonny tilted his head back and *screamed*, contending with the wind, and then sobbed. The sharp smell of ammonia filled the air, overpowering the ozone from the lightning that kept flashing in the windows, and Sonny let out a little sob of mortification. Ace's heart broke a little more, but oh fuck him, he didn't let go.

"Sonny!" roared a voice above their heads. "Open your mouth!"

Ace hadn't even heard the door open or slam shut, but suddenly a giant hand appeared in front of his face, then in front of Sonny's. He heard a muffled, indignant refusal, and then the hand closed over Sonny's mouth, his nose, and Ace closed his eyes and hung on. Jai grabbed more of whatever he'd just shoved into Sonny's maw, and this time Sonny didn't buck so hard. There was a moment of silence while the tension in Sonny's body remained high, but he didn't throw any more punches or connecting hits.

A moment passed as the storm roared by.

And another.

And another.

Sonny shuddered out a breath. "Were those gummy bears?" he asked, sounding surprised.

"Da," Jai said, and Ace realized Jai had sat down on the floor and was currently leaning against the couch, as wet as he and Sonny were, shell-shocked and exhausted.

Something clattered. Something in the auto bay clanged. But Ace couldn't think about what had just been freed and set loose to blow out into the desert.

"Ace?" Sonny said, his voice tearful and sad.

"Yeah," Ace croaked. Sonny had caught him in the throat and the kidneys. His ribs felt bruised, his face was swelling, his hand was on fire, and he imagined he'd have to piss blood in a few minutes.

"You gotta stay there a bit. Sorry."

Ace nodded, his body still on high alert, the tension between his shoulder blades and his neck setting a screaming pain in his head. "Sure, Sonny," he mumbled, his own voice a little shaky. He nuzzled the back of Sonny's head, glad Sonny had let his hair grow out from the military stubble he'd kept it at for years. Sonny smelled like motor oil and the shampoo they both used. And fear sweat.

Mostly fear sweat.

"Those gummies taste awful," Sonny confessed, resting his head against the carpet. Ace took advantage of that and settled his unbruised cheekbone on the back of Sonny's head. "If I puke rainbows on the fuckin' carpet, I promise I'll clean up." He let out a little sob. "I don't know what to do about the piss."

Ace let a smile slip through—and a few more tears.

"We have spray for the dog," Jai said matter-of-factly.

"Thanks, Jai," Ace whispered.

"Da," Jai said, as inscrutable as always.

The storm raged on and on and on. Muscle by muscle, Ace felt Sonny's body relax, and the storm was still going strong when he heard the faint sounds of snoring.

Very carefully, one aching muscle at a time, he started to move.

"Jai?" he asked, not sure if the big man had fallen asleep.

"Da?" Jai returned quietly.

"If I get up, can you... can you stand in front of the bedroom door and watch him? I gotta pee."

"Da," Jai returned quietly, getting to his feet while Ace was still counting his limbs. "Would you like help?"

"No," Ace replied. Gazing out the window, he could see a giant piece of debris cartwheeling down Hwy 15. He froze, waiting for it to hit the house, but it stayed on the highway, which was now looking more like a river. The sound of the sail-sized piece of metal was like more thunder as it passed. Ace took a deep breath and got shakily to his feet. "Don't... don't take your eyes off him," he rasped, glancing down at the sleeping Sonny. "And don't underestimate him. If he... if he gets scared again, he could take us all out."

"Da," Jai said heavily. Then, "He split open your face. Get an ice pack."

Oh. Was that blood on Ace's cheek? His lip? He felt with his tongue and realized some of his teeth were loose. Fucking awesome. "Gotta go piss out half my kidney first," he said with a grim smile. "Back in a sec."

He'd been in enough fights as a kid to know it wasn't the end of the world when you pissed a little blood. He had some bruised ribs, he reckoned, and grabbed a couple of rolls of ACE bandages to wrap around his torso; he'd need Jai's help for that. He carefully washed his hand, grimacing at the flap of skin Sonny had torn loose. That's probably what made his stomach sick, he thought clinically. Before he dressed it, he washed his face, used a butterfly on his cheekbone and one under his eye, and hoped the lip and the nose would stop hurting soon. His head ached fiercely, and he felt a little wobbly. He knew what concussions felt like too. Ibuprofen, he thought, swallowing two gratefully. It would help.

The hand was swelling and likely to become infected. Great.

He stopped staring into the mirror—it was just depressing—and finished wrapping the hand with gauze. He brightened when he found his and Sonny's sleep pajamas and T-shirts hanging carelessly on the towel rack, where they'd left them before their morning shower. Clean enough, he reckoned, and stripped out of his sodden clothes, then left them over the curtain rod.

When he got out of the bathroom, he saw Jai had dutifully not moved.

"Sit," Jai ordered, nodding to the corner of the futon.

Ace was too exhausted to argue. He sat and watched with incurious eyes as Jai stripped Sonny's rain- and piss-sodden clothes off and dropped them in a pile. He grabbed a towel from the clean laundry and wrapped an unconscious Sonny in it before scooping him up and depositing him in Ace's arms. Ace took him with a grunt, his ribs and body aching in ways usually reserved for wrecking a car, but he wasn't going to let his boy go.

"Jesus," Ace mumbled, stretching Sonny's legs along the couch and cradling Sonny's head to his chest, wet hair and all. "What did we give him? He's gonna wake up, right?"

"Just CBD and THC," Jai murmured. "Usually two will make you sleep easy. I gave him five."

Ace let loose a broken laugh. He couldn't even reprimand Jai since it had been a close thing between Sonny calming down and Ace's body giving out.

"So if the storm doesn't scoop up the house like Dorothy's," he said, "we might make it through the night."

Jai nodded. "*I* will get you the ice pack," he said. "And some food."

Ace almost whimpered. "Something soft," he begged. "My jaw's swelling shut."

"Da."

The storm was still loud, so Ace couldn't be sure, but it sounded like Jai was broken too.

It wasn't until Jai deposited a bowl of blessedly overcooked macaroni into his hands that he remembered to be grateful they still had electricity.

"Jai," he murmured, "we bought ice. A lot of it. It's in the two chests under the table. If the electricity goes out—"

"I know where the generator is," Jai said. "I will pack the freezer with the ice unless they go out. Till then, should we watch a movie?"

"Yeah," Ace said. "Something…." He let out a breath. "Something gentle."

"That I can do."

They watched a show about angels and demons that featured a Bentley. Ace fell asleep in the middle of episode three, wondering when the angel and the demon would break down and kiss each other.

Blessedly, while the storm raged—and the power cut out, leaving them in the sweltering dark—that's what he dreamed about.

THE LIGHTS had come back on, even before they'd needed the generator, when George texted. Ace was still on the couch with Sonny, looking like the survivor of a car wreck, dozing on and off. Sonny whimpered in his sleep, every now and then lashing out with his fists, and Ace calmed him down—a word, a hand on his wrist, some murmured orders. Whatever Ace said, it was magic.

You guys survive? came the text.

Depends on your definition, Jai texted back wearily. His heart was sore. The carpet by the couch, where Ace had thrown himself on top of Sonny and just *endured*, had been sprayed with pet-stain remover and sopped up with towels, but there was nothing to do about Ace's blood, of which there was more than Jai wanted to contemplate. What had happened in this place he loved like his home had been violent and obscene, and neither Ace nor Sonny had deserved it. For so long he'd carried a torch for Sonny, and when he'd let go of that idea, he'd had an inkling of the strength a man must have to love somebody as broken as Sonny Daye—but only an inkling. It was like this storm, he realized. You could hear about hurricanes on the other side of the country for years, but until one crashed overhead in the heart of the desert, you did not know.

Now he knew, and he wanted to weep for the both of them, and for a breaking of his heart he couldn't even define.

The phone rang in his hand.

"Jai?" George said softly.

"How are you, little George?" Jai asked, suddenly needing to know.

"Still at the hospital," George said. "Amal and I decided to stay." He let out a breath. "I hope the cats are okay."

He had left both cats—his own ridiculously fluffy, impractical cat, Jingle, and Amal's sleek minipanther, Bond—in a Great-Dane–sized dog crate, with a small cat box, food, and water from a giant bottle upended into a small dish. The cats should be good for at least three days, Jai thought, but George wasn't just worried about their health.

"The storm will be loud and scary," Jai said, voice rumbling. As he spoke he cradled Sonny's dog, Duke, in his arms. Duke had been beyond barking when Jai had finally gotten to him. He'd crouched in his crate, eyes enormous, and shivered in reaction. Jai had expected to be bitten as he'd reached his big paws in to pull the little animal out, but Duke had gone to this familiar human willingly and had huddled against Jai's chest.

Jai was fine with that. He could grudgingly admit to himself that he needed the comfort.

"They needed the walls around them," he said, trying to give the same thing to George. "The noise and the wind—it is scary for an animal. They will be safer in the crate than they would be bouncing around the house."

"Yeah," George said, like he'd needed to hear that. "What's wrong?"

Jai breathed out. "When the storm has passed, and the roads are not so bad, George, perhaps you could come here and check on Ace?" He glanced over to where Ace dozed, his face contorted in pain. "I think he bruised some ribs, and maybe kidneys, and his nose is broken. He has a laceration on his hand"—that may be infected, he thought—"and might have a concussion."

"Oh. My. God." George's voice had gone from a sort of warm drone to sudden, complete attention. "*Jai*. What. Happened? Did the roof come off? Did something blow over you? Are you bruised? Is Sonny okay? What in the actual fuck?"

Jai laughed softly to himself and settled on the recliner near the couch. "We are fine. I suspect Ace will be fine as well, but I worry. Sonny...." George knew Sonny, he reminded himself. This might come as no surprise. "Sonny—he didn't deal well with the storm. It is like the crate. The cats will do *better* in the crate, but they do not like being *put* in the crate."

"Cats and crates?" George asked. "The.... Oh."

Jai let out a breath, relieved that he didn't have to explain it.

"Ace was the crate," George finished.

"Da."

"Oh Lord. Jai, are you sure Ace is all right?"

"Da." He was, in fact, not, but he didn't want George to risk himself and knew Ace wouldn't either.

"How's Sonny?"

Jai let out a broken chuckle and was surprised at the spatter of water that blew out from his lips. "Stoned," he said, remembering shoving the handful of pot gummies into Sonny's mouth.

"Christ," George murmured. "Okay. As soon as the ambulances clear that road, Amal and I will be out there—"

"Only you," Jai murmured. "Little George. Please."

George sighed. "Amal will be in the car," he said. "We came together, remember?"

"Da." More brine down his cheeks. The wind blew overhead again, and he heard another part of the auto bay crash to the ground. "When you can, Little George. Do not put yourself in danger."

"Oh, Jai. It sounds like you've been in enough danger today for the two of us."

Jai let out another tear-spattering breath. "Tell me about your day, George. Tell me about the cats. About Amal. I... just talk."

George did, and Jai breathed through the tears that wanted to consume him. Letting people in, he knew. It could hurt. He'd known this—he always had—and he'd known Sonny was fragile. But this terrible day, this fear, all of it pressed down on him, and he used his lover's voice to escape.

THE MINUTE Burton realized that Ernie had been standing in their living room staring into space for *six hours*—from Burton's hurried kiss as he ran out the door into the blustery day in the desert until now, when he'd arrived at his target—he'd called for the helicopter to go back.

"What?" Jason demanded. "What in the fuck? Lee, we just *got* here!"

"It's Ernie," Burton told him, his jaw tight. He dropped his voice for Jason's ears only, although they were on a private com. "Jason, I think... I think the storm shorted him out. He lost time. He... he didn't even know the storm was coming. Should we call Cotton—"

"I'll call Cotton," Jason said sharply. "Jesus."

Their coms clicked off, and Burton glanced around him fitfully. They were monster hunting again, and this time their monster was in a sleepy little town known for raising prize cattle. He was leaning against a small outbuilding in the middle of a Mexican cattle ranch, which was where the Black Hawk had *just dropped* him. Jason had been stationed where the valley narrowed. The plan was, Burton would spot the guy— he had an ATV that he used to drive to a cabin nearby from the resort where he stalked tourists for prey—and chase him toward the mouth of the valley where Jason waited with a high-powered rifle.

This guy really *was* a monster—a clichéd one who liked young women who liked to laugh—and when their intel tracked the guy straight from a kill and a disposal to his cabin, Jason and Burton had deployed ASAP.

Ernie had known before Burton, like he always did, and Burton had grabbed his go-bag, kissed Ernie soundly, and said, "I'll be back before you know it."

"Love you, Cruller," Ernie said as Burton shut the front door and headed out to where Jason was waiting to take them both to the helicopter site in the desert.

And Burton had strode out, confident in Ernie's capabilities. But as the storm had begun to lash the Nayarit coast, Burton had worried. He'd called Ernie, fully expecting Ernie's competence, his gift, to have informed him, because Ernie was *unfailingly* competent.

Unless, Burton remembered now, his gift was frying his brain.

Fuck.

The trees were still whipping around overhead, and while the lashing rain had passed, leaving the stone outbuilding pretty serene, all things considered, Burton felt like the end of the storm here was just the beginning of their troubles in Victoriana.

He needed to be home.

He'd never considered himself gifted in any way, but his stomach was churning, and he felt the pull in his gut. His Club Boy needed him, and no monsters or killer cows or whatever were going to get in his way.

The thought of killer cows made him look around, though. The small valley he was in was on a giant plot of cattle-grazing land—he'd seen plenty of the beasts as he'd been heloed in—but he realized he don't know where they'd gone over the last few hours of storm. Ernie's dreamy, panicked warning was *still* a warning, nonetheless, and Burton couldn't get to Ernie if the killer cows got him.

The earth rumbled under his feet, and he had a moment of confusion. Hurricane, right? Not earthquake? Not—oh God.

He peered around the corner of the outbuilding he was standing beside and saw them coming down from the same direction he'd expected their killer monster to come from, heads tossing in confusion, frantic lowing issuing from massive throats.

Every goddamned one of them had horns, including the panicked bull, who was—oh *Christ*—wearing a man on his horns like a hood ornament, and they were *heading right for Burton.*

Burton was, by training and ability, insanely agile. He climbed the nearest support beam to the top of the outbuilding and crouched at the far end, the end closest to the giant oak tree that probably provided shade during the summer months, when its leaves hadn't been ripped off by an impossible storm.

Burton scrambled into the tree's whipping branches, feeling the sting of every lashing twig. He found a sturdy branch close to the trunk, wrapped his arms and legs around it, and *held on* like his Club Boy's life depended on it.

And watched, horrified, as a raging tempest of frantic animals passed underneath him.

The forerunner of the stampede, the bull with the amazing horns, passed first, and Burton got a good look at the unfortunate hood ornament, lying Christ-like on his massive head.

Oh. Well. Burton's sympathy faded as he recognized the features of their monster, a once-handsome man with a square jaw and blue eyes and artful stubble. He looked like he should be surfing in Baja, which was probably why women had spent time with him, flirted, met their deaths.

Burton would bet the weather started the stampede, but he had no idea how their monster ended up as the hurricane's martyr. He'd have to chalk the killer's death up to an act of God... and continue to hold on for dear life.

The horde of panicked cattle rattled Burton's bones; the trembling earth of their passage nearly shook him out of the tree. When the stampede was down to a few lone gravid cows trotting disconsolately after their peers, Burton carefully climbed down the tree, trying not to groan as the ground continued to loop under his feet.

Fuck. The tree itself was wedged into a couple of granite boulders, and since he didn't have to worry about being seen anymore, Burton managed to climb on top of one so he could perch there and let the wind blow some of the quaking from his bones.

Only then did he manage to check his phone.

Jason had texted, *Cotton says they're inside with all the cats. The garage is flooded, but they shored it up. Says Ernie seems panicked and a little shocky, but they're both on the couch, under blankets, watching cartoons. Yes, he says we should come back, but no, it's not urgent.*

Oh thank God.

When's our target coming?

Burton let out a small laugh. *Target has been crucified on the horns of a bull. I shit you not. Get the fucking helicopter here to bring us home.*

It wasn't until he heard the sound of the Black Hawk in the distance that he thought to wonder about the others in their little family. He pulled out his phone and texted Ace but got no answer.

And that was when he began to worry.

JASON'S ANGEL had really come through.

Jason and Burton crashed through the front door of the house, mindful of the fifty-dozen cats. The storm had passed over nearly seven hours earlier, so the cat boxes weren't too full yet, but Jason could see the towels pressed under the connecting door to the garage from the kitchen and knew that it would happen soon. Ernie and Cotton had apparently herded all the garage cats into the house to keep them safe.

Three cats reached out to claw Jason's leg as he walked through the feline minefield to the couch, where Cotton watched them with wide, almost amused eyes, so Jason could take Cotton into his arms.

"We're fine," he said softly, but he was looking at Ernie with trouble in his expression.

Ernie, who had slept through their arrival, which was unnatural to say the least.

Burton said he'd stood in place for six hours, head in outer space, apparently lost in the roar of the incoming hurricane, everybody's favorite witch blown off course on his figurative broom.

Burton had pulled Ernie up into his arms and was shaking him gently. "Ernie," he said gruffly. "Ernie, baby. C'mon, I need you with us."

Ernie squinted at him like a man with a hangover. "My head hurts, Crullers," he whined. "I… it hurts so bad."

"I'll get you some painkillers," Burton soothed. "We'll get you to bed."

Jason grimaced. Their original plan had been to come pick Ernie up—they needed his help at Ace and Sonny's—but whatever had happened with Ernie and his gift in the hurricane, it had obviously put Ernie out of commission.

"I can't… I can't walk," Ernie confessed, almost tearfully. "It's like a concussion. Vertigo. Cotton had to do everything. I-I'm sorry. I…. Ace and Sonny need you."

"Shh shh shh."

Jason Constance had seen Lee Burton kill men without batting an eyelash. But you couldn't see that side of him now as he nuzzled Ernie's temple and soothed him back down to the couch.

"I'll get you some painkillers," Burton repeated softly. "Cotton here will get you some crackers for your stomach. The power will be back on in a few. The humidity is probably killing you."

"Ace—"

"Me and Jason will go take care of Ace," Burton said softly. "He'll be fine. You know Ace. Tough as nails."

"Sonny didn't take the storm well," Ernie said, and his voice trembled. "It was like I thought about him and I was in it. The storm, his brain, all of it, bounced around the sky and the earth and a dark cave with a rotting body and—"

"Shh…."

Cotton struggled from Jason's arms and went to the bathroom, then came back with ibuprofen *and* some Benadryl and a glass of water.

"Here," he said to Burton. "Both of them. He needs to sleep. It's what I gave him when I got here."

Burton complied and then rocked Ernie softly, disentangling himself reluctantly as Ernie fell abruptly asleep and began to snore.

Jason met Burton's eyes bleakly. "What was he saying about—"

Burton shook his head and closed his eyes. "Sonny…. Sonny's seen monsters," he said, and Jason thought immediately of their bull-gored serial killer. "I think Ace knows them, up close and personal. May even have, uhm, gotten rid of them. But it's like… like the monsters we hunt, right?"

"They leave damage," Jason said bleakly. As they'd flown the helicopter over the impassible highway, both Burton and Jason had spotted what looked like human remains that had washed from a mud-filled hole. Bodies had a way of surfacing like that, even when it was probably better for all involved that they stayed put.

"Yeah," Burton said softly. George had called him, which was scary enough because George was always so self-contained. He'd said Ace was hurt, the garage had taken damage, Hwy 15 was a river, and the desert had turned into a mud floe. George and Amal weren't even allowed out of the *hospital*, much less permitted to drive to the garage, which probably would have been declared a disaster area if anybody even knew where it was.

Jason's first instinct had been to check on Ernie and maybe take him to help them with the garage, but obviously that was out. Ernie couldn't even get off the couch. George hadn't given specifics, and Burton had thought to ask Cotton to come with them to see to Ace's injuries, but obviously Jason's angel was needed here for Ernie.

"We can pick George up on the way," Burton said after standing rustily to his feet. He grimaced and peered at Ernie. "Cotton? You'll…?"

"'Course," Cotton said. He gave his gentle smile. "Me and Ernie get along fine. And you know, I think some of these cats may need to come home with me."

Burton chuckled. "He'll never know," he said, squeezing his eyes shut.

"Go," Cotton said, touching Jason's hand. "He's been fretting about Ace and Sonny. They need you. He'll be able to rest if he knows you're there."

"Roger that."

Jason was tired—bone-tired. He couldn't sleep on the transpo any more than Burton could. But somehow his entire day had boiled down to two garage mechanics and their mob enforcer in the middle of the desert.

Still, he'd spent his life dedicated to keeping people safe from monsters. The least he could do was make sure his friend's friends were safe from their own.

"OH GOD."

Burton crouched in the open bay of the Black Hawk, hand gripping the handle by the bay door tight as the pilot searched for a place to land.

Pickings were slim.

The road could be spotted as a smooth ribbon of flowing red-gold mud—the storm had washed sand and soil over it until it was mostly invisible. The good news was, there weren't any cars on it, but the bad news was, estimating how far down the copter would sink was a tough gig.

Burton heard Constance yelling directions to the pilot, and then he was at Burton's elbow.

"We'll jump down when it's a few feet off the ground. George? Amal? Wait for us. We'll help you down."

"Gotcha." Burton had figured as much. He hoped the mud wasn't too deep or he and Jason might end up with broken ankles.

George nodded, gray eyes wide and receptive to any direction. He tapped Amal's shoulder to get his friend and fellow nurse to nod too. George seemed particularly adaptive; he'd grasped immediately that Burton was there to take him and Amal to go help. He'd started to fill a medical bag with supplies and his own extra clothes before Amal had even nodded, still looking stunned.

They were going to be covered in mud and tired by the time they got to the front door of the little house off the road, but they might still be better off than Ace and Sonny.

The auto bay was mostly there, but a big chunk of the roof had torn off. God knows where it was, but Burton would wager somewhere in the middle of the desert. Tools and equipment had washed against the wall on the interior, and the mechanics well, used for working on the underside of vehicles, was full and floating with equipment Ace and Sonny would be hard-pressed to replace.

They have insurance, he thought, and while it should have been a comfort, the extent of the damage was still shocking.

And then he saw the cars.

"Oh dear God," he murmured.

Ace's baby, the Ford SHO, was parked on the leeward side of the garage, under a sturdy carport and out of sight of the road. It was fine.

But Sonny's car, a battered POS Toyota, and Jai's vehicle, the same but a Chevrolet this time out, had been parked on the other side, the side with the biggest wash from the road.

The mudflow must have been mighty, Burton thought, still stunned. It had washed the two vehicles down the slight drop from the road out into the desert, and the wash of water and soil had flooded into a plain of dirt and hardpan, combining to make a mixture like oatmeal.

Oatmeal that was quickly drying like concrete, the top of one car barely showing over the windows, the tires of the other peeking some yards away.

"Oh crap," George muttered after the Black Hawk had taken off and it was just the four of them, slogging through ankle-to-knee-deep mire. "Jai really liked that car."

Burton got it. The small personal things that they dealt with every day would be the hardest. Burton mourned the little patch of algae that Ace kept trying to grow, hoping it would turn into a lawn.

Jai had heard the copter and stood waiting at the door, which surprised Burton until he swept his eyes over Amal and Jason unhappily.

"You and George only," he said to Burton. His eyes rested on George's face for a moment, and Burton saw a moment of profound relief, of comfort, of love, cross the giant man's unlikely features before he swallowed as though remembering a duty. "Please," he said, sounding genuinely distraught. "Only Burton and George."

Burton frowned at him, not sure why this would be a problem. "Jai," he said uncertainly, not wanting to come to blows about it. "Amal and Jason are friends—"

"They don't know them," Jai said, his voice shaking a little, and George stepped forward to take his hand.

"Hey, big guy," he said softly, standing on tiptoes to raise his face for a kiss. Jai bent down, his huge hand resting in the small of George's back for a moment. Their lips brushed together, and then George murmured into Jai's ear.

Jai murmured back, his wide shoulders shaking, and George lowered himself to the flats of his feet and said, "Jai, they've helped all of us here. Nobody is going to hurt our friends, okay? Amal and I brought IVs for two. It would really help if we could both go in there."

Jai shook his head, but he stepped back. "Da," he mumbled. "I understand."

Uneasy—particularly because of Jai's reaction—Burton stepped into the little house first, expecting to find comfort there because he had so often. Ace and Sonny had been their nucleus for so long, giving Burton a safe house when needed, a haven for Ernie before Burton could claim him. Movie nights for Jai and Alba, Christmases and Thanksgivings, soft moments in the lives of two hard men who had not lived easy. As tiny as their house was, it had meant something warm and kind to all of them, and Burton sensed an unwelcome intrusion in it now.

The first thing to hit him was the pungent smell of urine, and he stared at the rug in surprise. Big towels were sopping up an even bigger mess, and while there was an undertone of carpet cleaner, it was clear somebody grown had voided themselves on Ace and Sonny's beige carpet. Staring at the pile of towels, Burton saw blood there too.

The cleaner hadn't done any better with the blood than it had with the piss.

The electricity was on—the television flickered gently against the wall, and the refrigerator hummed—but they'd turned off all the lights, probably to conserve the fuel for the generator if it had to switch over. Ace sat on the couch, as he had most nights Burton had stayed over, with a towel-wrapped Sonny-burrito stretched across his lap, head against his chest.

The last time Burton had seen Ace this badly injured, he'd almost died in an illegal street race when he'd swerved to miss a child running across the track.

Ace must have heard them enter because he opened his eyes from a doze and tried to adjust himself on the couch. "Oh God," he muttered—it sounded like he was short on wind. "I must look dead for you to stare at me like that. Jesus, Burton, did you bring the whole fuckin' army?"

"Just George, Amal, and Jason," Burton told him, moving to crouch next to him. Gently, taking liberties, he reached over to Sonny's head to smooth the dirty blond hair from his brow. "What'd you give him?" he asked.

"Homemade pot gummies from the guy across the street," Ace told him without remorse. "Supposedly just CBD and THC, but we've needed to give him a lot."

Burton grunted. Sonny's face showed a faint rug burn on one cheekbone, and the unmistakable paleness and swollen eyes of a crying jag. With his eyes closed, his interminably busy body still, he looked young. Hell, he *was* young, Burton realized. Younger than Ernie, Sonny's real age was probably closer to twenty-two than twenty-five. He'd faked his birthday for his recruiter. Ace had figured that out, but then, Ace had told Burton Sonny had a real devil to run from when he'd run to the hell of war.

"I think we should have George check him out in the next room," Burton said softly. "He knows George—"

"He needs a sedative first," Ace said flatly. "He'll never forgive himself if he lashes out and hurts George. He'll never be able to look Jai in the face either. No, Lee, you all treat him here and make sure he's calm before you move him." Ace swallowed, and Burton could see he was in considerable pain. "And then I sure could use some lidocaine for my ribs and something for my kidneys. I swear to God, if I piss any more blood, a whole chunk of kidney's gonna come out my peter and I'll be fucked."

Burton shuddered, thinking about that sort of pain, but in addition, Ace's nose was swollen, and his lip and cheek were split, and his hand, as it rested across Sonny's chest, was covered in a blood-seeping bandage. The fingers were stiff, as though the wound was infected, and Burton thought that if they didn't have to copter Ace to a hospital and handcuff Sonny in a psych ward, that was the most miracle they'd get for this gawdawful day.

SONNY WOKE up a little as George was tending him in the bedroom, but Ace's advice about the sedative turned out to be well-founded, because he only glanced around blearily, sighing with relief when he realized George and Jai were in there with him.

"George," he murmured. "You okay? You were dealing with a car crash a while back. Sad. The kids made it, but the parents didn't. Sorry 'bout that."

George froze. That had, in fact, been the emergency that had been blowing up the ER of the tiny hospital he and Amal worked in when Ernie had called, but he hadn't mentioned it to a soul.

"It's kind of you," he said softly, taking Sonny's temperature and finding it a little elevated—probably with stress. "But, uhm, how did you know?"

Sonny shook his head. "I dunno. Ernie told me, I think. He was talking to me as the storm moved in. He had to go, though, and things got… got fuzzy after that." His lower lip trembled. "George, I-I think I hurt Ace. Did I hurt Ace? I remember him lying on top of me, and I was fighting so hard to get my gun. I don't remember why I did that, though."

George took a long, shaky breath and peered up at Jai, whose eyes were shiny in his stoic face. "Same reason people reach for guns all the time," George said, hating the things with all his heart. "Because you were scared. You were scared and trying to make things not so scary."

Sonny gave a little smile. "Not scared now. You, Jai, Burton—you'll keep Ace and me safe. But I hope Ernie's okay. He was sounding a little freaked out when he had to leave."

"Ernie's fine," George lied. "He's got a headache is all, from the storm. He's asleep in his house, covered by cats. Cotton's with him."

Sonny gave a sweet, indulgent little laugh. "The kid who looks like an angel," he said. "Yeah, he and Ernie should get along. An angel and a witch. Keep the place safe."

He closed his eyes then, and George double-checked his heart rate and respiration. When he was sure Sonny was all the way out, he spoke again, his voice shaking.

"Jai?"

"Da?"

"Do you know where their gun safe is?"

"Under the bed," Jai said. "The knives are under the pillows."

George's eyes widened. "Okay. I want you to lock the knives in the gun safe and move the gun safe somewhere Sonny doesn't know about. Can you do that?"

Jai nodded. "Da. I'm sorry. I should have thought about—"

George shook his head and met Jai's exhausted gaze. "You and Ace did the best you could," he said softly. "I'm thinking Ernie did too. Burton said he spent six hours staring into space. I'm wondering if he didn't spend six hours staring into *Sonny*, trying to keep him sane until Burton called and snapped him out of it."

Jai's exhaustion dropped away at once, and he gaped. "That… that is *amazing*," he said. "But also—" He shuddered. "—we should have known. Sonny was too calm. Too… too focused as we were preparing. The minute I said 'sedative,' Ace seemed to know what was coming, so he saw it too."

George shrugged. "I don't know what to think about it," he said softly. The wind and rain had lessened considerably, and the thunder had long moved on. "I'd say we'll know what to do during the next hurricane, but…." He raised an eyebrow.

"But this only happens every hundred years," Jai said. Some of the shockiness had fallen away, and George was glad. He'd been disheartened to see his lover so terribly, terribly affected.

"But this…." George stroked Sonny's hair back from his forehead. "This—it happens inside Sonny's head every day," he murmured. "Jai, we should find a way to treat it. To treat *him*—"

"Working on cars," Jai said. "Having Ace. The dog. Ernie to talk to. Friends who know him. Do you think this is not treatment?"

"But he needs to talk to somebody!" George protested.

Jai sighed, like he was trying to get George to understand. "Last week," he said, "he was working a bolt. The bolt would not come. He started to yell at it. Ace and I heard him. He said… he said terrible things to it. Things I do not want you to hear. He broke the bolt loose, and Ace took him aside. He said, 'Baby, did somebody ever *do* those things to you?'"

George stared at him in surprise. "Why would he say that?"

Jai shrugged. "Because he knows the man who did those things. He *killed* the man who did those things. But Sonny wasn't ready to talk about them until he couldn't loosen a bolt. Do you understand?"

George swallowed, and suddenly he understood why Jason and Amal hadn't been welcome in this house. There were secrets here, kept by necessity, because the world was not always kind, and law and order did not always cover all contingencies. Sonny Daye's very existence, from his name to his age, was all a lie. But the person he had been—the *child* he had been—had probably been dead for a very long time. Who else was he supposed to be if not Sonny Daye?

"Until an impossible storm dumps rain in the desert," George said bitterly, "and Ace and Sonny and *you—you*, do you understand? Come very close to death!"

Jai regarded him with gentleness then, and George was suddenly swamped with anger. Gentleness meant yet another thing George didn't consider that Jai lived with every day.

"Little George," he said gently, coming close enough to cup the back of George's head and stroke his cheekbone with a long thumb. "You know that Ace and Sonny and I—we are very, very aware how lucky we are to not be dead already. You knew this when you moved into that giant silly house with me and your friend far away in the guest bedroom. You knew that our existence here, on the edge of the desert, it's impossible. There are no gay Russians. They are killed or imprisoned, and everybody in Russia knows that. There are no gay servicemen or witches. No children are ever sold by their mothers for bricks of drugs.

No, the government does not have assassins hunting down serial killers they have made themselves. None of us exist. You and Amal, perhaps. Cotton—perhaps not. I know for a fact that is not the name he was born with. Our lives together, in this town, are as impossible as this storm. That we survive the one to continue the other, that is so much impossible, it is a miracle."

George was sobbing by the time Jai was through, with sadness and stress, with anger and fear, and in the end all he could do—all he ever could do in the face of Jai's simple practicality about the worst things life had to offer—was to launch himself into Jai's arms and cry.

AMAL WAS kind and competent and nonjudgmental, but he also was comfortable enough with Ace to not mince words.

"I need to stitch up the hand," he said, no bullshit. "And you need a fuckton of antibiotics, only some of which I have."

Ace grimaced. "Well, hopefully by the time I need more, the roads are clear."

Amal blew out a harsh breath. He'd bandaged Ace's ribs and palpated his kidneys and then, to Ace's complete mortification, checked over his shoulder to see how *much* blood he peed. His assessment in the end had been the same as Ace's, with the caveat that he shouldn't do much more than wander around the house for the next week on the off chance that he poke a hole in his lungs or burst his kidney or rattle his brain out of his skull or sneeze and blow out his eyeball because his cheekbone was probably fractured or any one of a thousand stupid things that could happen when your body had been through a meat tenderizer.

"*How* did this happen?" Amal asked.

Ace and Burton exchanged looks. "It doesn't matter," Ace evaded, and Burton had apparently had enough.

"Sonny had a severe PTSD episode, and Ace had to stop him from—from what?"

Ace grunted. "Going for the guns."

"Fucking Jesus." Oh yeah. Jason was there too.

"Ace," Burton said softly. "You can see why we're worried. You... you live with a time bomb—"

"And he ain't more primed to explode than he ever has been," Ace snapped. He sighed. "Look, guys—what're we gonna do? Answer me that. Send him to a shrink who'll have to have the law look into his history?"

"What is his history?" Jason asked.

"Jason!" Burton snapped, and his CO stared at him in surprise.

"I-I thought this was a sensitive subject," he said. "But I didn't realize it was classified."

Oh for Christ's sake. "His history is he was sold to a fucking sexual sadist when he was probably ten years old, and he escaped into the army, where one of your goddamned monsters almost killed him," Ace snapped. "So no. All of you. I'm what he's got. I'll take all the help you have to give me, but—"

"You know Ernie was probably floating in his goddamned head for that lost six hours," Burton said, surprising Ace badly. Amal had been wrapping the ACE bandage around his ribs, and he stopped.

"I did not," Ace murmured. "Burton, I'm sorry."

"It's not your fault," Burton muttered. "And it's not Sonny's, and it's not even Ernie's. But Ace, what I'm saying here is—"

"He's dangerous." Ace gave the best kickass smile he had. "But Lee, so are the rest of us." He sent Amal an apologetic glance. "Except you, Amal. You're fine. So's George. Not dangerous at all. We have zero worries."

Amal glared at him flatly. "Thanks," he said. "I'm reassured."

Ace rolled his eyes. "Does nursing school make you people sassy or something? Is Cotton going to get all snarky and shit? Just warn me. Then I'll know."

"So far, no," Jason told him, lips twisting into a smile. "But I'll keep my eye out." He sobered. "Ace—"

"This is it, gang," Ace said, glancing around his little home, which felt violated with violence and sadness. Duke was sleeping in his crate, the door open, and Ace felt his blood pressure fall just knowing the animal was there. "This is my home. That there in the other room is my boyfriend. The garage bay, which is apparently torn apart, is my livelihood. Most days we can hold it together. Most days *most* people can hold it together. Today we didn't. Do you think Sonny's not going to watch me change out the carpet and hate himself? He's going to see the damage he did and cry. He'll watch me move the gun safe and change the combo and know there are things he can't have access to because he's too broken. But our life together, that's not one of those things." He swallowed. "Lee, I love you like a brother. Don't make me tell you to fuck off."

Lee wiped his eyes with his palm. "I love you like a brother too, Ace. I'm not gonna make you do a goddamned thing, but I'm saying. If you make me have to scrape your brains off the wall because one day this all breaks through, it's gonna put a dent in my fuckin' soul."

"Probably wouldn't do much for my day either," Ace said, chuckling a little.

"That's not funny," Burton muttered, and then, to Ace's complete surprise, he broke. Ace made Amal move so his friend—his brother—could rest his face against Ace's shoulder and cry.

A DAY AT a time, a healing bit at a time, they managed to put shit back together. Guns and knives—except Ace's hunting knife that he didn't leave far from his body—all went in the safe, which Ace hid in a place Jai and Ernie knew about. Sonny didn't watch him hide it, but then, Sonny had a hard time meeting Ace's eyes during much of that time.

The roads got cleared—and then fixed, because much of them had washed away—then used again. The shop got cleaned out and then fixed, and Burton had been right when he'd said insurance would pay for most of it, although Ace found himself dipping into the cash savings he'd put away from his last few street races. He didn't say anything to Sonny about racing again, but he and Burton met eyes a few times while he was dealing with that shit and Burton was there helping to put it back together while Ace couldn't. Burton knew.

The cars were left in the desert, because nothing was growing out there anyway, and replaced as well.

After a couple of weeks, Ace could finally lift more than ten pounds, the garage was almost ready to open again, and everybody was spending a rest day in their own homes, making love or petting cats or whatever. Ace had spoken privately to Ernie, thanking him for all he'd done—no matter how he'd done it—and promising that he'd had Amal leave a bottle of something that could knock Sonny on his ass within minutes, and the next time something like that happened, they had a better weapon than homemade pot gummies. He'd asked, carefully of

course, if Ernie was angry or bitter about those six hours he'd spent
battered by the storm, by Sonny's brain, by the elements at large, and all
the things they expected of him when he was, in fact, more sensitive than
any of them to the terrible vagaries of nature and fate.

"Ace, you all let me be useful here," he'd said after a minute. He
met Ace's eyes then. "You need to know—every day, *every minute* of
every day, Sonny makes an effort to be sane for you. Just don't think…
don't think because this one time the devils won, Sonny doesn't love you
enough to fight for his better angel."

Ace smiled at his friend then. Had, in spite of healing ribs and
kidneys and everything, embraced him with all he had. "Thank you," he
said, eyes burning. "So many people are wondering why I'm not scared
of him. Wondering why I'm not running away. I know he fights for us.
Every day. I-I cannot be grateful enough that he has your help."

Ernie's own eyes had grown red-rimmed, and he'd returned the
hug gently. "He always will," Ernie said. "Lee needs you too. Not every
man finds his brother, you know."

"I know it," Ace rasped, and someone had come into the room
then, and they'd dropped it.

But Ace knew his boy, knew his boy's demons, and on this one
day when nobody was there but them, they sat on the couch and ate ice
cream—probably the same ice cream Jai had brought that terrible day,
because it had eventually made it to the freezer—and watched a silly
children's movie.

Sonny's voice in the middle of the movie made Ace hit Pause.

"I'm broken," he said.

"Yeah," Ace agreed, because to not agree would be an insult and
a lie.

"Why do you want me when I'm broken?"

Ace turned toward him then and stroked his cheekbones with his
fingertips. "Because I love you," he whispered. "I think the guy you
could have been unbroken—he would have been too bright and shiny
to be human. 'Cause you are such a good, amazing person with all the
brokenness, you're the best human I could ever hope to love."

Sonny's eyes grew glossy, and for the first time in weeks, he
touched Ace's face back, his fingers tracing the healing scars, including
the broken skin of Ace's nose. "I hurt you," he said, voice cracking, and
Ace took his fingertips and kissed them.

"It was an impossible storm, baby," Ace said. "There were so many ways we could have died that day, and we didn't. You came back to me."

They'd let him wake up fully after the rain had moved on. They'd hidden the gun safe and the knives, and he hadn't had nearly the injuries Ace had. Sonny had been there again, his partner, his friend, his lover, the man by his side. He'd come back in every way but this—the reckoning.

"I love you, Ace," Sonny said. "I… I love our life. Our dream. Our friends. How do I not lose all that?"

Ace swallowed and sighed. "Look, Amal's got… he's got a friend. A friend who spent too long on deployment and not all of him came back okay. Would you want to talk to his friend? Just take his number? You fight against your demons most days, Sonny. On the days you think you might lose, could you call him? I'll… I'll understand if you say no. We are, all of us out here in the desert, broken. But maybe talking to someone else with your brokenness, he can help you fight."

Sonny swallowed, nodded, and rested his head on Ace's shoulder. "You still want me, Ace?"

"God yeah, Sonny Daye."

"I'll talk to anyone you want me to if you still want me."

"Good."

Ace wrapped his arm around Sonny's shoulders and drew his head to Ace's chest. He didn't have any good words, so he hit Play again, and Sonny held him, close and tight, like he should, while their dog curled up in Sonny's lap and breathed softly.

Impossible storms. His world was made of dreams that shouldn't happen, men who shouldn't be, hope that shouldn't survive. But Sonny Daye loved him, loved him enough to fight for his own sanity, and that was the most impossible miracle of all.

Epilogue

IT TOOK Ernie a month to be able to wake up and sleep again in his normal, lopsided, loopy schedule. Burton had helped Ace put his garage back together for part of that and occasionally got called into work. Cotton was a godsend because the roads were still bad and Cotton simply stayed, petting cats, doing homework, playing video games, and making sure Ernie actually made it back to a bed if he got up.

One day when Burton was elbows deep in a mostly complete socket wrench set that needed to be reassembled on the neat pegboards on the auto bay walls, his phone rang, and Cotton spoke quietly on the other end.

"Burton? You got a minute?"

Burton grunted, "Let me see," and looked over to where Sonny was doing the same reassembling thing with small containers of different sized bolts and gaskets.

"What?" Sonny asked irritably. "Am I growing fangs? Threatening to turn into a goddamned lunatic again? What's wrong?"

"Nothing," Burton muttered, trying not to be unsettled. For a little while he'd almost forgotten that Sonny was the equivalent of the bunny in the Monty Python movie. He *looked* cute and helpless, but he was literal dynamite. "Just need to take a call from Cotton."

Sonny scowled. "I'm fine. I have no homicidal plans at the moment. Jai?"

"Da?" Jai said from where he stood in the mechanic's well, taking a scrupulous inventory of what was missing *there*.

"Tell Burton I'm not gonna go murder anyone while he takes a phone call."

"Sonny will murder nobody," Jai said, and then, incongruously enough, gave Burton a wink. "Myself, on the other hand, there are no guarantees."

Burton gave them both a flat glare. "You two are hilarious. I'm gonna go get some more water and have this conversation in front of

Ace, who isn't such a comedian." He huffed and then added into the amused quiet on the other side of the phone, "Go ahead, Cotton." He went through the door and into the August heat of the desert that awaited when the partial shade of the auto bay was gone. "I'm listening."

"I.... Burton, he keeps calling out to you in his sleep."

Burton stopped still in the middle of the brightest ray of sun in the world. "I, uhm, should I come home?"

"No," Cotton told him gently. "He doesn't want you to, and it's not really urgent. He... he's worried about a killer cow?"

Burton blinked and remembered to keep moving. "Killer cow," he said. He got to the house and opened the door, making sure Duke didn't escape. The little dog had been as rattled as his owners in the past week, and Burton didn't blame him. Usually Duke was happy to stay in the house unless his leash was on, but they'd needed to stop him from fleeing out the door a couple of times that week, and it had become a family project.

"Does that mean anything to you?" Cotton asked.

Burton let out a short laugh as that moment—which normally would have been the most notable thing about his month—came thundering back. "Yeah, kid. The next time he wakes up, tell him he saved my life. Warned me about a stampede. And, uhm, a bull that killed the guy we were after, so, you know, killer cow, but also a really useful colleague."

Cotton's chuckle was truly amused, and Burton smiled tiredly.

"I'll tell him that," he said. "I'm sure there's more, but if I tell it that way, he'll laugh and probably sleep better. Thanks."

Burton sighed and opened the refrigerator, mostly to stick his head in the freezer and get a blast of cold air.

"Hot out there?" Ace asked from the couch, his tone of voice indicating he was very aware of what a stupid question that was. Poor Ace—he'd been one of those kids who hadn't done well in school, not because he was stupid, but because his sturdy body and practical mind hadn't *wanted* to sit still, dammit! Recovery was hard on him, especially when he knew all his people were outside working.

"Yeah," Burton said, grabbing the pitcher of chilled water and dumping thirty-two ounces into a plastic cup. He refilled the pitcher, put it back in the fridge, and then wandered into the living room and sat on the recliner, willing to spend a minute or two keeping Ace company.

"So," Ace asked, obviously dying of curiosity. "A killer cow who's a useful colleague? You know, I'd never get this clue in a crossword."

Burton laughed softly and took the opening. Truth was, all of the fuss about Sonny had sort of put this story on the back burner, and he realized he was *dying* to tell Ace. In fact, he wanted Jai and Jason there too, because Jason hadn't gotten the full story, and he knew these men wouldn't get squeamish about the dead body and would find the idea of a "killer cow" to be *hysterical*.

Ace laughed until he coughed and grabbed his healing ribs. "Oh God," he rasped when he'd calmed down. "Oh my heavens, what a way to fuckin' *go!*"

"Right?" Burton chuckled. "Nothing like a killer stampede to really put the weird in the day, you know?"

"Serial killer was probably real surprised," Ace agreed. "Nothin' like a hot beef crucifixion to fuck up your day."

Burton was so shocked he snorted water out his nose.

"How dare you?" he choked. He laughed and snorted more water, and then, seeing the innocent look on Ace's face, he laughed some more. He coughed and laughed and snorted and giggled, all of the stress and fear and sadness of the last week cutting loose in one hysterical, ugly laugh.

When he finally came to, barely breathing, Sonny and Jai were in the living room, drinking their own water, staring at Burton like he'd sprouted wings.

"Funny joke?" Sonny asked.

Burton and Ace—who had hooted and hollered a lot himself—both nodded.

"Care to share?" Sonny prompted, sounding irritated and a little hurt from being left out and, well, very much like himself.

That quickly, Burton remembered that he *liked* Sonny Daye. He wasn't just the dirty bomb who had tried to kill his friend. He was the funny, grumpy little man who had worked like a champion to overcome his demons, and who gave solace and shelter to a little dog, a giant mobster, Burton's dreamy witch, and Burton himself.

"Oh my God," Burton said, letting his laughter color his voice. "You guys are not going to believe this. I… it happened on the day of the hurricane, and I totally forgot."

He told the story again, and Sonny and Jai laughed with them, and Ace laughed all over again. While he spoke, Jai moved about the kitchen, making sandwiches, and when they were done laughing, they all got to eat a sandwich and drink some more ice-cold water and tell their own funny stories or crack their own awful jokes. After an hour, Ace was almost asleep in his corner, and Jai, Ernie, and Sonny got back up to go work.

As they stepped outside, with a pat to Duke's head of course, Sonny closed the door behind them and said, "Thanks, Lee."

Burton turned to him, surprised. "For what?"

"You forgot for a minute. You know. That I'm scary."

Burton thought about it for a minute. "Sonny, considering what we all find funny? I'm thinking we're all a little scary."

Sonny grinned at him, bright and shining, and Burton's heart crumbled at the edges a little. Sometimes he could see it—a lot of times he could see it—the Sonny Daye that Ace loved with his heart and life. "Yeah, but I'm terrifying, right?"

Burton laughed and, gingerly, threw a companionable arm around Sonny's shoulders. Sonny didn't flinch or dodge; he just kept grinning.

"I'd trust you over a killer cow any day, Sonny."

"Righteous," Sonny said, proud of himself.

Together they followed Jai to the garage and continued the long job of putting together the thing that had been broken. After the last hour, Burton felt like they were a little closer to making it possible, like a little more of it had been repaired.

The Coldest Fish

*It's funny how some of your best characters start off as a lark.
There I was, writing what I thought was a Christmas
ficlet in the Fishiverse, when suddenly, I had an
assassin. A very intriguing assassin.
And 45,000 words later, I had a character in need of
a love interest and a plan for a whole other book.
But first, we had to see this character as he
entered the Fishiverse—he is The Coldest Fish.*

Part 1—Declined

"SO WHAT do you think?" Ellery asked quietly as the door closed behind their next potential client.

Jackson shook off the soul-deep chill that had been left near his heart after the interview. Eric Christiansen—probably not his real name—had been handsome in a pale-eyed, blond way, clean-cut, pleasant, cordial, empathetic, and soft-spoken.

The interview had started off well enough—the man had been helpfulness itself.

"Here's the numbers of all the people who saw me giving a speech when my business partner was killed," he'd said, producing a folder that Ellery had passed to Jackson without a word. "That also outlines the nature of our contracting business, the various contracts we've signed, and the jobs we've carried out—everything there will prove that Mike Chesney and I were completely square at the time of his death. There were no disputes, no owed money, no philosophical disagreements."

"No motive," Ellery said dryly.

Christiansen shrugged. "As long as the police see it that way, our association will be very brief." His smile then was so charming it made Jackson's blood run cold.

"We'll need to discuss it and do some digging of our own," Ellery said. He gave a nod toward the chaos Jackson was aware loomed outside the office. "As you can see, our preholiday work has been somewhat... unusual."

From the other side of Ellery's impressive oak door came the sound of kittens mewling, coupled with the frantic scratching of tiny claws on cardboard.

For the first time there was a chink in Christiansen's armor. "I, uhm, *did* notice," he said, sounding disconcerted. "What the... erm, may I inquire about all of our furry little friends?"

Jackson arched an amused eyebrow but let Ellery field this one. The more invisible he was to Mr. Christiansen right now, the better.

"One of our clients," Ellery said. "He was charged with taking kittens from a kitten mill. In the course of the, erm, investigation, it was determined that the mill was not run legally, and the kittens were scheduled to be euthanized. Our staff, uhm...."

"Disagreed with that assessment," Jackson supplied, taking pity on him.

Ellery nodded. "So they are in the process of, uhm, relocating the company's stock."

Christiansen cocked his head. "To where?" he asked.

Jackson and Ellery exchanged glances. "Since the shelters are all full," Ellery grossly understated, "that remains to be seen."

"Oh." Christiansen held up his hand and appeared to have a quick, quiet conversation with himself. "Well, I can see you're busy—and with such a worthy cause," he said, rising gracefully. He wore a slick business suit, and his dark blond hair was coiffed perfectly back from his stunning ice-blue eyes. "I'll take my file back, and if my concerns remain after the holidays, I'll come visit you again."

Ellery had his mouth open, probably to protest, but Jackson held out the file to Christiansen, pretending he hadn't rifled through it for most of the pertinent information.

"Allow me to walk you out," he said mildly, and Mr. Christiansen inclined his head but refused the file.

"That's kind—but on second thoughts, you keep it."

Jackson glanced at Ellery over his shoulder and tried to give him some eyeball semaphore to "Stay away from this guy, he'll gut you with a stapler," or, "This is a very bad man, and he'll never touch you again," but Ellery just scowled at him for helping a client get away. Oh well. If Jackson made it back into the office with his head and all his internal organs intact, he'd be able to tell Ellery about their near miss on their way to the cabin in Tahoe, which was their Christmas present to each other this year.

Well, and Jackson had gotten Ellery some very sturdy wooden picture frames with pictures of the cats who had broken all of Ellery's not-so-sturdy mantelpiece tchotchkes, necessitating the change in décor.

But the Tahoe cabin thing was definitely their present to each other. Four days of walking in the snow and fucking in front of the fireplace. The walking in the snow part was optional, but Jackson thought it could be fun too, as long as that other thing took priority. He wanted Ellery so liquid he forgot he had knees when they left. His poor Counselor had endured some *very* harrowing moments this year, and Jackson wanted to start the next year off with nothing but sex and scenery.

And he had the feeling that taking Eric Christiansen's case might have put a crimp in that plan, so he was glad Christiansen seemed to have withdrawn.

Mr. Christiansen allowed himself to be escorted down the hall and toward the front door of Ellery's nicely planned office. The place had a children's corner with toys and tablets, and magazines and books for the adult's corner. Everything was clean and comfortable, and there was even a television with children's programming in the corner.

Which nobody could hear right now due to the racket of all the misplaced kittens. Jackson had to resist the temptation to put his hand up, blocking out the sight of all those pathetic little cardboard crates as he and Mr. Christiansen passed.

Still, he couldn't resist when their would-be client paused to open one with a red X on it. He peeked inside, surprised.

"These kittens are... amok," he said, and Jackson grimaced. He couldn't do it. He had to look in. Sure enough, there were the last two of the Cornish rex litter, the one that had been inbred enough to produce numerous birth defects.

"Did you hear that, Katie?" he asked a little calico with a back leg that stuck out at a ninety-degree angle from her hip. They'd done a quick consult with a friendly veterinarian, who'd assured them that the kitten wasn't in any pain, but she wasn't going to win any races either. "You're amok."

Katie was destined to roll her way between her food bowl and her litter box, and she used that skill now, flopping over to her back and kicking out uselessly with her mismatched feet.

"What's wrong with her?" Christiansen asked in wonder.

"A sense of entitlement whenever a human passes by," Jackson replied dryly. He held her unresisting little body up so he could see the hip deformity. "Her whole litter was riddled with genetic defects. The staff found a volunteer to place three of them, but this other box has a bonded pair. Katie and her brother, Oliver, tend to get very upset if they're separated."

At that moment there was a frantic, "Meow! Meow! Meow!" from the box, and Jackson reached in and picked up Oliver, Katie's twin.

Oliver, as far as Jackson could see, didn't have more than three extra toes on one foot and two on the other. Unlike most polydactyl cats, Oliver wasn't particularly adapted to walking on the extra digits, and he, like Katie, was going to spend a lot of time on his side, contemplating the glory of dust motes. They still did use the litter box and could make it to the food and water—they were just not as active as most kittens.

Jackson held a kitten in each hand, close enough for Oliver to groom his sister, since she seemed to be the one who got all the attention.

"What… what are you going to do with them?" Christiansen asked, sounding almost afraid of the answer, which was funny given that Jackson had pegged him as a violent sociopath from the moment he'd entered the office.

"Well, we'll place them," Jackson said. "Somehow." He gave them both severe looks, which they ignored. "I would take them," he said, touching noses to each kitten. "I would. In a heartbeat. But we already have two three-legged cats, and they're destroying our house. I… I couldn't do that to Ellery. It's bad enough he has me. I don't want to saddle him with a whole animal shelter."

"Two three-legged cats?" Christiansen asked.

Jackson eyed him warily. "Yes. One lost a leg during a drive-by—a toaster fell on it and we had it amputated. The other one was born with a withered limb. They still manage to break the place. Why?"

Christiansen shook his head. "No reason." Something about his face shifted then, the creepiest thing Jackson had ever seen. It was like watching an alien presence drain out of all his facial muscles and a human being take its place. "I'll take them," he said, staring almost wistfully at the creatures in Jackson's hands. "Do I need to fill out any paperwork?"

Jackson glanced at Jade. "You filled out the initial consultant papers with Jade, right?" he asked, because that would have all his information. Not that Jackson trusted any of that to be true.

"Of course," Christiansen replied smoothly.

Jackson had planned to play this next part cool, to insinuate and intimidate and intimate. But as this cold-blooded man—and, Jackson suspected, cold-blooded killer—took the two kittens from Jackson's hands, Jackson realized he couldn't let the kittens go without making sure they weren't going to be used as target practice.

"We will," he said, "expect updates. This firm has worked very hard to make sure these animals haven't been sent to kill shelters or out-and-out euthanized. We need to know we're not sending them into danger."

Eric Christiansen's eyes shuttered. "I'm a simple businessman, Mr. Rivers. What sort of danger would I be?"

"The kind that uses babies as target practice," Jackson retorted, hoping Christiansen wouldn't open fire here and now in the office. Jackson hadn't seen anything provable in that file, but he'd seen enough. Christiansen had very thoroughly laid out a defense, not just for his business partner, but for a number of otherwise seemingly natural deaths that Jackson had seen in the news and vaguely suspected. There'd been no reason to set up his defense for those dates unless, Jackson supposed, he had actually *done* something on those dates. There'd been four that Jackson had seen, and he would put money on that being a good month for this guy.

"Only human babies," Christiansen murmured softly, and Jackson sent him a glare.

The man gave a "just kidding" smile that practically sent Jackson's *balls* back up into his stomach.

"Not feline?" Jackson asked, wondering how honest he could get the guy to be. Sociopaths could lie so easily.

"I've never killed an animal," Christiansen said, and suddenly the man behind the mask was meeting Jackson's eyes. "Most animals don't need killing."

Jackson stared back. "Most humans don't either," he said.

"Some do." Christiansen's eyes went to half-mast, and Jackson's stomach knotted. "You have to admit. Some do."

Jackson swallowed. "I know people who can take care of that," he threatened, and Christiansen's eyes widened.

"You mean that outfit down south?" he asked. "I'd heard rumors about you and Mr. Cramer, but do color me impressed. Are you going to tell them that I came and… adopted kittens?"

"I repeat," Jackson said, his voice flinty, "do you plan to hurt the kittens?"

"No," Christiansen said, and Jackson got the feeling he was telling the truth. "And not your precious little law firm that would sacrifice its holiday *rescuing* the kittens. Are you satisfied now?"

Jackson nodded. "I am. Sir, I'm afraid we can't take your case, but you are very welcome to take your furry little friends there." Katie and Oliver seemed to have found a second mother—Katie was nursing on the guy's $1000 suit.

Christiansen smiled thinly. "Will you keep my file private?"

Jackson gave him a level gaze. "I'm afraid I'm going to share this with my friends down south. Will that be a problem?"

Christiansen sucked in a breath. "No," he said after a shocked moment. "My new friends and I shall simply need to make some travel arrangements." He had big, capable hands, but the tenderness he used stroking the fur between Katie's ears made Jackson feel better somehow. "We'll enjoy some open spaces and greener pastures," he said gently, before giving Jackson his own level look. "Of course, they'll be kept indoors— the greener pastures are only figurative for our little furry friends."

Jackson nodded... and hoped.

"I'm glad to hear it," he said. "Would you like to take their cardboard crate?"

Christiansen nodded. "That would be kind, sir," he said. "Don't worry about escorting me outside. In fact, I'd rather you wouldn't."

That, Jackson thought, was a direct threat.

"I have plenty to do in here," he said, offering the crate to his new enemy.

Christiansen tucked the two kittens into the crate, cooing to them and stroking their little whiskers through the vents in the sides, and bid Jackson good day.

Jackson watched him go for a few heartbeats after the door clicked before turning back to Jade, who had been staring at the two of them with her hand on the gun she kept under the counter.

"Who in the fuck is that?" she asked, her voice low and level and frightened.

"I do not know," Jackson said, handing over the folder in his hands. "But I need you to scan this to Jason Constance yesterday, because whoever he is, I think the only thing that saved mine and Ellery's asses was kitten rescue."

Jade sucked in a breath. "On it, boss," she muttered, which reassured him because she was just as scared of Christiansen as he was.

"Excuse me," Jackson told her, "while I go tell Ellery why that man wasn't a good bet for a client."

She made the sort of humming sound in her throat that alpacas use when they're trying to calm themselves down. "I'm surprised he didn't take Ellery with him since he seems to like helpless creatures so much."

"Let go of the gun, darlin'," Jackson told her soberly. "We don't want to accidentally kill any *real* clients, right?"

He heard the distinct sound of the gun getting locked back into its little safe.

"Understood," she said.

"Now let me go tell Ellery why we're giving each other our Christmas present a day early."

They'd been planning to spend Christmas Eve with Jade and Mike and then go up on Christmas Day, and her grimace let him know that she understood—but she'd miss him.

He paused to hug her and kiss her temple. "We'll do New Year's up right," he promised. "Maybe even get your brother down here. I plan to visit him while we're up there."

"How'd you know what I wanted for Christmas?" she asked, and he smiled before turning back down the hallway.

"I always know! We'll drop your gifts off on our way out!"

"So, what do you think?" Ellery asked when Jackson closed the door behind him.

Jackson had never been shy about telling Ellery *exactly* what he thought.

Ellery remained unimpressed with Jackson's assessment, but he did concede to leaving for Tahoe early, although he claimed that was mostly to get ahead of the traffic. Ha! Traffic to Tahoe had started during Thanksgiving and hadn't let up yet. But given that the entire office had been busy redistributing the kittens from the busted kitten mill, they really didn't have any other clients to worry about until after the New Year's holiday.

"So tell me again why we ran screaming from Sacramento a day early?" Ellery asked as he piloted the Lexus—outfitted with chains after their stop in Auburn—up the hill.

"Because that Eric Christiansen guy was terrifying," Jackson told him. "And I wanted to be far away when he decided that two kittens that somehow melted his icy heart were not enough to compensate for the contract on our heads I think he dropped."

"He was *hired*?" Ellery squawked.

"Oh yeah," Jackson confirmed. He and Jason and Burton had initiated a tense three-way conversation, during which Burton and Jason had an active argument about whether or not to send a man—Burton—to go defend Jackson and Ellery while they were at the cabin.

Jason was the one who'd eased Jackson's mind a little by saying, "Look, there *was* a hit on you two, but now there's not. The chatter is… weird. And a little scary. It's like Assassins 'R' Us has a product it can't sell."

"Our heads?" Jackson asked, appalled.

"Yeah," Jason said. "Basically. We'll send somebody up there tonight—no, Burton, not you. I promised Ernie—but we purchased a cabin in the area as a safe house, and I've got some guys who'd love a week in the woods. We should have this sorted before you go back to Sacramento, so nobody you know will be in danger. As long as you save your visit with your brother—"

"How'd you know?" Jackson asked, surprised, because he hadn't mentioned it.

"Please," Jason said, and Jackson could *hear* the rolled eyes. "Do you not remember I've been there before? Twice? Save the visit until the end of the stay, when you get the all clear, and let Burton hook you into the security system. I'll let you know who your bodyguard team will be, and as long as you don't tell Ellery, nobody will be the wiser."

"Why wouldn't I tell Ellery?" Jackson asked, suddenly very unsure on this point.

"Uhm, Jackson?" Burton said, and Jackson could picture Burton having eyeball semaphore with his friend and superior officer. "I assume this was a… uhm… *romantic* getaway?"

"Yeah," Jackson replied slowly, suddenly seeing where this was going.

"How romantic do you think things will *be* if Ellery knows what may or may not go down?"

Jackson swallowed. "Gotta be honest here," he said. "I'm not sure how romantic they can be now that *I* know what may or may not go down. I'll tell him. If it kills the romance but keeps the lawyer safe, it's a fair trade."

"Ugh," Burton said. "So healthy. You'd make a lousy assassin."

"Sweet talk will get you nowhere," Jackson said. "'Cause I'm taken. Now about that security system…."

Burton had helped Jackson transfer the entire thing onto his phone, and now Jackson was in the car with Ellery wondering if maybe not mentioning the whole thing might have been better for their planned Christmas weekend.

"How do you *know*?" Ellery challenged. "You can't just call somebody an assassin based on your gut, Jackson. Not that I don't trust your gut because it's kept both of us alive."

Well, better for romance, Jackson decided with a sigh, but not better for their relationship.

"See," Jackson said, "I had Jade scan that file he gave us to compare dates of events and of people he knew etcetera, etcetera, etcetera, and each date was the date of something shady that went down in the part of the state he was in. Nothing too obvious: One politician died of natural causes the same week he was there. Another lobbyist drove his car off the road. The only reason I recognized some of the dates is because he claimed to be in town for a couple of concerts that I really loved—like when U2 was in Las Vegas in the dome thing, right?"

"Yes," Ellery said hesitantly.

"Well, the chief of security for the concert got food poisoning that night and almost died. But the key there is *almost*, and he was well enough to foil a kidnapping plot on a political speaker the day after the concert. It made the headlines because U2 was so impressed, and, you know. Bono. The Edge. I'm a fan."

"They're not Kylie Minogue," Ellery said dryly, and Jackson rolled his eyes. Every now and then their tastes clashed like this, and it had stopped outraging Jackson, but it still took him by surprise.

"She was playing too, by the way," Jackson said with a sniff. "Anyway, Burton's crew put together a lot more dates with a lot more potential hits, and they came up with a handle. Not a real name, but a handle of someone who is mentioned a lot but not discussed. It's like all the people who look the guy up and pay him then stop talking about him. They show up on forums to talk about *other* things, but never this guy. He scares the bad guys."

Ellery gasped a little. "And he's after *us*?" he asked, and Jackson couldn't blame him for the slightest little bit of panic.

"Maybe?" Jackson replied. Then he relayed Burton's and Constance's assessment that he'd declined the hit and called off the contract, but they weren't exactly sure if it was cancelled or not.

"The person who issues the contract is supposed to call it off," Jackson said. "They're afraid somebody might ignore Christiansen's protective order on us."

"Why did he issue that again?" Ellery asked, and while his hands were steady on the wheel, his voice pitched a little.

"I think," Jackson said slowly, "because we were rescuing kittens?"

Ellery groaned a little. "That? The whole kitten rescue debacle? That's what's going to save our asses?"

Jackson had no good answer to that. "Maybe?" he said.

"Oh God," Ellery muttered. "So much for a romantic getaway."

"We could still have sex," Jackson told him. "That security system Burton set up there while Jason and Cotton were using the place is top-notch. You can see a beaver getting beaver from a mile away."

"Charming," Ellery muttered. "Can you see a hitman in the snow? 'Cause that would *really* impress me."

"Only one way to find out!" Jackson said cheerfully. "Who's ready for the weekend?"

Part II—Accepted

ELLERY GLANCED around the cabin and tried to be optimistic. It really *was* pretty.

Set in a clearing with just enough snow to make Santa think about landing there, it had the traditional log-cabin exterior, with a sharply peaked roof to shed snow and a porch that could be enclosed with storm windows and heated so two lucky people—such as Jackson and Ellery—could sit next to each other on the love seat and watch the snow falling on the lake.

And not talk about the assassin's contract, oddly enough.

They had dinner in the oven—a brisket and vegetables with the promise of lots of leftovers, although they had a whole other meal for the next evening—and somehow the smell of cooking food and the peacefulness of snow didn't lend itself to talk of fear and strategy.

Instead, they talked about the presents they'd gotten Kaden's kids, Diamond, River, and Anthony, and then about the air fryer they'd gotten Kaden and Rhonda. Jackson had maintained that any appliance was a pretty shitty gift and they should have gotten Kaden video games to play with the kids, and Ellery had done the unthinkable and actually *called Rhonda* to ask her opinion on the thing.

She'd called Jade, who'd hinted to Jackson that an air fryer would be an awesome gift, which led them to this peaceful moment right here during which Ellery was leaning his head on Jackson's shoulder. Then Jackson said out of the blue, "You know that was pretty dirty, Counselor, going around my back like that."

Ellery's face heated, and he struggled to sit up, but Jackson had an arm around his shoulders, and he didn't give an inch. "I have no idea what you mean," Ellery said with dignity.

"Sure you don't," Jackson replied dryly. "I'm just saying, going to Rhonda was pretty slippery—"

"How do you know it wasn't Kaden?" Ellery asked archly.

"Because Kaden would have wanted the video-game system," Jackson said with a snort. "All I'm saying is next time, we should maybe get them separate presents."

"No," Ellery said, knowing his tone was persnickety but not caring.

"What do you mean, no?" Jackson asked, sounding more amused than put out.

"Couples get couple's presents—it's etiquette."

Jackson made a dissenting rumble. "But Kaden and Rhonda are my people. Shouldn't I get them presents?"

"No," Ellery said. "Last year we got them a garden ornament, remember? Why are they suddenly 'your people'?"

"I don't know if there's a rule book for that sort of thing," Jackson defended. "Last year we got them a garden ornament because I hadn't gotten them a housewarming thing and I was lucky to be alive, so combining Christmas and housewarming and a couple of birthdays wasn't a big deal. But this year I'm healthier—"

"You were in the hospital in November," Ellery told him dryly.

"I'm still more alive than I was last year," Jackson retorted, stung.

"Okay, fine. You're more alive. That's reassuring. But we still get them a couple's present."

"And I ask again," Jackson growled, "why?"

Ellery snuggled in, reassured that this wasn't a real fight, because Jackson still kept his arm around Ellery's shoulders so Ellery couldn't move from his embrace. "Because we're a couple," Ellery said smugly. "We're a couple, and couples give other couples gifts."

He couldn't *see* Jackson, but he could almost *hear* him roll his eyes. "So what if their *couple's* gift to us is a new video-game system?"

"Then we'll be thankful and excited, and we can buy them one on the DL so you and Kaden can hook up over the internet and play together. And in the meantime, Rhonda gets an air fryer, and since you say she's the one who does all the cooking, everybody will be happy."

Jackson let out a little harumph that made Ellery wonder if there wasn't a video-game system smuggled in with all the presents in the Cameron family bags, and then he sighed softly against Jackson's shoulder. It was warm under blankets on the porch, and watching the snow was so soothing after the long, stressful drive. Leaning on Jackson's shoulder made him feel safe and cared for.

His eyes were closing, and he was fine with that. The brisket would be done in forty-five minutes and the stove would click off, leaving the meat to rest, and he could get to that too. In the meantime it was his vacation, and unlike Jackson, he'd always been brought up to believe you should get as much happy as possible on your vacation. The week had been a nightmare of chaos, cat crap, and tiny little mewls that broke the heart, the drive had been a muscle-clench of hurry up and wait, and now? He was in his favorite place in the world.

Jackson, apparently content for the moment, pulled his phone out of his back pocket and started to play while Ellery slept.

Part III—Horror Theater

JACKSON HAD hooked his phone up to the security system before they'd even left Sacramento. Every time Ellery thought he'd been texting someone in his family, well, he *had* been, but he'd also been restlessly scanning the cabin and its surrounding areas, including the lake and the shore across the way.

He'd known the minute the helicopter had dropped off Jason's men and they'd moved into the nearby cabin Jason had purchased and then scattered, surveying the surrounding areas.

He knew when the bear lumbered through, obviously grumpy and ready for hibernation, and when a mama deer and her one-year fawn had picked their way across the snow, foraging for the choice green bits hidden underneath a bush. He knew when an owl flew to his home, presumably just a few feet above the camera, because *that* moment had startled the shit out of him.

And now, Ellery asleep trustingly against his shoulder in a way nobody in his life had ever slept, he knew when the assassin arrived.

"Zz…," he murmured. As in "assassinzzzzzz." As in, "assassins" *plural*.

As in more than one.

The first one was good. Not, Jackson suspected, Eric Christiansen good, but good enough. He was wearing a white Tyvek suit, and he carried a gun done in a matte metal of some sort. Jackson didn't study guns because he hated the things, but he recognized a special order. This one was made to disappear in snow. The assassin moved quietly on the edges of most of the cameras, not as though he knew where they were but because he naturally gravitated to the least likely places to be seen. He skirted underbrush and whispered behind trees on principle, and Jackson could admire the fluid way he moved.

Jackson had literally pulled up the number of the military contact Jason had given him when he saw the hint of something else while his eyes were glued to the guy moving soundlessly toward the cabin.

Just a breath. Not a white blur but.... Jackson squinted. A dark green sweater, dusted with snow, light-colored pants, fawn boots. Not disguised but subtly camouflaged, and not *skirting* the cameras, but blending in so thoroughly with his surroundings that the cameras literally didn't see him. Until—oh God.

Jackson was not expecting Eric Christiansen to spot a camera—the one the owl nested above—and turn toward it, fingers to his lips, staring Jackson in the eyes like they were standing across the room from each other.

Jackson stared at him, and his phone buzzed in his hand. A message from Calvin Briggs, one of Jason's men, scrolled across the top of the phone.

Are you fucking seeing this?

Yes. Do you see both of them?

...

...

DO YOU? he texted, panicking, at the same time Briggs texted, *BOTH?*

Jackson blinked. *Which one do you see?*

The bozo in the gleaming white Tyvek with the ceramic gun.

Oh.

On his phone, in the little corner display, Eric Christiansen rolled his eyes, shook his head, and showed his watch, where apparently Jackson's text string with Lieutenant Briggs was showing up.

I see him, Jackson replied carefully. *But hold up.*

Christiansen was pointing to Jackson and then pointing to himself and then making his fingers like a duck quacking.

What am I waiting for? Briggs asked.

I need to have a conversation, Jackson replied, watching his phone screen.

Christiansen nodded.

With who? Briggs asked.

A friend? Jackson replied.

On the screen, Christiansen held out his hand and wobbled it back and forth. Suddenly the view on the phone changed, which meant something had activated the motion sensors, and the screen showed the white-coated assassin pausing as though he'd heard something.

Quicker than film—quicker than *digital*—quicker than blinking, a… what? Blade? A knife? A throwing star? A goddamned *batarang*? Flickered through the air like a twinkle light and then flickered away.

The assassin in white Tyvek was lying on the ground, a spreading pool of crimson melting the snow underneath him and congealing into ice as Jackson breathed.

Jackson's screen changed again as Christiansen deliberately activated the motion detectors by pointing at his watch and arching his eyebrows at the camera he was staring into.

Jackson texted Briggs. *Give me ten.*

The actual fuck just happened? Briggs asked, obviously seeing the body now.

Like I said, give me ten. Jackson wasn't sure how Christiansen had tapped into the system, but he'd been subtle about it, giving Jackson's phone the whole feed and keeping the military out of some of it. Given that he could have killed Jackson and Ellery ten times while Jackson had stared at his phone and Jason's men wouldn't have seen a thing, Jackson was going to take it on a little bit of faith that maybe, just maybe, for this Christmas Eve, the only thing he and Ellery had to worry about was how mad Kaden would have been if Jackson hadn't snuck him a new gaming system in the box under the one carrying the air fryer.

He yawned and stretched and then scooted out from under Ellery, who pouted in his sleep and rested his head on the throw pillow Jackson had pulled from the corner of the bench.

"Where you going?" Ellery mumbled.

"Bathroom," Jackson lied, pulling the blanket up under Ellery's chin. Ellery had been awake for much of the last week, trying to get real office work done in between finding homes for all those kittens in his office, and for that matter, so had Jackson. But Ellery had driven, to satisfy his control issues, Jackson assumed dryly, and the drive was always a little nerve-racking with icy roads, unrepentant logging trucks, bumper-to-bumper traffic, and zero pit stops between Auburn and anywhere else in the Sierras. They'd taken Ellery's Lexus because, frankly, they were a little afraid of the minivan's temperament and figured deep snowdrifts weren't the place to test out the thing's seeming affection for Jackson and his tendency to feed her premium fuel.

And Jackson didn't want Ellery to see the body currently stiffening on the mountainous side of the cabin's property. Jackson paused for

Ellery's expensive snow jacket and his own worn water-resistant boots on his way out the door. The jacket would have gloves and a scarf in the pocket, and it was made for skiing, not that they planned to do any this week. Jackson also grabbed a water bottle from the flat of them on the inside door of the foyer, because basic survival said you didn't go anywhere without water, and Jackson wasn't sure if he'd have to run for his life in the middle of the frozen Sierras.

If so, water would be prudent.

Jackson had been to the property in the fall—had, in fact, assisted in an op, using the wilderness setting and uncertain footing in his and Henry's favor as they'd tracked down killers and helped Jason and his boyfriend, Cotton, survive an attack. He wasn't Grizzly Adams, but he did know the places to walk that kept his own face out of the cameras and minimized the footprints he'd leave in the snow. Nevertheless, his phone buzzed.

What are you doing? Briggs asked, obviously frightened.

Conferencing, Jackson replied. *Stay tuned.*

It took him about ten minutes to arrive at the copse of trees about a hundred yards south from where the first assassin lay, his blood freezing into the snow.

He spotted Eric Christiansen about the time Christiansen spotted him, and he tried not to let his vanity make a big deal out of that.

"You've got some skills," Christiansen said, but he sounded unsurprised. "Sure I can't tempt you to my side?"

"Positive," Jackson said. "Should I thank you for, uhm...." He gestured into the clearing.

Christiansen grimaced. "Naw," he said, and his measured, cultured tones had faded, leaving the gruff, flat tones of a working-class East Coaster.

Interesting.

"Can I ask what happened?"

Christiansen gave a shrug and gazed off into the distance, and if Jackson didn't know better, he'd say the man appeared... hurt. Christiansen's shoulders gave a jerk and the impression went away, but Jackson filed the expression away for future analysis.

When he spoke again, Eric Christiansen's voice was once more that of the college educated businessman. "I told my employers that it was unwise to take this job. They were... deciding on a course of action when my young protégé decided to carry out the contract anyway." He let out a sigh. "It's not good to let people countermand your orders. You let that sort of thing stand and people think it can happen all the time."

Jackson blinked—particularly over the word "protégé." "He looked young," he said.

Christiansen swallowed. "He was—but only in years. Don't let the sweet little face fool you. He'd done many... unsavory things."

Jackson heard it again. Sorrow. "He was a friend?" he asked delicately.

"I had plans," Christiansen said, the way someone might announce their plans for lunch had been changed. "They involved a motor home, two cats, and some peace."

Oh wow. "That's rough," Jackson said, and he felt a legitimate sympathy for the guy. He'd been willing to lay down his sword, but his partner had picked it up and waved it in his face. "I'm sorry."

"Plans change," Christiansen said, but Jackson might not ever buy his insouciance again.

"I'm sorry," Jackson said softly. "Change is hard." He knew this in his bones. If he hadn't had Ellery to help him change, he wasn't sure he would have had the strength to do it.

Christiansen shrugged. "The kittens will be fine. They're predators, you know. They've already torn the shit out of a couple of catnip mice. We get along."

Jackson grinned, surprised at how much he meant it. "Ours are destroying our house. Enjoy." And then he sobered. "So," he said, "do I need to know about the contract?"

Christiansen's expression was pure disgust. "Alexei Kovacs. Did you know him?"

Jackson's eyebrows went up. "*Did* I know him? No, I did not."

"Do you know who killed him?" Christiansen asked.

Jackson's blood, breath, entrails—all of it turned to ice, but he kept the expression on his face that of polite interest. "It's my understanding," he said, as though thinking, "that the military took him out."

Christiansen frowned. "See," he said, that working-class accent haunting him again, "that's what I heard too. The op was clean and big. It's what most of my people have been saying all along. But someone seems to think there's some sort of... I don't know. Elite force operating down south. They've taken out meth labs, petty criminals. It's like a quiet law enforcement agency, but I've got to tell you, LEOs are usually not that slick. I mean, entire *branches* of the Russian mob have just disappeared."

Jackson nodded, agreeing with him that law enforcement was not that slick. Privately he didn't think an auto mechanic, an off-duty military assassin, a psychic, a seven-foot ex-mobster, and an occasional psychopath were what one would term "slick," but he wasn't going to tell Christiansen that. "So the word out is that was *us*?" he asked, and the surprise was legitimate. "Ellery and I were involved in our own shit up here when that went down."

Christiansen gave him a long look from those almost colorless eyes. "You were," he said. "But your 'shit,' as you call it, seems to dovetail nicely with Alexei Kovacs's death. And word is you gave his brother a pretty sweet deal to talk."

Jackson shrugged. "We treated him like a human being," he said. "The guy lost his entire family while he was in a coma. He wanted to smell the ocean. He was willing to talk about the dead so we could put pieces together. Was hardly a sweetheart deal."

Christiansen nodded. "I heard that too," he said, surprising Jackson. He guessed criminals really *did* talk. "People were afraid of you two. They put out the hit. I said I'd talk to you first. I talked to you, and I said no. My word needs to matter." He glanced out into the clearing again, although darkness had fallen and his, what? Boyfriend? Little brother? Student? Was now hidden from sight.

"I'm so—"

Christiansen shook his head. "Not your concern," he said brusquely. "What *is* your concern is what you're going to tell the military people who are about to come running for your ass."

Jackson raised his eyebrows. "All of it," he said. "I'll say that the man we know as Eric Christiansen appeared in my feed, that he wanted to talk, and that I came out here to talk to him."

Christiansen regarded him narrowly. "You need to tell them I killed the Snowman," he said. "That needs to get around."

Okay, then. "Of course," Jackson said.

"Are you certain," Christiansen asked, his cold, educated demeanor descending, "that you don't know who killed Alexei Kovacs?"

"Yes," Jackson said. All he knew was that Ace, Jai, and Burton had somehow blown the place up.

Christiansen smiled suddenly. "You're lying," he said, almost jovially. "Excellent. You keep lying like that, my friend, and you'll protect whomever you're protecting."

Jackson shrugged. "As long as I don't end up bleeding out in the snow," he said casually.

Christiansen shook his head, looking wistful. "I don't think so," he said. "Are you certain you… you would like to stay here? In your current situation?"

It took Jackson a beat to recognize this as the come-on it was, and when he *did*, he was shocked into absolute honesty. "I left him *sleeping!*" He thought of Ellery's closed eyes and the trusting way he'd curled up on the love seat in the heated porch. Nobody could betray that much goodness. *Nobody*.

"It's a shame," Christiansen said philosophically. "You and me, we could have had fun."

The blood around Jackson's heart congealed, almost as certainly as the dead man's did in the snow. Would he have taken this offer before Ellery? In spite of a plethora of sexual partners, he'd been so very, very alone.

But the promise of Ellery had been there, he thought with relief. Jackson could hear Ellery's persnickety voice back then, scathing in its superiority. *I would have thought even you had better standards than that.*

"Probably not," Jackson told him frankly. "But I'm flattered." He shivered, and his watch buzzed unmercifully. "Listen, if you're not going to kill me—"

"I'm not."

That was reassuring. "Then I have to go. But, uhm… I do have a word of advice."

The man appeared ready to listen. "Back in the day," Jackson said carefully, "I spent a lot of time in bars, looking for a way to not be lonely."

"Like you do," the man replied, seemingly unfazed by the cold.

"I didn't find him in a bar," Jackson said. "That's not where people go when they're serious about not being lonely anymore. I, uhm, wherever you found the unfortunate Snowman?"

Christiansen's eyes widened with understanding. "Not the right place to fish," he said.

"No," Jackson told him. "I've got to go tell all the people all the things. Thanks for not, you know."

"Killing you?"

Oh yeah, Jackson had to get out of there. "Yeah, that," he said.

"Thank *you* for being interesting enough not to kill," Christiansen said.

"Uhm, you're welcome. Merry Christmas."

And with that, Jackson had started the kind of deep shivers that wouldn't stop with a trip to the bathroom. Goddammit, he was going to have to tell Ellery about this. With a little wave, he turned around and started back to the cabin, waving also at the nearest security camera and pointing to his destination.

Since Ellery was going to have to be alerted, everybody might as well come in out of the cold.

Part IV—Hot Chocolate and Hot Beef

ELLERY HEARD tromping up the stairs to the front door first, and the murmur of voices second. With a yawn and a stretch, he glanced around for Jackson and realized that the spot he'd occupied when Ellery had fallen asleep was empty and cold. The heaters kept the porch tolerable, but night had fallen, and it was chilly enough for Ellery to stand up, turn the heaters off, and go inside.

"Jackson!" he called, shutting the door behind him and moving into the house proper. "Jackson, how long have I been ou—oh!"

Jackson was standing in the foyer, stripping off Ellery's good skiing jacket and his own boots. Behind him was a young military officer, his skin a pale clay color with a sort of unbearable earnestness around the eyes that didn't seem to befit a man in Jason Constance's secret unit of assassins and support.

"Hey, Ellery," Jackson said softly, and now that he was in his moccasins, he moved forward to touch Ellery's hip gently and give him a peck on the cheek. "Can we go into the kitchen for some hot chocolate for Lieutenant Briggs here, and he can call in Daniels and Medina? We've got some shit to discuss."

Ellery stared at him, mouth opening and closing, and Jackson gave him a gentle wink.

"You'll yell at me later," he said, "but right now it's Christmas Eve, and these guys gave up whatever leave they had coming to watch our asses. They don't have transport home until tomorrow, and the least we can do is give them some hot chocolate and—"

"And brisket," Ellery said quickly. "We've got a roast in the oven, and I made enough for plenty of leftovers. We might as well share. There's pie in the refrigerator too." He gave Jackson a resigned look, and Jackson inclined his head in thanks. Yes, they'd planned to have leftovers and an intimate Christmas dinner together; they'd fled Sacramento because, in spite of how much they loved family and friends, they wanted, just for a little bit, to have time to themselves.

But Jackson was right, as he was so often right about people. Whatever he'd done that Ellery wouldn't like, he'd obviously called in backup. Yeah, sure, they could do this as crisply and efficiently as the military op it seemed to be, but why? Jackson had called their friends to have his back, and these were the men Jason and Burton had sent. It didn't seem right to turn them into the cold after a mechanical debrief and tell them to have a nice night.

"Ooh," Jackson said. "I'd forgotten about the brisket. Seriously, Briggs, did you guys have anything better going down?"

"Pizza," Briggs said, sounding haunted—and hungry. "And hot coffee. And no hot chocolate—"

"Or pie or cookies or Jackson's sister's fudge," Ellery told him, winking. "Bring your men in. I assume the crisis has passed."

Briggs gave Jackson an assessing stare and nodded. "It has," he said. "But we've got lots to discuss."

Which they did after the others had arrived, removing their own camo jackets and snow boots in the foyer, following Jackson's lead.

Jackson moved around the table, putting down winter place settings while the young men—all of whom had worked together for a long time, it seemed, and with Jackson too, apparently—bantered about the snow and the animals they'd seen on the security system. Meanwhile, Ellery took the roast out to rest, prepared a vat of hot chocolate with some coffee thrown in for good measure, and made the salad.

When everything was ready, he had the young soldiers go wash their hands, and he turned to Jackson, who was serving up the chocolate in mugs he'd been pleased to find above the stove. Ellery's mother had bought the cabin for the both of them and had it outfitted, and every detail—the enamel-coated tin mugs, the sturdy stoneware plates, even the giant roasting pan—was absolute perfection.

"How bad is it?" Ellery asked, and Jackson grimaced at him over the hot chocolate vat.

"What makes you think—"

"So far we've heard about snowy owls, a giant bear, and how Daniels's sister thinks he should settle down in a throuple but he's not sure how his military benefits would work with that. Which is interesting, but none of it explains where you *were* for half an hour while I was asleep."

Jackson grimaced. "They're trying to spare you, at least until dinner's done," he said softly. "Also, they really want to hear the parts in the middle. Christiansen hacked the security system, Ellery. There were whole chunks they didn't see. So as impatient as you are, they're *more* impatient, and they're trying to be chivalrous."

Ellery mulled this over for a moment. "Is it going to ruin my roast if we talk about it?" he asked.

Jackson seemed to consider. "No," he said after a moment. "I mean, there was a death, but at no time was I in danger."

Ellery's eyes narrowed. "I'm pretty sure that's a lie," he said. "But as long as it won't turn my stomach, I say let the conversation flow."

Jackson looked worried, and Ellery thought that was probably a sign of dawning wisdom.

The young soldiers returned, and everybody dished up some food. The roast was exquisite, and the vegetables had cooked up nicely if Ellery said so himself, and in a few moments, there was the quiet hum of happily eating people.

Ellery met Jackson's eyes as he toyed with the food on his plate and cocked his head. "Eat," he said softly.

Jackson rolled his eyes. "It's good," he said apologetically.

"I'm not breaking up with you on Christmas, Jackson. Eat."

Jackson shoved a bite of food in his mouth, chewed—appreciatively, it was true—and swallowed. "But the day *after* Christmas?" he asked delicately.

"Probably not," Ellery said dryly, and to his relief, Jackson took another bite. The soldiers looked from one of them to the other, decided it was *not* a domestic dispute, and kept eating. Ellery breathed a sigh of relief and dug into his own food, almost losing himself in the pleasant side talk of the younger men, to the point that when Briggs actually broached the subject, he was neither tense nor surprised.

"So," he said, wiping his mouth with an air of contentment, "that was amazing, Mr. Cramer. We can't thank you enough."

Ellery's heart, already mellowed by the meal and by Jackson's obvious remorse, melted even further. "You're more than welcome," he said. "Now, is anybody going to tell me what happened?"

"Well," Briggs said, sending a nervous glance at Jackson, "like your man here suspected, you were followed."

"By Christiansen?" Ellery asked, still amazed that the seemingly mild-mannered, handsome businessman had been an assassin.

"Oh no," Daniels said. Daniels was California-boy handsome, with gold-streaked brown hair, a square jaw, and an easy good ole boy smile.

"Or, I mean, Christiansen was *here*, but you were followed by a guy we only know as the Snowman. It's our understanding that Christiansen followed *him*." He sent Jackson a look. "Isn't that right, Mr. Rivers?"

Jackson nodded. "That's about it. Christiansen—or whatever his name is—was supposed to carry out a contract on us. He met us and decided we didn't do what he was supposed to kill us for. Also, I suspect"—he glanced at all the young men—"he's wary of crossing your unit, because he knows what you do."

"But how would he even know we were involved?" Medina asked, and Ellery was glad because it had been on the tip of his tongue.

"Because we were being targeted for the death of Alexei Kovacs," Jackson said, and eyebrows went up all around.

"We had nothing to do with that," Ellery blurted, and then he remembered who *had* something to do with that, and he blinked slowly. Did Burton's unit know what he, Jai, and Ace had done?

The faces of all three young men went carefully blank, and Ellery assumed word got around.

"Ex*actly*," Jackson said.

"Does he know who did, now?" Briggs asked.

Jackson shook his head. "He knew I was protecting somebody," he said apologetically. "But he didn't dig into who. He wasn't there for that. He'd declined the contract, put out word that we weren't to be targeted, and he was there because the Snowman defied his orders. What can I say—the man has a reputation to protect."

"Wait," Ellery said, suddenly aware that there was only one way Jackson could have gotten this information in the span of half an hour. "How do you know this?"

"You know," Medina said suddenly into the silence, "I'd love to clear the table and do the dishes and dish up dessert and maybe vacuum—"

"Sit down, you cowards," Jackson said dryly to the rest of the young men, who were making "getting up" motions. "He'd rigged the cameras. Briggs and the others saw Snowman go down, but they didn't see Christiansen. The only one who saw him was me, and he wanted to talk. So I went out and talked to him."

Ellery's stomach, which had been all happy-fine with the wonderful meal, threatened to rebel. "You what?" he asked faintly, and when Jackson spoke next, it was exclusively to him.

"He could have killed us at any time," Jackson murmured. "The way he had the cameras fixed, we would have been on our own. Ellery, I didn't even see what took out Snowman—"

"It looked like a tiny scalpel, fired with an air gun—but something small," Briggs said. "It was silent, almost invisible, and deadly."

Jackson waved his hands in agitation. "*See?*" he said, as though that one word held all of the speculation and fear he'd been living with for the last two hours. "If he could do *that*, in full view of the best of the US Military covert ops, *I* didn't stand a chance. But he didn't want to kill us. So I went to talk to him to find out why."

Ellery swallowed. "You left me sleeping," he said, feeling helpless.

Jackson bit his lip. "I didn't want you to be scared," he said softly. "He wasn't going to kill us, but we needed to talk."

"I would have come with you." Ellery felt perilously close to tears.

Jackson grimaced, and Ellery frowned for a moment. When Jackson met his eyes again he seemed… embarrassed.

Wait. Ellery knew that look. *That* was the expression Jackson had worn when he'd—in his words—"hit that" in his previous life of lonely manwhore and "that" still had a yen.

Oh wait. "Really?" Ellery said.

Jackson shrugged. "I had a feeling."

"He *hit on you*?"

The three young men at the table were now staring at Jackson in appreciation.

"Really?" Daniels asked, sounding *very* impressed.

"His last companion was, uhm, no longer available," Jackson told them meaningfully, and Ellery knew when his full meaning had sunk in because they all gasped.

"*Really?*" said Briggs and Medina in concert.

Jackson gave a sheepish glance at them. "Yeah. I, uh, gather the Snowman was his retirement plan. It, uhm, didn't work out. He was wondering if I'd, uhm, consider… you know."

"Did you?" Briggs asked, and Medina—who was sitting next to him—smacked him in the arm.

"I left him *sleeping*!" Jackson protested, gesturing to Ellery with his empty hot chocolate mug, and all three young men nodded.

"Yeah," Daniels said. "Of course you didn't."

Ellery had to admit, the pervasiveness of that sentiment made him feel better about the young men guarding them.

"So what was the upshot?" Ellery asked. "He told you why the hit was taken out and then tried to get you to run away with him?"

"More importantly," Jackson emphasized, "he told me *it wouldn't be carried out, period*. Don't you get it? If he'll kill his own boyfriend for trying, nobody else is going to take the contract. We're safe, the situation is over, and, well, he's lonely, but I think the kittens are going to a good home."

Ellery's brain shorted out, and Medina said, "Wait, kittens?" and Briggs really *did* clear the table while Jackson and Ellery told the kitten story to the appreciative young men.

THEY STAYED for dessert and some quiet conversation in the living room, after having cleaned the kitchen with military precision. Ellery had to admit, if it hadn't been for the assassins, he would have enjoyed the young squad's company immensely.

But Jackson—with some help from the soldiers—had built a small fire in the hearth and set up twinkling lights on the mantel. As charmed as he was by their help decorating, he was relieved to see them go so he could curl up in Jackson's arms and have the privacy they'd tried to give themselves for Christmas.

The soldiers bid a quiet, grateful goodbye, and after escorting them out, Jackson returned to the couch to regard Ellery warily.

"I'm still not breaking up with you," he said dryly, and Jackson's relieved smile made him laugh. "Come," he said, patting the spot on the couch next to him. "Sit. Let's try this again."

"Sure," Jackson murmured, and Ellery sat up so he could lean against Jackson's strong and battered body.

"Why didn't you wake me?" Ellery asked after a moment of silence. He was careful not to let recrimination seep into his tone. *He was sleeping*! Jackson had protested, and every soldier there had nodded. There was a level of protection in that, of seeing your partner as vulnerable, of wanting to make sure that moment was preserved. Ellery didn't think of himself as the weaker partner, but that begged the question. Why not involve him?

"Another year," Jackson murmured, settling back against the corner of the couch. "Another year that was *not* easy on you, Ellery. Where you lost sleep over me again and again."

"If I didn't want this life," Ellery said softly, "I wouldn't be here."

"As you've informed me," Jackson said, and Ellery could hear the wry laughter there. "And I'm taking you at your word. But this time... I had a hunch it would be okay. That this *could* have been a crisis, but Christiansen, or whoever he is, had decided against it. Because if he hadn't, we'd already be dead."

Ellery grunted. "He can't possibly be that goo—"

Jackson shook him slightly. "No," he said. "Don't make that mistake. Ellery, we were in very mortal danger tonight, but... but when I saw Snowman go down, I felt hope. I wanted you... asleep. Dreaming of what we were doing tonight. Content. Not afraid. Not scared for my life. Just once... my Christmas gift to you, I guess. I wanted you to be dreaming of peace and not planning for battle."

Ellery's eyes stung. "Please tell me you dream of peace too, sometimes," he said wistfully.

"I dream of our wedding day," Jackson said, surprising him, because Jackson had made few plans or demands, leaving most of it to Ellery. True, Ellery *loved* it, and Galen relished helping him, as did Jade and most of Jackson's family, but Ellery had assumed that meant Jackson didn't think about it.

"What do you dream?"

Jackson *hmm*ed. "I dream of it being outdoors—you said you reserved a day in the rose garden in front of the capitol?"

"Yeah. June seventeen," Ellery said. They had court the week after, so they wouldn't be leaving on a honeymoon right away, but Jackson loved Sacramento, and one of his few requests had been natural flowers during an outdoor wedding. Another request had been that it be near the evening, so no matter how hot the day, the delta breeze would, in all likelihood, cool them down.

"I love the idea of being there, releasing butterflies, being a part of something beautiful. I-I've never felt like that before. That I could be part of something beautiful. Not until you. I dream about that. Not of a perfect day, because...." He shook his head, and Ellery gave thanks for somebody who anticipated disaster, as he did.

"Same," he said, and Jackson chuckled.

"But you'll be looking good in a suit, and I'll…. God willing, no major injuries next year. I'll be cleaned up and pretty, here's hoping. At least I'll be shaved."

It was Ellery's turn to chuckle. "You'll be stunning," he said, meaning it. The man was stunning in ill-fitting jeans and whisper-thin T-shirts. In a suit, shaved, his hair water-combed and trimmed, he was irresistible.

"You're easy," Jackson teased, and Ellery felt his eyes burn.

"No," he said softly. "I'm not. I… I never trusted anybody to watch my sleep before. I never wanted so badly to be in somebody's dream."

Jackson nuzzled his temple. "So I let you sleep," he said softly. "Just this once. I wanted you to have a peaceful Christmas so we can share a brave new year. Is that okay?"

Ellery's tears spilled over, but he didn't care. He captured Jackson's mouth, feeling like he'd captured more. He'd captured the heart of a rare and precious creature, and he had to treat it carefully.

Jackson poured himself into the kiss, and suddenly careful wasn't a word.

They kissed until clothes became unbearable, until skin to skin became necessary. Jackson tore himself away at one point, leaving Ellery dazed and sprawled naked on the couch, his cock aching and wet from Jackson's mouth, his body trembling on the edge of everything if only, only, Jackson LeRoy Rivers would touch him again.

Jackson came back with a thick sleeping bag he'd stashed in the spare room. Ellery had wondered at him bringing it at the time, but now as Jackson—naked in the firelight—straightened the thing out on the carpeted floor in front of the fireplace and threw a couple of pillows from the spare room at its head, he understood.

When their bed was ready, he turned hopefully to Ellery, who allowed himself to be borne to their makeshift bed, their bodies stroking against each other, the light of the flames bathing their skin.

Ellery thought foolishly that he could have kissed Jackson forever, their bodies touching like that, but Jackson's hands, his mouth, his skillful touches, brought Ellery closer and closer to his peak again, and urgency swept him like the unrelenting waves of time.

"Jackson!" he begged, relieved when he felt a lube-slick finger penetrate him. The lube didn't surprise him—it must have been brought in with the sleeping bag and the pillows—but the touch! Oh, that almost sent him rocketing into the night.

And again, and again, and before Ellery could shout and grovel, his hand on his cock as he ground himself into climax, Jackson was slicked up and poised at his entrance.

"Ready?" he asked, and Ellery nodded at him mutely. Jackson's face was damp with the sweat of lovemaking in the orange light, and his eyes—so damned green they defied logic—took in Ellery's face, his nakedness, his need, with a grateful sort of hunger. He'd never wanted anything so bad in his life, Ellery thought. He'd never been so happy that the very thing he craved was there, welcoming him inside.

And then Jackson was in, moving seamlessly, his every breath a wordless cry. When he threw his head back, body trembling, Ellery tried to keep his eyes open, to see the expression on his face as he came, but he couldn't. His own climax washed over him, and he had to squeeze his eyes shut and trust, trust, that Jackson's immersion into their lovemaking was as complete, as all-consuming, as his own.

Jackson moaned softly as he poured his come into Ellery's body, and Ellery cried out as he convulsed around Jackson's cock. As Jackson collapsed against him and kissed his neck, his jaw, his shoulders, Ellery had no doubts.

They were each other's. Their dreams, even, were one. Jackson wouldn't desert Ellery when he was sleeping unless it was to secure his safety, because Ellery's safety, his sleep, and his dreams, were Jackson's to hold.

And Jackson wanted peace and health for the next year. He wanted a day in the sunshine with hope. Ellery would die to give him these things, just like Jackson would kill to keep him safe.

So much work to do—always so much work to do—but here, in this isolated cabin over Christmas, they had earned a sweaty, sexy, *peaceful* rest.

THE SLEEPING bag was big enough to cover them both when Jackson pulled one side of it over their bodies. They'd probably move to the bedroom—the floor wasn't as comfy as it could be—but for the moment they were naked in front of the fire. And replete.

"Jackson?" Ellery said softly.

"Yeah?"

"So we trust each other, right?"

"Oh yeah." Jackson nuzzled his temple, hoping the night held no more surprises, because he was unbelievably content.

"Do you trust me enough to, say, tell me what you *really* got Kaden for Christmas?"

"An air fryer," Jackson said dryly.

"And...?" Ellery teased.

"And you'll see when we visit them for Christmas," Jackson said primly. "Are we going to fight about it?"

Ellery chuckled. "No," he said. "You're incorrigible, and I love you like that."

Jackson held him close, his back to Jackson's front, and together they watched the fire burn itself down.

They had plenty of fuel for the future.

A Perfectly Sonny Daye

FUCKIN' KIDS. Who thought giving rich kids a nice car was a great idea? I got no idea who thinks you should cut a kid loose with no responsibilities or any fuckin' thing and a fine automobile and goddammit, it was Jai's day off and Ace was workin' the window and I want someone to swear at.

"Ace!" I hollered from the well under the goddamned fucking Mazda3.

"Yeah, Sonny," he called back. He was doing shit too, but he lets me do the hard stuff 'cause he says I'm better and faster at it, which sometimes I think is Ace just being nice, and sometimes I think it's Ace being lazy, but most of the time I think it's Ace being practical, because he's solid with cars and a right fair mechanic, but he's right. I'm faster. And in this case, getting this fucking thing done—somebody had put some fucking low-grade fuel in this fuckin' car, and I needed to rebuild the fucking catalytic converter, which I'm not supposed to be able to do, but God, how stupid do they think I am.

"I gotta rebuild this bitch. Them kids across the street?"

"Not sure."

"You wanna go tell them I can either rebuild this thing, or they can pay to have one shipped out here, or they can pay to have this fuckin' car towed to civili-fuckin'-zation?"

"You sure *you* don't want to tell them?" he asked. "You got such a way with words."

"I swear to fuckin' Christ if I gotta tell one of them douchey college kids how to not fuck up their car, I will clock him across the face with a tire iron, and you keep telling me that shit is *bad*."

Ace made a sound suspiciously like laughter, and that put me in an even fouler mood. "You're right, Sonny, that shit is bad. I don't like leaving you alone, though. You come outta there so you can see what's doin', okay?"

"Yeah. I need a soda anyway."

"Want me to get us some sandwiches?" he asked, probably to jolly me out of what I had to admit was a shitty mood.

"We got leftovers," I said reluctantly, but he did have a way of breaking up my cooking with takeout so we didn't get bored.

"Yeah, but they just started carrying a new sandwich," he said with decision. "Now unhook the catalytic converter and bring it up here, and I'll go tell them kids to get comfortable or call their daddies."

"You mark my words," I replied sourly, "one of 'em's gonna offer you a blowjob before that conversation's over."

Ace snorted. "Oh, I don't think it was me they were all soft on," he said. Then he smirked. "Or hard on."

I let a grin slip through. I did love me a good dirty joke, and Ace was pretty sharp that way, but he was crazy if he thought them kids were all hot and bothered for my scrawny ass. Every now and then someone thought I was cute, sure. Jai sure had held a torch, and I was glad he'd found George 'cause it's hard from your best friend, right? But Ace? Ace was… what's the word? *Incandescent*. He was all lit up inside with sex and heat, and that was before people even saw his cock, which was somethin' special.

Naw, if them kids wanted anyone, they wanted Ace.

I finished up detaching the damned converter and came up out from under the well so I could take the thing apart and clean it and put it back together again and not die from heat, because it was *hot* down there.

Ace took it from me when I got halfway up so I could use the handrails on the concrete stairs, and it was all I could do not to stare at him, all soft and shit, 'cause… 'cause he was Ace, and he did nice things for me without thinkin'.

I set the converter on the workbench and then turned to him, feeling trouble in my soul.

"What?" he asked.

"You… you do good things for me," I said. I knew this, but I was not good at saying thank you. I think you get used to taking crumbs of good things—most of them thrown in your road like trash—and running away like a feral raccoon, clutching the good thing to your chest. *Mine*

mine mine! Mine mine mine! That was me and Ace—he was *mine!* And I was clutching him to my heart and not letting go no no no no no no.

But he was *Ace,* and he did a thousand and one miracles for us every day. This place, this garage, our house. The people around us— like *family,* but better 'cause we got to pick 'em, and my family threw me away for meth. Our fuckin' *dog.* One day on our day off Ace just up and took me to a shelter in Santee. Said he'd been lookin' on the computer for a little one, since we were afraid a big one would run into the road, and we couldn't fuckin' fence the whole goddamned desert. And there was Duke, almost a baby and scared we'd hurt him like he'd probably been hurt before and…. Ace *did* that for me. And he saved kids and helped people, and then he came back and did for *me,* and who the fuck was I? Some thrown-away street trash who looked at him one day and said, "Mine!"

"What you thinkin', Sonny?" Ace asked, and I came aware that I been staring at him as he shucked his coveralls to the waist and grabbed his wallet from the lockbox.

"I'm thinkin' you're mine," I said, and then I hated that. "But more. I'm thinkin' you do nice things for me. I need to say thank you."

He has this way of smilin' at me—his eyes crinkle, his lips curve gentle-like, and we been in this desert nearly three years, which means we've known each other for five, and it's only now, this last year, I been realizin' that smile is *shy.* That when I say something nice to him, it embarrasses him 'cause I *mean* somethin' to him.

My eyes burned. "I ain't never said thank you enough," I murmured, embarrassed. All this time and he ain't complained once.

"You do," Ace said, and since we were alone, no Ernie, no Jai, he moved into my space like if we were in the house together, and we got sweet.

I gazed up at him, so bright, so shining, and he lowered his head for a kiss. I didn't get skittish like I might've once. I raised my face and let him kiss me—but I didn't agree with him.

"Do not," I argued softly.

He pulled back and feathered his lips along my temple. "Your brain is doing other stuff," he argued. "Trying hard not to beat up the stupid kids who drive their cars into the ground. Remembering to get up and turn your face to the sun and feed the dog. And then most of the time, you feed me, which I'm getting real partial to." His voice dropped even further. "Staying in the here and the now and not getting lost in all the dark places. That's my favorite thank you, Sonny. You being here with me."

God, I loved him. We'd made a resolution, me and him, to say it more often. To make it real all the time. "I love you," I remembered to say, and that smile again.... I kissed him, hard, no apologies this time, no holding back.

He kissed in return, and that's where we were when we heard the crunch of gravel as a car skidded down the hardpacked dirt drive and around to the entrance of the garage.

Ace jerked back, frowning, and I was with him on that, because dammit, we were getting somewhere with that kiss. But Ace's frown was more of his military frown, the thing that said something wasn't right and he had to fix it, and I tried to focus. Then I realized that the car's motor was still on and we could hear footsteps crunching on the gravel, like somebody was running from the blind side of the garage to the window.

Goddammit, were we getting robbed again?

"Stay here," Ace said, and I did it 'cause he said it, and he always wanted to protect me, but part of me was still fuming because *that kiss*!

Ace went striding out in that way of his that said, "Ain't no threat, just a simple country boy here, no worries 'bout me, folks," that stupid people bought. When he didn't call to me, though, didn't let out a peep that he wasn't the only one there, I knew something was wrong. I did what came natural, I picked up a tire iron and peeked out of the garage.

He was facing me, which meant he'd managed a little bit of magic there, because he should have had his back toward me. There was a guy in front of him. All I could see was the crown of his head, and he had a greasy brown mullet, brand-new jeans, and a zip-up hoodie in deference to the March cool of the desert.

"Why here?" Ace was asking, sounding irritated. "There is a gas station and a sub shop and a convenience store right across the road. Why's it always gotta be *here*?"

"No cameras," the man in front of me said. "If you don't want to get robbed, you need cameras."

Ace's expression turned to disgust. "You think cameras are gonna save you? That's the dumbest thing I've ever heard."

"Save me?" said the would-be thief. "Save me from *what*?"

And that's when I brought the tire iron down on the back of the man's head. Three or four times.

"GOD, HEAD wounds bleed a lot," Ace said as he took his position at the guy's head and reached under his arms.

I got his feet. "He's still breathing, right?" I asked, a little concerned for Ace's sake. Ace wasn't fond of killing people. He'd do it if he had to, but most of the time he'd just rather they go the fuck away. Although he didn't seem to mind victims of their own stupidity, which I thought was some common ground between us. Anyways, I wouldn't have minded if this asshole was dead since he'd been *holding a gun* on *Ace*, but Ace, like I said, got concerned.

"Yeah. He'll recover. Why'd you hit him so many times?" Ace asked, grunting, as together we hauled him toward the Sportage he'd driven in. Not bad, really—I was going to enjoy refurbishing it, filing off the VIN numbers, redistributing some of its parts, and hauling it off to Maaco for a pretty new paint job. Ernie seemed to like blues and greens, and I thought maybe we'd do this one up right for him.

"Tire irons don't got the heft I need to feel real satisfied with the job," I told him, feeling my nose wrinkle. "When I'm pissed, I need to feel like I'm moving some metal."

He blinked and nodded, like he was filing away a new thing he'd learned about me, and together we moved the guy on top of the tarp Ace had set up, and then we grabbed the tarp and hauled it to the passenger seat of the vehicle. It was hard to get blood out of upholstery, even leather, and since we'd decided to keep the Sportage and ditch the felon, we figured we'd keep it clean.

"How far you going with him?" I asked.

"Primm," Ace said, and I nodded. There wasn't a sorrier stretch of land than Primm, Nevada. Its only real claim to fame was having a foot in Cali and a foot in Nevada and some of the saddest giant casino hotels backing up against the desert that the world has ever seen.

"Sand dunes?" I asked, feeling a little bit evil, but Ace shook his head.

"Naw, back parking lot. I don't want to kill him, Sonny, I just need someone to find him without getting on camera."

I grunted. "What if he tells the police what happened to him?"

"What's he gonna say?" Ace asked. "'I'm sorry, officer, I was holding up a gas station, and suddenly my head exploded. I have no idea how it happened? No, he'll be fine as long as we get him some medical attention. After that, maybe his bad life choices will be his own."

I grunted. "With any luck, he lost the brain cell that remembered us when it ran out his ears."

Ace made a sort of snerking sound that said he was both highly amused at me and also horrified. It was the sound he made at something only he and I thought was funny, and that made me proud.

Together we loaded the guy up into the Sportage, and Ace grabbed the guy's keys from his pocket. He checked the gas and water before he hopped in, pleased when the car, at least, seemed to be well-kept.

"Think he stole it?" I asked.

"No doubt in my mind," Ace said. "Let me pop the hood and we can disable the GPS."

Took me five minutes.

Ace sighed as he started the thing up and peered at me through the open window. "I was gonna get you lunch too."

"Well, let me work on the fuckin' converter," I told him. "Ernie and Burton got a day off. I don't want to call him in, but maybe Jai can back me up for a few."

"Yeah, I think George is on shift until later tonight," Ace agreed. "Tell him I'll bring…." He paused. "What kind of food you want?"

"Steak sandwiches," I said, feeling like we'd earned it.

"I'll get extra," Ace said, nodding. He glanced down at himself; he'd shed his overalls after we'd moved our robber into the back seat, and now he was dressed simply in an OD green T-shirt and blue jeans. When you had that much sexy, simple was all you needed.

I suddenly didn't care about who was watching, even though we were in the open drive of the garage. I leaned in through the window and kissed him, suddenly just as het up as we'd been before the asshole with the head wound had shown up with his gun.

Which reminded me. "Did you put the gun in the lockbox?" I asked, pulling away a little.

"Yeah, it's in under the safe."

Burton and Ace and Jai had built the place—it had a cunning little door under the regular safe. Money we could lose, but the cache of weapons we'd picked up from guys like this asshole over the years we really couldn't afford to have found. Burton could only make so many trips to the military munitions dump without making people all nosy.

I kissed him again, and he winked at me and drove off, and I went back to the garage to ask Jai for help and to rebuild the catalytic converter.

Them damned kids were in my face before Jai arrived, and I scowled at them. There were three, and I don't think it was just 'cause I liked guys that made me think two of 'em were crushing on the other and that one didn't have any interest in boys at all.

But one of the crushing ones was the one who owned the car and had the daddy who made lots and lots of money and thought he owned the place.

"What's taking so damned long!" he yelled, waving his arms, and I thought longingly of my tire iron and the gun Ace had put in the special lockbox.

"What's taking so long is that spoiled little rich kids don't know how to drive a fucking car," I snarled. Maybe I should have gotten a peanut butter sandwich—I've been known to get hangry. "You feed it crap, you drive it too fast on the straightaways, you hard-brake it all the fuckin' time. You're lucky the damned thing hasn't rolled over and died to escape you, you little college puke! Now I'm in the middle of rebuilding your catalytic converter. You can either call a tow truck, which'll cost you a thousand dollars, have me order the part instead, which'll take you three days, or *leave me alone* to fuckin' rebuild this thing and install it! Which'll cost you five hundred but won't be done until tomorrow!"

"Five hundred dollars for a day's work?" the kid asked, sounding super put out.

"Well it was gonna be two fifty until you treated me like shit. Keep being an asshole and I'll push your stupid car to the side of the road and let you sort it out."

I glared at the kid, unmindful of the money I could lose. I know it was stupid—Ace and I were always working on a shoestring. But God! That sense that he could be mean like that to me because I was working for him. I felt like I should have a T-shirt that said I've Killed Men for Less, even though mostly I leave the killing to Ace.

The kid got a sly look on his face then, and with a sidelong glance to the one kid who *wasn't* gay, said, "You know… I could do *other* things to, uhm, pay."

I stared at him for a minute. He was probably only a little younger'n I was, agewise, but in life?

I started to cackle, 'cause it was really the funniest thing I'd ever heard, and the kid slunk *backwards* until he was even with his friends.

"It's okay, Kev," said the kid who *was* gay—and who was suddenly regarding his friend with the sort of kindness that meant maybe this whole little enterprise wasn't doomed. "Me and Freddie'll help pay. There's a little hotel 'bout two miles down the road. I looked it up. Let's grab some subs and some sodas to go and walk there. We don't need to be back until tomorrow night as it is." The kid glanced up at me with the expression of a little kid talking to an elder. "I'm sorry. We didn't mean to be disrespectful. We just spent more money than we planned on the trip is all. We got it to spend."

He glanced at "Kev" and then at the straight kid, who also looked earnest, and they all nodded.

I let out a growl of frustration and then let it drop. "You walk to the hotel now, we can drop off the car tomorrow 'round eleven. Fair enough?"

"You know where it is?" said the nice kid.

I stared back at him. "Is there another hotel in Victoriana that I don't know about?"

"What's Victoriana?" asked the kid.

"This town," I said. "And if you go past the hotel, there's a street with some fast food and some restaurants on it that you can't see from the highway. Get water, take a hike. You don't need to cart your shit all over hell."

"Can we grab a shaving kit and some underwear from the back?" asked the kid.

I gestured toward the auto well and told the little assholes not to fall while they were popping the trunk. They got their stuff and a small backpack to carry it in and were ready to go by the time Jai pulled up. He slid his Crown Vic in front of the house, where company parked and where we sort of hid the SHO, and strode up to the kids, who were staring at the highway dispiritedly.

"Jai," I said. "Can you give these kids a boost to the hotel? Their converter started blowing smoke, and they've had a shit day."

Jai looked them over, rolled his eyes, and gestured with his shoulders. "You will all sit in back. I will be your chauffeur." He laughed then, because it was a pretty good joke, and I went back to work on their damned car.

Jai came back and started to help. About a half hour in, he said, "That was nice thing you did. I would have let them walk."

I shrugged. "At least one of those kids was gonna be heartbroke by the end of the night. That's no fun. Besides. I broke another guy's skull today. I was trying to get it to balance out."

We kept working, and Ace texted me when he stopped for food. I told him Jai was there to help, and he got his order too. He was about fifteen minutes out—he should have been an hour out, but damn that man could drive—when our last customer came in. Jai and I rolled our eyes at each other because this was the guy our little Mazda3 kids were *trying* to be.

"It's making a knocking noise," he said, like we couldn't have heard that coming in. "How long to fix?"

"Three days for a new engine," I told him bluntly. "Or call for a tow to your dealership. Or abandon the car, tell your insurance it was stolen, and hitchhike home."

The man blinked. I remembered the first one of these who showed up at our door and who had tried to pick up on Ace. Didn't make me any friendlier toward this one, but still he cracked his nicotine gum 'cause who did he think he was foolin', lifted his sunglasses, and gave us that used Mercedes smile. "You saying you can't fix this?"

I shook my head and glanced at Jai. "Where's a fuckin' tire iron when you need one?" I asked, feeling surly.

Jai shrugged. "Is okay. Either way he will have to walk two miles to find a place to sleep tonight."

The man's cocky swagger leaked out of him, and he almost swallowed his nasty gum. "You really can't fix it?"

"You heard the knocking?" I asked him.

"Yes. Started about twenty miles ago."

"Look at your car's trail as you pulled in. What do you see?"

The man obeyed, his thick lips opening into a juicy little O. "Is that oil?"

"Yessir. That is the look, smell, and sound of you reducing that fine Audi to a useless pile of slag. Now, we are a *waystation*. I *do* know how to fix your engine, but I would have to order parts, and they would have to get here. Did you see the Audi dealership on your way into town?"

"No," said the man, very confused.

"Neither did I. The closest thing is down in LA, which would be"—I made a "gimme" motion with my fingers—"how far away?"

"About two hours," he said with injured dignity.

"Yessir. And what time is it?"

The man checked his watch, which I didn't need to do because it was getting close to dark. "About six."

"Yessir. Now me and my friend are gonna finish this job, and in about fifteen minutes my boyfriend's gonna show up with takeout, and you, sir, will have a decision to make. Fish or cut bait. Sleep in the hotel two miles away or call a cab or a tow truck or wait three days for the fuckin' parts because everybody at the Audi place has already gone home, and I can't order them until tomorrow. But no matter what you choose? Me and my boyfriend are going to go and shower and sit and watch some fuckin' TV and pet our goddamned dog, 'cause it's been a shitty day. So you let us know. Just understand that *absolutely nothin'* is getting done tonight."

The man swallowed, close to tears. "Oh God," he muttered. "I'm going to miss work tomorrow."

"That's too bad," I said, turning my back on him.

Jai and I worked in silence before we heard him clearing his throat. "Uhm... is the sandwich shop the only place to eat?"

I started searching for my tire iron, but Jai gave the man directions and saved me the trouble. I'd gone back to the catalytic converter, which was just about ready to reinstall, when the asshole—erm, potential customer—started his own trudge down the road to the hotel after getting *his* small suitcase from the trunk and paying a fee for parking his vehicle here while he arranged for a tow.

As he made the mad dash across Hwy 15, Jai said, "This one I am not driving to the hotel?"

"This one needs to contemplate his goddamned navel," I said shortly. "George is almost off shift, and I've had about enough of people today."

Jai grunted. "A Sportage, you say?"

I smiled, 'cause besides me and Ace making out in the garage, that was about the best part of my day. "It's nice," I said. "I know Ernie's been hoping for a luxury SUV. It's not a Chevy Tahoe or a Navigator or nothin', but it's a notch above our usual piece of shit."

"You are sure the owner won't come back looking for it?"

I shrugged. "If he can remember where he left it when he recovers from the concussion, he'll still have to tell the police what he was doing when he left it here. I'm thinking he's going to remember he stole it and live his life."

"Fair," Jai agreed.

We had put the finishing bolt in place when Ace pulled in, parking right in front of the garage so the Sportage was out of sight.

"I took it to get detailed," he said. "So hopefully any blood trace is gone." He grinned. "Thanks for coming in, Jai. You guys about done?"

"I have time to shower before George gets home," Jai said happily.

"Here's some steak sandwiches for the two of you," Ace said, handing him a separate bag. "You two have yourself a good night."

Jai took the bag and smiled. "Thank you. It was a good day."

He left, and Ace turned to me as I closed the auto bay and locked the place up. "What about you?" he said. "This a good day?"

"Shower," I said. "Steak sandwich. Pet the dog. Watch the movie. Eat the ice cream. Have the sex. We still got a ways to go."

Ace let out a positively filthy chuckle then, which should have been my warning.

I was still surprised when, after our showers, and after we'd each had a turn taking Duke out for a run behind the house and then giving him his treats, he moved up behind me as I was shutting the door.

"Sonny?"

"Yeah?"

"You starving?"

I felt his breath in my ear, his hands splaying across my stomach, the warmth, the strength, the kindness that was always my Ace when he was being sweet.

"Not for food," I whispered. He was going to take me to bed and use me and give to me and suck me and fuck me and come inside me, and I'd earned that today by only picking up the tire iron once and stopping when it was time.

"Me neither," he said, running his lips along my neck.

I wanted him more than steak, more than ice cream, even more than violence.

We raced for the bedroom, shedding our sleep clothes as we went, and all of the rest of the day disappeared, and it was this—me on the bed, hips in the air, Ace slicking up my asshole and getting ready to drive out all the demons in my soul with his cock.

Any day that ended like this, me crying out, coming all over my own goddamned chest, ass clenching on Ace's erection as we used each other the way only people who loved fierce and hard could—

That was a good fuckin' day.

The Coldest Fish Goes South

Part I—He Did What?

"HE DID what?" Burton asked numbly, not sure he'd processed that right.

Jason pinched the bridge of his nose. "Uhm, Jackson Rivers *talked* to the assassin, the guy told him he was leaving the job, and, uhm... he left. After, I guess, killing his boyfriend for trying to take the Rivers/Cramer contract off his hands."

"And Rivers just... *talked* to the guy," Burton said, wondering why he couldn't seem to understand that. According to Jason, the entire thing had gone down over Christmas, and they were just hearing about it now. Of course, Jason had taken some personal leave to purchase his house and get it set up so he could ask Cotton to live with him, and, oh yeah, impossible fucking storms and their aftermath...but... but... but that had been over a month ago, and they were *just* hearing about it *now*?

"And... Rivers simply talked to the guy," Jason replied. "And then he and Cramer and Daniels, Briggs, and Medina all had a nice Christmas dinner, and they left the next morning, and, uhm...." Jason wasn't immune to embarrassment. "Uhm, if our surveillance is accurate at all, nobody went knockin' 'cause their cabin was rockin'."

Burton stared at him. "I didn't need to know that."

Constance glared back. "Neither did I, but they told me anyway, and I had to share."

They both shuddered in an attempt to shake it off, although part of what they were probably shaking off was the embarrassment of thinking of Jackson Rivers naked and doing the thing. Now that Burton knew he himself was bi, he'd been able to admit when some guys would have done it for him if he hadn't been devoted to Ernie. Rivers was one, and even Ernie called him "sex on legs" sometimes.

"So...," Burton muttered, "this guy... this, uhm... *guy*. The actual fuck?"

"We don't have a name or an ID or even confirmation he exists," Constance said. "And we've been looking since this went down. But

Medina's been going through the chatter on the dark web, and…." He gnawed his lip, and Burton had a chance to process how young his friend had seemed since he and Cotton had moved in together. Of course, Cotton still went to nursing school during the week, but Burton knew from experience that sometimes it was the *hope* that your person would be there to greet you. Jason managed to make it home about two days a week, mostly to see Cotton, and Burton had no doubt that even that small amount of time had given his CO and friend a longer, happier life.

"And what?" Burton asked, curious because Jason Constance was *never* this uncertain.

"And there are… blank spots," Jason said grimly. "It's hard to put it any different than that. Like, one minute we can *see* the contract on Jackson and Ellery, and the next minute nobody is asking about it. Now, you and I know that's because our cold fish put a stop on the contract and then backed it up. But the internet chatter doesn't show us the real-life stuff. If anybody lived to see it, nobody's talking."

They both met eyes. "If anybody lived to see it," Burton said darkly.

Jason nodded and then took a few steps around Burton's quarters, where they were currently conferring. It wasn't that their association with Jackson Rivers and Ellery Cramer was secret, but Burton's boyfriend *and* Jason's boyfriend were definitely on the down-low. Some people in their unit might have met Cotton, but nobody knew he was currently at Jason's place on the weekends. Ernie had saved every deployed member more than once by telling Burton to "watch out for the girl in love with a schoolteacher," or, "Hey, that guy with the godlike chest and Adonis blue eyes is going to run into trouble tonight." (Burton hadn't been excited by that one, but he had passed the tip along as "chatter," which ops used a lot to keep their sources secret.)

"Or maybe…," Jason murmured, pausing his pacing. He grimaced and shook his head. "Well, I wouldn't bet my life on it," he said.

"What?" Burton asked. "Bet your life on what?"

"Lee… what do you think Victoriana looks like to someone in the intelligence community?"

Burton stopped breathing, his face taking on a perfect mask of neutrality. "I have no idea what you're talking about," he said.

"Um-hum…. Sex-trafficked children found on the side of the road next to their coyote who apparently committed suicide. Ring any bells?"

"You're the one who got them to safety, sir," Burton said.

"Remains of mobsters revealed during flood in the desert—any clues?" Jason pressed.

"I wasn't there when they went into the desert, if that's what you mean," Burton said. This time, he tried for guileless, but he wasn't sure he was good at it.

"Mm… yeah. How about, a serial stickup felon who turned himself into coyote kibble for no apparent reason? What about that guy?"

"From what I heard, he just swerved into a cactus and kept going," Burton said. He *had* been there for that one, but then, so had Jason's car, which had been taken into Ace's garage to get its brakes fixed.

"Come off it, Burton. *Three* entire *branches* of the Las Vegas mob scene have disappeared into the black hole between Vegas and San Diego—"

"And meth dealers," Burton said, giving an evil little smile.

"Whose children were saved by random strangers hauling ass through the house," Constance muttered, but his admiration was unmistakable.

"You should have seen Ace," Burton reminisced, beyond pretense now because he was so proud of his friend. "He was like one of those action heroes on the big screen, running through the house, throwing kids out windows, clocking bad guys, leaping out in a shower of shattered glass barely ahead of a fireball. It was *epic*."

Jason gave him a droll look. "And yet funny how none of those things is ever picked up on chatter," he said drily, and *then* Burton got it.

"Oh," he said softly.

"Oh yeah," Constance said, but he was much grimmer. "And you know, our cold friend up north actually mentioned us. For all we know, he thinks your people in Victoriana are related. According to Medina, he sounded, well, impressed."

"We don't know this guy's agenda," Burton said thoughtfully, "but we know it might not be all bad."

"That's right," Constance said, but then he shuddered. "But I'd hate to be the one who has to make the decision as to how bad it really is."

"Does anybody but us know about this guy?" Burton asked, suddenly worried.

"Only this unit," Jason said, obviously thinking what Burton was. Jason's unit kept a *lot* of secrets, and Burton felt safer about the world because of it.

Burton blew out a breath. "Should we keep it that way?"

Jason gnawed on the inside of his cheek. "Maybe…. Look, I'm just playing the percentages here, but maybe you should, maybe, tell Ernie and have him talk to everybody else."

"And I would do that because?" Burton stared at him.

"Because there's no telling what will happen when two blank spots in the chatter overlap and…." Jason rubbed his stomach. "Could you… could you text Ernie *now*?" he asked.

Burton's entire body went cold. "Yeah. Yeah, how about, uhm, how about I just go home early today, how's that?"

"Great idea," Jason said. "I…. Shit." Burton understood—Jason had at least five, six hours until he could leave the base. Burton could admit without conceit that he was Jason's best operative and his most trusted friend in the unit, but Jason had a lieutenant colonel who was his titular second-in-command. Given the sensitivity of the mission at the base, *one* of them had to be in attendance at all times. "I'll get out of here as early as possible. But text Ernie *now* for me, could you?"

Burton caught Jason's urgency and, like he did on an op, fought through the cold and into action. He was texting Ernie before he thought about it, and he and Jason waited breathlessly for him to text back.

And waited.

And waited.

Earlier that day

OH! COTTON was so excited! He'd managed to pass his first three big tests, and while his workload hadn't diminished one bit, he was going to drive to the unfinished neighborhood outside of Victoriana to spend the weekend with Jason. He could get lots of homework done between swimming in the pool, visiting Ernie and his cats, and banging Jason stupid.

Cotton hadn't forgotten his priorities, but he'd rediscovered the joys of having a lover he actually *loved*, and he didn't intend to forget about it anytime soon.

He shared a congratulatory soda with his roommate before packing his clothes and his schoolbooks and hopping into the little sedan his friends at Johnnies had bought him before his semester started. Jason's friends Sonny and Ace had checked the thing out during his last weekend in Victoriana and pronounced it sound, so he *and* Jason were both okay with him driving it across the desert to visit, which was nice, and being that it was a crisp March day in Death Valley, the trip promised to be exhilarating rather than exhausting.

Or it did until about halfway there, when the steering wheel gave a sudden lurch and the car began to list as steering became impossible.

Oh shit. Oh shit oh shit oh shit.

Cotton got the thing to the side of the road and killed the engine, his heart pounding. His hands were sweaty as he pulled out his phone, and he was about to text Jason when he remembered what his boyfriend did for a living.

Saved the world.

Jason Constance saved the world.

And Cotton Carey could change his own damned tire.

Still, his hands were clammy and shaking as he hopped out of the car and surveyed the driver's side tire, which had apparently given up the ghost in transit.

Checking for service, he was grateful for the three whole bars. He took a picture of the tire and texted it to Ernie, who replied almost immediately.

D'oh! Sonny and I will be right there.

Where's Ace and Jai? Cotton asked, mostly because Sonny usually stayed behind and minded the fort. Cotton thought it might have something to do with how easily Sonny could get spun up if he wasn't in his comfort zone.

Something came up, Ernie texted, and Cotton realized that might be all he ever knew about that. He was surprised how often something "came up" for the people of Victoriana.

I'm about an hour out, he sent back. *I could probably change the tire myself.*

No!

He stared at his screen, a little surprised.

I'm sorry?

Sorry, Cotton. Got a feeling. Can't really explain it. Hang tight. Don't take any rides from strangers, okay?

Cotton stared at the text, a little bewildered, but Jason had told him once to trust *everything* Ernie said. He'd trust this too.

Sure. I've got water, snacks, and a little light reading. That last one was a joke, because he had several chapters of his anatomy textbook that he had to be up on by the end of the weekend, and he figured this would give him a chance to get to that without inconveniencing Jason.

You do that, Ernie replied, and Cotton wasn't sure if he got the joke or not, but he'd already pulled out the textbook and gotten into it, so he forgot to ask.

About a half hour in, around the time he was ready to get out of the car and take a piss on the side of the road, he saw a vehicle approaching in his rearview, slowing as it drew near. With a sigh he got out of the Toyota and stretched, ready to tell this nice civilian that he was fine, just waiting on his friends who would help him change his flat.

The vehicle was bigger than he'd anticipated. In fact, oh my God, it was an entire *Winnebago*, and the man who got out of it was good-looking in a very blandly handsome way. He approached Cotton genially, hands in the pockets of his worn Levi's, a colorful scarf wrapped around his face and shoulders to fight against the brisk desert wind. As he got near, Cotton saw he had ice-blue eyes and dark blond hair, and he gave Cotton, in his sweater and jeans, an appreciative glance.

Cotton returned the smile in that neutral way he'd been learning since he quit porn. His body wasn't readily available anymore, and wanted to convey that message along with the same basic friendliness that Cotton had always possessed.

"Heya," the man said. "Do you need some help?"

"No thanks," Cotton said, remembering the almost panicked tone of Ernie's texts. "I mean, it's nice of you to offer, but I've got friends on the way. They should be here soon. I'll be okay."

The man barely contained a grimace. "Are you sure?" he asked. "I've got hot chocolate in the RV, and a couple of kittens who would *love* for you to entertain them!"

Cotton gnawed his lip, sorely tempted by both things. He glanced at his phone screen again and politely declined. "Sorry, if my friends drive by and don't see me, they'll panic."

"Good friends?" the man asked, leaning up against Cotton's vehicle with his arms crossed.

"Yes," Cotton said. "New, but good. I sort of, uhm, inherited them from my boyfriend, really. He's deployed a lot, so they keep an eye out for me."

"Deployed?" The stranger's relaxed position on Cotton's car didn't shift, but Cotton was aware of a... coiling. A muscular tension in the man that hadn't been present before. "He's in the military?"

Wait! Jason had rehearsed how he was supposed to answer this. "Yeah, he's in a troubleshooting squad for training sites. You know, accidents, injuries. He goes and assesses the site and works with the insurance adjuster to decide if it was human error or a trainee mistake. They don't like people getting hurt on the military's watch, right?" He nodded earnestly. He remembered asking Jason if there was really such an office in any branch of the military, and Jason had shrugged. "Hell if I know, Cotton. I just know there's usually ten layers of bureaucracy to get anything done, *including* money for training facilities. I'm going to be charitable and assume some of that would go there."

"Sounds... boring," the man said, none of that coiled tension leaving his body. "Is he?"

Cotton stared at the man in outrage. "No! He's smart and funny, and we read books together and discuss them, and—" He paused in his vigorous defense of Jason when he realized what was going on here. "Oh. You're hitting on me."

"Well, uhm, *yes!*" The man laughed. "I don't know if anybody's told you this, but you're *stunning.*"

Cotton grimaced and told the truth, which was guaranteed to get a man like this—average, vanilla, arrogant—to back off. "I used to be an adult performer," he said. "I've heard it a *lot.* I tend to go deeper now. Beauty fades."

The coiled tension disappeared as the man's absolute surprise registered. "An... an adult performer? Oh my God. You were a *Johnnies model?*"

Cotton raised his eyebrows. There was "porn" and there was "Johnnies," and the second one was specific enough to know he'd found a viewer.

"You know my work?" he asked pleasantly.

"You're...." The man stared at him, helpless and a little bewildered as he adjusted his stance—and his pants. "Uhm, yeah. I've...." An absolutely *livid* blush swept up from his neck, and he had to clear his throat a few times. "Uhm. Wow." He shook his head. "I am having the *weirdest* week. So, uhm, your boyfriend works a boring military job, and you were an, uhm, adult performer. What do you do now?"

"I'm in nursing school," Cotton told him blandly, and the guy's eyes bulged.

At that moment, a car—one of the few out on the road at this hour—approached from the east. Cotton peered at it and then grinned at his friend who'd helped him pass the time.

"Hey!" he said. "My friends are here. One of them has cats—like, *lots and lots* of cats, so you two can talk about that when they get out." Cotton smiled in anticipation. "Petting his cats is one of the best parts of visiting my boyfriend on the weekend. Surrounded by that purring… it's *great!*"

At this point his friend was a little bit dazed. "Wow. Okay. I can't wait to meet your friend who has cats."

Cotton gave him an indulgent smile before turning to watch as Ernie's latest POS arrived on the road's shoulder. It had no sooner stopped than Ernie and Sonny got out—Ernie had been driving—and while Sonny went for the jack and the power tools and the new tires, probably two if Cotton knew his friends, in the back of the POS sedan, Ernie got out and strode toward him and his new friend from the Winnebago. Not wandered, Cotton noted, *strode*.

"Ernie!" Cotton said in genuine pleasure. He really *did* love Jason's friends. "Come meet this nice man who pulled over to help me." He looked expectantly to the stranger. "I'm sorry, I didn't get your name."

"Eric," said the man, extending his hand to Ernie. "Eric Christiansen."

Ernie took the man's hand with a certain resolution, and then his shoulders twitched as though something not entirely painful—but definitely anticipated—shocked him.

"I'm Ernie," he said, and his dreamy black-lashed indigo eyes were suddenly very, very sharp. "And what brings you to the desert, Mr. Christiansen?" He paused, and to Cotton's surprise, his friend's jaw was square and hard. "And think *very* carefully before you answer."

Christiansen's eyes were suddenly as hard and as cold as a glacier, and Cotton glanced from Ernie to this stranger who'd approached him on the side of the road and was very, very afraid.

ERNIE SLEPT with an assassin—some of his best friends were mobsters and psychopaths. He'd even killed a few men himself.

He did not rattle easily.

But "Eric Christiansen"—not his real name—had rattled Ernie since Cotton had texted, probably twenty minutes before the Winnebago had even pulled up.

Ernie had sensed it coming, like a glacier on a freight train, a speeding tonnage of absolute ice.

He'd had to steel himself to shake Christiansen's hand, and he'd been expecting bugs—giant beetles with frozen feet—but he'd been surprised.

The cold, yes—but it was the snow crust on the pelt of an Arctic fox. There was a warm-blooded mammal underneath the snow, but ice was its element, its home, its life force, and killing was a necessity, a thrill, and a means of sustenance all in one.

Ernie wasn't sure he'd ever met a more emotionally *efficient* killer in all his life, and he'd been drafted by an illegal branch of the army to evaluate assassins as a *job*.

"Cotton, needyerhelp here," Sonny called. "You got muscles, boy, let's put 'em to use."

Ernie saw Sonny, crouched in front of the car with the jack, and suppressed a smile. He'd told Sonny to distract Cotton from the interloper before they'd pulled up. Sonny had asked, "Is this a witchy thing?" and Ernie's "Pretty much," had been all he needed. Sonny's absolute trust was a magical commodity, and Ernie would *not* take it for granted.

Cotton hustled off in an earnest desire to help, and Christiansen watched him in what seemed to be honest bemusement. "That boy," he said conversationally, "has a nine-inch penis with a two-inch diameter. It's stunning. Usually that sort of thing comes with a proportional ego, you know, but I've had apple crumbles with less sweetness and more pretension."

Despite his internal warnings—and they were going off with full impact—Ernie smiled.

"You won't find a kinder, more grounded person than Cotton," he said. The indulgence in his tone cut off. "We'd kill to keep him safe."

Christiansen's bemusement failed. "Why would you even—"

But it was pretense, and they both knew it. "Zero crap, Mr. Christiansen," Ernie said. "What are you doing on this stretch of the desert? Your answer matters."

"I was on my way to—"

"No," Ernie said.

"Las Vegas is—"

"Nuh-uh."

"And the Grand Canyon is—"

"Please stop jerking me off. I don't need a nine-inch penis to find it offensive and personal."

"What would you do about it if I were?" Christiansen asked as though legitimately curious.

"Do you know what borderline personality disorder is?" Ernie asked as though talking about the weather.

"Yes," Christiansen said, blinking rapidly.

"That nice man changing Cotton's tires is a textbook case. If I whistled him over here and told him what you are, he would brain you with a tire iron before I was done speaking, and then he and Cotton would help us hide the body."

Christiansen's eyes widened in surprise, but Ernie kept talking.

"And I know you're thinking that the scalpel in your pocket could kill me, Cotton, and maybe Sonny—but probably not because he's got skills you'd never guess—before Sonny got to you with the tire iron, but remember this." Ernie's voice dropped, and Ernie was effectively in the present in a way he only usually was when having sex with Burton. "Sonny is the least dangerous person Cotton knows."

He saw the moment, the actual moment, when that registered. Christiansen swallowed *almost* imperceptibly, and his pupils widened the tiniest bit, and his nostrils flared as though he were scenting prey. "Where would the *most* dangerous person Cotton knows happen to be?" he asked.

Ernie gave an insouciant shrug. "Maybe he's a quarter mile away with a sniper's scope on us," he said airily, although he knew Burton wasn't *that* close. He was aware that Burton *and* Jason were currently scrambling for a helicopter. "And maybe he's taking care of something that the law would not," he hazarded, although he knew *exactly* what Ace and Jai were doing. "And maybe he's simply caring for somebody who's been injured through no fault of their own." Which is what he was pretty sure George was doing. "And maybe, just maybe, he's having a pleasant conversation with a stranger about the two kittens currently batting the windshield of the man's Winnebago." Deliberately, Ernie turned and waved at the little darlings. "Aw," he said, legitimately charmed. "One of them has club feet. Good for you, adopting special kittens. Points in your favor."

He turned deliberately back—not moving quickly, not showing any of his own military self-defense training, not doing anything to spook the professional killer who had shaken his hand. "If you'd like some pointers for dealing with kittens with special needs, I have a friend who specializes in three-legged tomcats who like to destroy living rooms."

Eric Christiansen's eyes grew *very* wide at this. "In fact," he said, his voice a little thready, "I got these kittens from a man named Jackson Rivers. Do you know him?"

Ernie was lucky he'd seen the association in the shake of hands. "I do," he said pleasantly. "We consider him and Ellery Cramer to be *Very. Good. Friends.*"

Mr. Christiansen nodded carefully. "What did you say the most dangerous man you know is doing?"

"Any of a dozen things," Ernie told him, his gift responding to the *whap-whap-whap* of the helicopter blades when it was undetectable to his ears. "Why do you ask?"

"I think," Christian said, "that in answer to your earlier question, 'What am I doing here,' I might want to talk to this man. One dangerous man to another."

"Hm...," Ernie murmured. "Then perhaps you want to follow us? I'm in the mood for a soda—there's a mini-mart about half an hour away." By Winnebago, it was half an hour away. By Ernie, who was driving like a NASCAR racer, channeling both his gift and his friendship with Ace to get him and Sonny to Cotton *ASAP*, it was closer to fifteen minutes.

"I have soda in my—"

Ernie sent him a hard glance, knowing that to his left, Sonny had changed Cotton's tires in record time and was currently putting his jack and power tools into the trunk of Ernie's POS, along with the two tires he'd removed, because Sonny was that fast.

"The mini-mart," he said, smiling thinly. "Your kittens are awfully cute, sir, but I don't need to see them in person just yet."

Christiansen swallowed. "For the record," he said, his cultured voice masking the tiniest edge of hurt, "none of the people here would be in any danger in my RV."

Ernie took that for what it was. "That's reassuring," he said. "But *so* many people would be in danger should it become convenient to go back on that promise. I'm choosing the safest option for all involved."

Christiansen's hurt faded. "How many people are we talking about?" he asked, suddenly sounding a little alarmed and *very* curious.

"You don't have to worry," Ernie said. "Odds are you'll never have cause to meet all of them at once."

"And where are—"

Ernie gave a slight smile, and now the *whap-whap-whap* was actually audible. "I suggest you get in your vehicle and make your way to the mini-mart with the sandwich shop inside, right across from the garage. Trust me, they're the only buildings you can see from the road for quite a ways. You can't miss them."

A faint look of panic crossed Christiansen's features as he heard the helicopter too. "Are you *military*?" he asked, surprised.

"Me?" Ernie laughed. "No. And you're not on any military radar at the moment, so don't panic. But *do* get in your RV and follow us." Ernie smiled indulgently at Cotton, who was getting into his vehicle and waving. "But not Cotton. He needs to get home."

Christiansen waved too, his bemusement never fading. "He has no idea who I'm dealing with, does he?"

Ernie laughed softly. "Oh, he knows. He just doesn't understand violence, not in any meaningful way. We would like to keep it that way, and we don't mind leaving a few things out to do that."

Sonny was approaching now, his toolkit still in his hand when it should have been thrown in the trunk already. "We ready to go?" he asked, giving Christiansen an unfriendly stare.

Christiansen bowed slightly. "I'll follow you to the mini-mart," he said respectfully.

Sonny nodded back curtly. "That's fine," he said. "Someone'll meet us when we get there."

"Someone?"

Ernie tilted his head. "I know you think you need to meet with the most important person we've got," he said, keeping the illusion that they were an actual organization. "But what you don't realize is we are *all* the most important person we've got. Don't worry. Somebody who can answer your question will meet us there."

"What's my question?" Eric Christiansen asked. "How would you know what it is?"

"That was the easiest thing to figure out," Ernie said, and it was true. The minute he'd sensed Christiansen's true nature, he'd known what it could be. "You want to know if you're safe here or if you'll be treading on any toes. You want to know if there's a territory, if you need to mark a space. You don't want to set up shop here—you want to *live* here, and you need to know if it's safe to do so."

"Is it?" Christiansen asked, sounding wistful.

"It could be," Ernie said thoughtfully. "But we'll talk there." He gave a faint smile. "Bring the kittens inside in their crate—I'd love to say hello. Sonny, one of them's got club feet, can you see?"

Sonny glanced to the front of the RV, his face splitting into that impossibly young and excited grin. "Ain't he cute," he said. "Why they call 'em club feet? Or club foot? 'Cause that'd be a pretty sucky club right there. Why isn't it 'unique feet'? That'd work better on account of it rhymes."

Ernie gave Christiansen a real smile. "Well, sir, you heard him. We look forward to meeting your kitten with the unique feet." His smile turned businesslike. "Later."

"Who will we be waiting for?" Christiansen asked. "Our friends in the helicopter?"

"It depends," Sonny said. "We got some folks doing a thing today. They're done with the thing, you might meet them instead." He gave an evil smile. "Maybe you should wait for the helicopter."

Christiansen looked like he'd had more shocks today than he was used to, so Ernie guided Sonny back to his vehicle and loaded in, telling Sonny that he'd drive if Sonny could text, because they'd need a guy on coms.

"What'm I doing?" Sonny asked as Ernie took the wheel and pulled smoothly onto Hwy 15.

"Checking to see if Ace and Jai are done," Ernie said grimly. "I'd rather not give away Burton and Jason yet, although they're the ones in the helicopter."

Sonny's chuckle was as evil as his smile had been. "I think Ace and Jai are having a banner fucking day, you think?"

Ernie chuckled back. "I sure do hope so."

A Banner Fucking Day

Very early that morning....

"GEORGE," ACE said, not wanting to doubt the man but not wanting to commit his full fury until he was sure, "tell us how you know."

George swallowed, glancing from Jai to Ace again and shuddering.

It wasn't often you put out a hit on a fundamentalist preacher with multiple family ties to law enforcement, now was it?

"Started a year ago," George said softly, sipping coffee at Ace and Sonny's much abused kitchen table, "before me and Amal started working at the hospital. But one of the other nurses, Barb Clemmons, she told me about it." He shook his head. "She was terrified. But little girls—between four and eight so far—have been brought in with the same symptoms. Abdominal pain, pain in urination, rash on the thighs."

"Chlamydia?" Ace hazarded, and George nodded.

"The first time, the doctor called social services before antibiotics were administered. The parents got wind and grabbed the kid and disappeared. The next time we saw her, she had a fever of 105. She almost died." He grimaced. "She'll never have kids. At the age of nine, we had to make that decision to save her life. I *was* there for that one. It's why Barb told me the story. So the next time parents brought in a kid—same type, blond, blue-eyed—"

"In this area?" Ace asked, surprised. Victoriana was close enough to the Mexican border for the population to be *very* much brown/brown/brown.

"Yeah," George said, his pretty face hardening with disgust. "Made the similarities really easy to spot. So with the next one, the doctor prescribed antibiotics first, after giving the kid the first shot. Had the parents wait in the exam room and sent Barb in to chat with them, keep them at ease. Asked about teachers, babysitters, crazy uncles—"

"Priests," Ace said darkly.

George touched his finger to his nose. "Bingo. Barb's good at sounding like a brainless chatterbox, so she managed to keep them from getting up and walking out, at least until they mentioned their local revival-tent preacher and their daughter started to cry. They were going to leave without meds, but the doctor came in then with the prescription and promised to bill them later, and they blew out of there, dad threatening to kill anyone who stopped them."

"Ugh," Ace muttered.

"So they finally had something they could report, but when the Doc—Barty Krebbs, he's a good guy, one of, like, ten this hospital has on staff—got back to social services, he found out the worker who'd reported the incident had been let go."

"For what?"

"DWI," George said darkly. "Barty actually knew her name and had her personal contact info—she'd been associated with the hospital forever—and the first thing he said was, 'Do you even drink?'"

"My guess is no," Ace murmured. Jai was behind him, nodding in time, and Ace glanced around the little kitchen itchily. "Do you see him?" he asked Jai, who was peeking out the window.

"I can see his feet," Jai muttered. "He seems to be in the zone, but he will start looking for us. I will go out now. You keep talking to George."

Ace nodded and Jai left. When Jai had approached him about helping with this matter, he'd mentioned, very soberly, that Sonny shouldn't hear the particulars. It's why nothing George said surprised Ace. Sonny's history being what it was, the thought that a rampant pedophile had been enabled by an entire community would be enough to send him on a rampage, and Ace barely survived the last one. Sonny had been "in therapy" in a rough sort of way to the guy Jason had hooked him up with, but that meant his temper was even more uncertain some days. He needed a good two days to come down from those moments on the phone with a virtual stranger, and while he was much more even-keeled for the rest of the time, Ace was just not ready for him to be triggered again.

"So she lost her job?" Ace said, turning around to George. "How's she doing?"

George shrugged. "Apparently the hospital took up a collection so she could feed her kid. Barty's going to have her over for dinner, and we'll see what else we can do for her. Why?"

Ace shook his head. "No particular reason. Had Burton put some money down on us racing is all. We took a couple pots home." It was cheating, and he knew it, particularly when Ernie was telling them he wouldn't crash. But Ace liked a cushion, and after the big storm, he'd gone racing for a number of weekends, and now they had a good one. He felt bad for this nice social-work lady who had lost her job for doing it. "But that's not what's up now. How many kids so far?"

George made a face. "Five that we know of, and by the way, it would be great if this guy would get his chlamydia treated. I'm fucking saying." He swallowed and then put his hand over his mouth, and it occurred to Ace that he'd sounded *just like* Ace in that moment.

Ace nodded. "These men don't thrive on kindness," he said softly, and George lost his self-consciousness and nodded. "Do we know who the social worker contacted?"

"Yeah," George said. "We got that much. Sheriff's Deputy Roy Kuntz. The social worker's supervisor told Barty that on the DL. She said that Christine—our worker—had done some cross-referencing and found that he was the brother of—"

"A local revival-tent preacher?"

"You're good at this," George said. "You should be a cop."

"That's just mean," Ace retorted, stung. "So we know the deputy at least is using influence to shut people up, and the preacher man's...." He swallowed. God, this did not sit right at all. "He's doing awful things to little girls. Do we got any other... I don't know. Proof? Evidence? Something?"

George sighed. "No. It's enough for us to know, but not enough for us to, you know, *prove*. Not with the guy in the sheriff's office silencing everything up."

Ace grunted, nodding. "What we need," he said after a moment, "is a—"

"We could ask Ernie," George said, and Ace shook his head.

"No. I mean, yes. We *will* ask Ernie before we put together a plan. I'm just... I'm not a cold-blooded killer, George, as much as this guy deserves it. I mean, I was *once*, but most other times it's been in the heat of battle, that sort of thing. But before we take out the preacher, we gotta see if his brother's in it with him. And once we've got some *evidence*, I got no problem taking 'em both out."

George's eyes were as wide as saucers, and Ace realized that Jai might not have prepared him for this level of criminal honesty.

"You'll kill them?" George asked in a tiny voice.

Ace stared at him. "Unless you were wanting me to turn them over to the police." He paused. "With all that that implies." He tried a winning smile then, and George stared at him some more. "Were you not prepared for me to tell you what we do?" he asked delicately.

"I just...." George floundered. "I *knew*," he said after a moment. "I-I just never had it put into so many words. And when I thought about it—" He shrugged. "—I gotta be honest. I sort of assumed Jai went and did it for you."

Ace gave him a kind look. "Jai's not our sin-eater, George. I mean, he's got no problem with some things, but I'm not sending him out to do anything I'm not prepared to do myself. Besides, Jai's easy to spot. Whether we assassinate them in blood or in reputation, it's gotta be a thing nobody here can be tied back into. But first...." He had some shit to think about.

Ace gnawed on his bottom lip for a second while George seemed to be getting his shit back together. "Listen, George," he said after a moment, "how about you take some cold sodas out to everybody. Send Ernie in here for some snacks, 'cause I'm gonna need him in a sec, but talk to Jai and Sonny about nothin' in particular, all right?"

George nodded. "What's your... what's your plan?" he asked after a moment.

"Rivers has people who do computers," Ace said briefly. "And Alba knows the law enforcement in these parts. What she don't know her family does. I'm gonna make a couple of calls and see if I can get some... I don't know. Confirmation. I believe you—and your social worker friend and all your hospital friends—don't get me wrong. But it would really suck if I decided to stick a knife in some guy's ribs and it was the wrong goddamned guy, you understand?"

George's nod got much more pronounced. He paused for a moment after standing up and walking to the refrigerator. "Ace?" he said softly.

"Yeah?"

"That's five little girls that we know about. In a year. God knows what we don't know about. I… I'm fine with killing if it comes down to that."

Ace peered up to Jai's "little George" and saw his gray eyes were troubled and red-rimmed. "I… suppose that makes me a bad person," George said. "I have faith in you, in Jai, that I just don't have in anybody else."

Ace smiled gently. "It's kind of you to say," he murmured. "This thing we do, where we 'take care' of the bad things around us—me, Jai, even Burton and Jason—we don't want it to touch you all, you understand? I wish you didn't know these things about me, even though you're a friend to me, a good partner to my friend. I wish you thought I was a nice guy and your boyfriend was just really fuckin' huge."

George laughed a little. "Yeah, I can see that. But I think my really fuckin' huge boyfriend wouldn't have been able to love me if I hadn't seen him for who he is. Even the scary parts. So it's fine."

Ace nodded. "Fair," he said. "So let me do some research and then talk to Ernie and get his take. I don't think we want Burton in on this. This may be a little too vigilante for him, particularly with Jason on his six. We try not to scare the civilians."

"But Ernie's okay?" George asked, perplexed.

"Hell, George, Ernie's *dead* for all the government knows. Ernie's the most Bat-Bastard of the lot of us, you think?"

George stared at him, but then he grabbed the cold sodas and walked outside toward the auto bay so Ace could get on the horn.

His first call was to Jackson Rivers.

"'Sup?" Rivers sounded like he was running, and Ace had to check the clock. Well, it was eight in the morning in Sacramento, in March—maybe not cold as balls but definitely brisk.

"Hey, you alone?"

"Yeah. Ellery had to go in early to prep for court. Henry's coming by in an hour to get me so we can go to the office. You got nothing but time, Ace. How they hanging?"

Ace grunted at the traditional male greeting. "They are trying desperately to crawl back into my body," he answered baldly. "I need some help here. I got nothing to steer by."

Jackson listened patiently while Ace outlined the situation, and somewhere in there, Ace heard sounds like Jackson was opening and closing a door. "Hello, No-thumbs," he called out. "Lucifer, for fuck's sake stop trying to jump off the couch. It only ends in tears."

Ace paused to chuckle. "How's he doing?"

"He's an idiot." Then there was some crooning of the type Ace only heard when Sonny was cuddling their tiny dog. "Aren't you, bubba? So stupid. If Billy-Bob didn't whack you upside the head, you'd forget you had to breathe."

Ace heard a very distinct "Meow" on the other end of the phone, and then Jackson spoke, his voice clear, and it sounded like he was sitting down. Ace could picture him in front of a computer or something, as he *hmm*ed.

"Okay, Ace. I got info on your scumbag preacher and his scumbag brother. What do you need to know?"

"Are there, I don't know," Ace said, "any signs that they've done this before? Is there any reason to, uhm, take direct action?"

Rivers grunted. "You mean like the preacher getting arrested twice in Mississippi and let off with a warning? That kind of thing?"

"Oh God," Ace muttered. "Yeah, like that."

"Or his brother getting accused of... oh God." River's voice, sarcastic and angry, dropped. "Yeah. Accused of—well, it says 'impropriety with a minor,' but it was enough to cost him his job in the same county his brother was arrested in, so it had to be something. Yeah, Ace. There's something here. Question is, what do you want to do with it?"

Ace grunted. "What you don't know, you don't gotta tell Ellery," he said. "Just, you know, if this goes south, I hope he'll still represent me."

"I did not hear that," Jackson said crisply. Then his voice dropped again. "You sure you want to go at it that way, Ace? I mean, we've got law enforcement. We could arrest these guys, and they'd live long, miserable lives in jail—or short, miserable lives—"

"Or they could be let out again. Chlamydia, Jackson. Babies with STDs." At that moment, the front door opened, and Ace saw Ernie slip in, glancing outside to where George was in earnest conversation with Sonny while Jai got to work on the red Kia with the replacement alternator that Sonny had been working on. "Hey, Ernie."

"Tell Jackson it's all good. We've got it handled." Ernie's eyes had that dreamy look that sometimes came with his gift. "Tell him there's a stranger he knows. Tell him the kittens in the RV are coming to town. It'll be fine."

"Did you hear that?" Ace asked.

"Oh dear God. Tell him to be careful!" Jackson gasped. "Oh shit, both of you be careful, you know? I gotta shower, but I can come down there—"

Ernie took the phone from Ace's hand and spoke firmly into it. "Jackson," he said gently, "this is an us thing. Don't worry. It'll never come knocking at your door."

And then he hung up.

Ace stared at him. "So, uhm, what do you know?"

Ernie's eyes were big and black and depthless, almost like an alien's when he looked at Ace. "I know you'll all live, and nobody's going to prison," he said. "And... and Cotton is coming to visit Jason, and something is coming with him that'll be a big help to what you and Jai have to do today."

"Have to?" Ace asked, because God—if God was out there—he needed to be sure.

Those depthless black alien eyes barely rippled. "Oh yes, Ace. It has to be done."

Ace grunted. "Well, we gotta figure out how so that jail thing isn't an option for anybody, you understand me?"

Ernie's irises receded a little, and he yawned. "Yeah. Can't go flying blind. I get it. Here, let me do some research on my laptop. You go out and spend some time with Sonny. We'll come up with a plan. Don't worry, Ace. Sometimes killing's got to be done. You were right about Jai—he's not our sin-eater. You are. Doesn't make you a bad person. Just makes you one of the people who does what's gotta." Ernie patted Ace's cheek. "Go outside. I'll do some surfing. You checked with Jackson, you're checking with me. It'll all be good."

Ace brightened, which must mean the decision had been made in his heart without his brain to guide it. "You know, if Jai and I treat this like a military op, we can pretend we're as good as Burton, right?"

Ernie's face softened. "You *are* as good as Burton," he murmured. "Now go."

Ace paused. "We're, uhm, not asking him in on this, right? He... I don't think he or Jason could get permission, and once they started asking, the whole thing would go south."

Ernie nodded. "I think he'll appreciate it when he finds out when it's done."

Oh wow. "Well, that's a weight off my mind," Ace declared. "Let me grab my own soda, and me and Sonny'll have a talk."

Part II—Preparation H and Goose Shit

SONNY TOOK Ace's Coke right out of his hand, chugged it all down, and gave him back the empty can.

"So there?" Ace asked, wondering if that was the extent of Sonny's pushback.

"So there," Sonny said sourly. "What am I supposed to say to this, Ace? No, don't get the bad man who's hurting little girls? 'Cause that would make me a complete asshole."

Ace fidgeted. "Technically, Sonny, I'm the one who's going to go do something illegal here. Doesn't that make me the asshole?"

"That makes you the hero, jackass," Sonny snapped. "And yeah, I gotta let you go be the hero. You're taking Jai?"

"If he wants to—"

"Da," Jai said from behind Sonny, as he finished up on the car Sonny had been badgering him about all day. "Ace doesn't go into danger without backup."

"That's kind of you," Ace told him, meaning it. "But you know us. We don't force nobody to do nothing, right?" He grimaced. "Particularly not with something like this."

Sonny scowled. "There you go, getting all noble. See, if it was me, I'd walk into that man's home with an AK-47 aimed at his nuts, and I'd shoot until there weren't no nuts. You probably got something quick and clean planned cause you're a goddamned humanitarian."

"Yeah, that's me," Ace said dryly. "I'm a murderer, Sonny, that's real fuckin' noble."

Jai popped up from behind the fucking car then like a goddamned jack-in-the-box. "Nyet," he said, and it was great for him that his voice sounded like the hammer fall of doom. "There is a difference between a murderer and an... an administrator of justice," he said, sounding proud that he'd gotten "administrator" right.

"A what?" Ace shook his head. "Never mind. What matters here is that no matter what happens, these little girls gotta be kept safe, and this guy, he can't hurt them no more. I wish I could say arrest him, but...." They'd seen how these things had gone in the press. The pain the parents went through, the pain the kids went through.

"That is not always the humane option," Jai pronounced. "No. I think this is our service to the public." He gave a smile that was downright disturbing. "Perhaps it is a calling."

Ace stared at him, not sure whether to be relieved or horrified. "You know, I'm done talking. While we talk, this guy is probably teaching a preschool class and thinking about his next meal. That don't sit well with me. Let's go make sure it's not what happens, okay?"

"Da," Jai said. "Which car?"

Ace sighed. "Ernie's." From a strictly bureaucratic point of view, Ernie had been unalive for a number of years. In the spirit of that, Ace, Sonny, and Burton had kept him in a series of vehicles that were also... unalive. They'd been rescued in parts from local auto wreckers or sold on the down-low or patched together by hope and faith and bubblegum. Between Sonny, Ace, and Jai, the vehicles were always safe to drive, but they were never traceable. They'd tried at the beginning to have a dedicated vehicle for Ernie and one for Sonny and Jai as well, but they seemed to go through cars, SUVs, trucks, minivans, what-have-you, at a truly astounding rate. As long as Ernie's current vehicle was unalive and untraceable, whatever could be found of the thing when its final adventure occurred would remain a mystery to the authorities forever and ever, amen.

And they always—always—had one if not two of them in the wings, waiting to be Frankensteined into unlife. And in the meantime, there was always Sonny's vehicle of choice—right now it was a small blue four-door sedan—that Ernie could drive until they had him another Ernie-mobile all prepped and ready to go.

"Do you think it will survive?" Jai asked, and Ace shook his head.

"No. If George is right—and we don't got no reason to doubt him—and the brother-in-law the deputy is in on this, I have a feeling we'll need to get rid of him too."

Jai's smile literally stretched from ear to ear. "You are a truly good friend," he said. "Do you have ideas?"

Ace glared at him, because if he did have any ideas, he wasn't going to share them in front of Sonny. Sonny worried enough about him as it was, and Sonny's agitation could be a dangerous thing.

"We'll make something up as we go along," he lied blandly. "We always do."

SONNY INSISTED on making them a good lunch, and then on putting ghost chips in Ace's and Jai's phones, which were a little gift from Burton and Jason for no particular reason. Jason had no idea really why any of them might not want to be tracked sometimes. What an entirely unexpected idea.

"Okay," Sonny muttered, "we're set." He scowled at Ernie. "Are we set?"

Ernie opened his mouth, closed it, cocked his head. "They're going to be fine," he said almost absently, "but you and I will have unexpected company." He waved a hand at Jai and Ace. "It's going to be okay. Is George going back to work?"

George was currently sitting in the front room in the air-conditioning, petting the dog disconsolately.

"I think we're going to have George stay here," Ace said. "If you're going to have company and all. I have a suspicion we shouldn't split up a lot today."

Ernie smiled, nodding. "I think that's a good idea," he said. "I think George will come in handy. I'll have him bring Duke out to the front office, and we can chat while Sonny gets to work on that damned minivan."

At this point in the garage, all minivans were "that damned minivan." Something about the chassis and the weight distribution made them prime candidates for needing things like new bushings and getting their belts replaced all the fucking time.

ACE AND Jai had the location pulled up on the tent-revival church— and yes, the main part was a big circus tent where people attended, but it was a parking lot away from the preacher's house. Ace had done a little bit of reading before he talked to Sonny. The preacher had a wife, a brittle middle-aged blond who was listed as the head of childcare and prayer meetings. Ace was pretty sure the house was being used as the church offices and day care—it would make sense—and he and Jai loaded into the car with nothing more than Ace's service pistol, Jai's favorite Glock, and Ace's knife. Ace assumed Jai had his own knife, but that had never been his style. Of course, Ace was fine with breaking tradition, as long as it got the job done and got them out of there without being recognized.

"You know," he said before he got in the vehicle, "this whole plan goes south if it turns out they've got some serious security and shit."

"They don't," Ernie said, cocking his head in that way he had when sometimes his gift answered shit he hadn't even thought of before. His eyes went blank, and when he blinked he said, "Do a little recon, find the secret staircase. It'll be fine. I think you'll be able to get shit done."

Ace and Jai met eyes. They'd planned to do a little recon. What soldier didn't? But they'd keep what Ernie said in mind and keep their eyes extra open.

The revival tent was on their side of Barstow, which was good, because even if there'd been anybody out, nobody would have seen them approach. Ace knew there was enough suburban life in Barstow to feed into a place like this: a giant white tent under a hazy spring sky, on top of a lawn made of mostly hardpan and crabgrass. He took perverse satisfaction at the crabgrass, though. After the impossible storm, when the desert had been flooded like a big muddy swimming pool, his own attempts at a lawn had died a muddy death. The only good part was that he'd rented a rototiller during the sweet spot, when everything was soft, and rototilled the area in front of the house, away from the road. It had been hard work in the evening, his body still recovering from… things… but he'd been able to plant some drought-resistant grass seeds there. A little bit of light watering and he was starting to get some hearty saw-tooth-edged blades of grass that were at least tall enough for the dog to piss on without stickers getting caught between its toes.

This asshole's entire driveway had turned to hardpan. There were even rocky little outcroppings of tire tracks from the last rain. Somehow this made Ace feel like his little lawn was a reward for clean living.

"Park behind the house, da?" Jai asked, studying his phone and interrupting Ace's musings. The hardpan driveway wrapped around the enormous newly painted Victorian mansion that seemed completely misplaced. Was this built here upon hope of water? Ace knew that at one point in time, all the water coming to this area had been diverted to Los Angeles. Had this once been a successful farm? Or had it hoped to be?

He had no idea, but as he followed Jai's directions and parked in front of an obviously added-on garage, next to a couple of dispirited minivans and one battered and ancient red Ford Fiesta, he did wonder what kind of car was inside the four-car garage. These were employees here, he thought, or parishioners here on church business.

"Recon?" Ace asked softly, and Jai nodded. "I'll go inside looking for my wife," he decided.

Jai nodded, then reached into the glove box and pulled out a small kit—multiple pairs of nitrile gloves, a packet of bleach wipes, and a distinctive red baseball hat with a deplorable slogan that nobody in their little group of people would be caught dead wearing, with the charming addition of little blond curls peeping out from under the edge.

"No," Ace said mutinously, glaring at the hat.

Jai glared back. "You are handsome," he said, but not like this was a good thing. "Women will notice you. You wear the hat, they'll be sorry they're married to another man who wears this hat."

"It's so dishonest," Ace whined. "And then I have to remember to bring it with me because it'll have my DNA all over it."

Jai stared at him as though bored.

"Fine," Ace muttered. "Let me go look for Sherry."

"Good name," Jai said with a nod. "You could be married to a Sherry."

"If I wasn't a gay assassin," Ace muttered, and Jai's chuckle followed him as he put on the hated ball cap and exited the vehicle.

He kept his head down as he walked up to the entryway with a sign that proclaimed Church Business and included an arrow. He noted two security cameras as he did so, one of them aimed right out in front of the house but not catching most of the parking lot by the garage, and one of them aimed at the foyer.

Yup. He was glad for the ball cap after all.

He thought about knocking and then figured Church Business probably eliminated that sort of need and simply pressed the old-fashioned lever on the front door. He slid inside and walked down the hallway, listening for sounds of people.

The interior of the house had been completely redone. The floors in the kitchen he passed were tile, and the hallway he was in boasted a bright, cheery laminate. The walls were white with brightly colored art—much of it featuring children playing or wearing adult clothes and looking somber or sleeping in flower costumes or….

Ace shuddered. Great. What was supposed to be a wholesome—if cloying—niche of commercial art had been rendered totally creepy by this man.

Fucking. Eww.

Then he heard it, what sounded like a large room with lots of space and the high-pitched chatter of children.

He kept walking and stuck his head in briefly, taking in several things at once.

It was a good-sized playroom, with kids in it from crawling-in-diapers age to reading-cardboard-books age (because what would Ace know about kids?) and a couple of women minding them. One woman, a little older, was setting down a tray with food and juice on it, along with little paper cups on a child-sized table.

"How's your Anna doing?" she asked one of the other women. This woman was cradling a girl, about five, looking like she'd stepped out of George's description. Blond, blue-eyed, precious as a porcelain figurine.

"Well, she stopped crying," the obviously distressed young mother said. "It was the darnedest thing. I told her that if she couldn't stop crying, we'd go get the pastor to see if he could make her feel safe, and… she went dead still. It was like his name was a magic spell."

She smiled at the older woman with troubled eyes, and the older woman gave her a carefully neutral stare that froze Ace's soul.

"We don't like to talk about magic," she said gently. "It's not Christian, you know."

Oh God. She knew. This woman knew what her husband was doing.

Ace had seen and done some awful shit, but he didn't ever remember having to repress his gag reflex with such absolute force. Some of his hesitancy about this whole enterprise drained away. This woman deserved to be caught up in the cleanup. Even if it just embarrassed her, caused her some inconvenience—or some nightmares—she deserved to have her husband's monster exposed to the world.

So women and children were there, got it, and after that the layout of the house was pretty easy. The playroom was a grand ballroom of sorts in this big old house. Next was a smaller place, an office, and that would be the—whatzit? The rectory? Whatever it was, Ace paused before walking down the hall to the door because he spotted the security cameras right above the doorframe.

Yup. This was the private office, Ace bet, and no doubt the preacher had the equivalent of a bell over the threshold to keep people from interrupting him.

At that moment the women started talking again.

"Is the reverend busy right now?" murmured another woman. "My second grader has been having some terrible nightmares, and I thought I'd talk to him about her. He's so wonderful with the children—I'd really love his guidance."

"I'm afraid he's deep in his afternoon prayer time," said the wife, who knew damn well why the children were crying and screaming in their sleep. "I'll wait until the red light over his office door goes off and then ask him if he's ready to see you."

"Thank you so much, Maureen," said the other mother. "You're a treasure."

Yeah, sure. Maureen was a fucking peach, Ace thought murderously. But one monster at a time.

The camera over the office door was the fish-eye kind, but Ace stood right outside its span if he knew his security—and at this point, he did.

He pulled out his phone and, glancing around to make sure there weren't any more of those little goodies parked inside the house, texted, Fisheye camera outside the hall of his office. Ideas?

Jai texted back, Secret staircase. Go back outside and climb to second window.

Ace blinked. How in the hell did you know that? he asked, although he was already doing what Jai told him. Ernie had mentioned the secret staircase, but Ace couldn't fathom the where to save his life. He burst outside, hoping the soft-soled boots he'd changed into had kept his steps from being too loud, and took a hard left after clearing the camera range on the front porch. Jai was on the other side of the house, hugging the shadows next to a chimney, holding a phone image that he must have taken while Ace had gone inside.

Yup. Ace could read the relatively simple infrared schematics, as well as judge the difference between the outside dimension and the inside dimensions.

"I'll be damned," he said, staring at the infrared image. "Why didn't you tell me you had this toy?"

Jai shrugged modestly. "I've been playing with it," he admitted. "Jason is a very helpful neighbor."

"You think?" Ace said, not entirely sure he was comfortable with how high tech they were at the moment, even if he was grateful. "All right, then, think you can give me a boost up the side of the chimney? See the ledge up there? Give me a running start and a boost up, and I can hook my fingers in that and pull myself up to the open window."

"Now who is bragging," Jai said sourly, but he'd tucked the phone in his pocket and was shooing Ace back to where he could make the run.

The trick to doing this sort of thing was to run balls out toward the wall you were planning to climb, without hesitation, and then use the springboard—in this case Jai's laced fingers—to change all that forward momentum to vertical momentum. The decorative ledge to the chimney was a good twelve feet off the ground, but Jai's laced fingers were held about three feet above the ground, and Ace was around five ten. A good hard run, a foot down to vault, and perfect trust in Jai, of course, and Ace found himself catapulted into the air and grabbing at the ledge with hands made hard and strong with manual labor. Whoop, whoop! A few swings of his legs and hips and he let go of the ledge and grabbed the window, hauling himself up into what appeared to be a guest bedroom with a few grunts and a plop onto a hard-tiled floor.

Ace glanced around the room itself and had to fight his bile again.

It was a kid's room. It had clowns and circus tents and rainbow colors on the walls, on the drapes, on the sheets. And stains on the sheets that Ace didn't want to think about, ever.

The staircase—little more than a crawl space between the back of the house and the brick chimney that probably never got used—was accessible through what looked like a closet door from a kid's movie on the outside but didn't even pretend to have stuff hung in it on the inside.

Who would go inside?

The space was wide enough for Ace's shoulders and chest as he walked quietly down the stairs, his boots not even creaking the carpeted planks underneath them.

He got to the bottom of the stairs, saw the closed door, and paused to put on his gloves.

Somebody was in the office. He could hear somebody making dog noises to himself—little grunts and ohs like a dog finding the perfect position, not to mention a repeated licking noise…. No, was that flesh on flesh? Or was that…?

Eww.

"Baby…." The voice was a man's, whispered harshly like somebody calling out in passion, and Ace looked through the old-fashioned keyhole and sucked in a breath.

The man was sitting with his back to Ace, staring at the computer screen and, Ace was pretty sure, jerking off.

The images on the computer screen were taken from that horrible room upstairs, and….

Ace saw enough to be sickened and then closed his brain.

This man had to die.

It was so easy. Frighteningly easy.

The preacher man had his earbuds on, which helped a lot. Ace opened the door quietly and slid out into the room, aware when the man—midforties, innocuous "white middle management with a comb-over" kind of guy—saw his reflection in the computer screen, because he jerked right before Ace put his hand over the good reverend's mouth and whispered, "If you scream, everybody will see what you're looking at."

The man relaxed in his grip, which made everything easier.

He was wearing a short-sleeved button-down shirt, and Ace kept one hand over the guy's mouth while he sighted the blue artery on the inside of his white arm, creeping into his elbow.

Ace pulled his knife out with his other hand, spun it open and made the cut so quickly the man barely had a chance to struggle, to moan against his hand. He stopped, satisfied when the wound started to spray.

"Shh…," he murmured, using the preacher's body as a shield as his lifeblood pumped out alarmingly. "I'll let you go in a second. I will. But first I'm going to have you unlock your phone for me. Don't scream or I'll slit your throat, okay?"

He got an excited nod in response, and Ace watched as that wound kept spraying the desk, the computer, the terrible images on the screen. It didn't matter. Reverend… Kuntz—that was what George had said the pastor's brother's name was, Ace remembered—probably thought he would get a chance to clean up, but he wouldn't. Ace had nailed his brachial artery dead to rights, and the good reverend wasn't going to be all right. And soon, another minute, maybe, he would realize he was dead.

He had enough juice left now to grab his phone from the desk and punch the code into the screen. Ace kept his position, one hand over the mouth, the other on the knife, as he memorized the six-digit code. Keeping the hand in place, he grabbed the phone and used one hand to pull up what he needed.

"Okay," Ace murmured, scrolling through recent contacts. "Donald Kuntz, your brother?"

He got a weak nod in return.

"Ooh," Ace said, finding the text stream that featured stills of some of the same dirty work that the preacher had on his computer. Well. Nothing like knowing your next target. Ace had to swallow bile again before taking a deep breath and moving on.

"You feeling a little woozy there, champ?"

He got another nod, and he felt the tension in the man's body begin to drain. He knew bleeding to death was supposed to feel like a burning cold sensation as the life trickled out, followed by a terrible lassitude. He hoped this fucker could think of all the ways people would see him, naked, helpless, and corrupt.

"You should be. See all that blood pooling on your lap, on your limp little STD wiener, on the floor?"

"Yeah," croaked his victim.

"That's gonna be about three pints, going on four. You're about thirty seconds away from bleeding to death there, champ. And you're naked and jerking off to kiddie porn featuring that same tiny little white wiener. Everyone's going to know. Everyone."

And with that, Ace stepped to the side and took a picture of the sorry sight, including a side view of the computer screen and what was on it and the man's limp, blood-pooled penis. He held the camera away from his body, away from his face, and out of the reflection of the computer, because some of those crime shows got it right.

"No!" cried the preacher, but he'd lost enough blood to hamper his organ function, and his lungs were already laboring for oxygen.

"I'll just send this to your brother," Ace said, doing that. "And to the AP news and the staties."

Ace had only just learned that California had its own bureau of investigation. It tickled him to text them the picture. He thought momentarily about dropping the phone in Kuntz's blood-soaked lap but changed his mind at the last minute and used a bleach wipe to clean it off before slipping it into his pocket and sliding back through the doorway and up the secret stairs.

He took the stairs three at a time, taking off one pair of gloves and replacing it with another, putting the soiled gloves in the plastic bag provided in the little kit. He double-checked his body then, pleased. The knife had blood on it, but he'd moved quick enough—and stayed on the far side of the victim enough—to have avoided most of the spray.

Of course Ace knew there was always a mistake—had he left a hair follicle on the premises? A skin cell? Those cop shows made it look like all they did was dump evidence in a processor and get out a result. But Ace had always suspected—and Jason had confirmed it—that the machinery for DNA tests and fingerprints moved very slowly. Ace and Jai would be on the far side of the county before the first cop car got there, and since Ace had a plan for that, he thought that maybe what the good reverend had been doing when he got killed would be far more interesting than his death.

In fact, Ace sort of wished he'd been able to leave his beloved knife behind to make it look like a suicide, but they'd been through too much together, him and this blade.

After stashing the bloody gloves in their plastic bag in his pocket, he approached the open window from that gawdawful bedroom on the top floor cautiously. When he peered out, Jai peered back, curiosity writ large on his broad face.

"So?" he asked.

"So, think I can jump down without breaking my ankle?" he replied.

"You have new gloves?" When Ace nodded, Jai added, "Then wipe off the ledge from your trip up, and then dangle. I will help you down. Like circus performer, yes?"

Well, better than waiting here for screams and such.

After doing the wiping off thing with the bleach, Ace crawled out of the window and hung by the ledge for a moment until he felt Jai's hands around his ankles.

"Keep legs locked until you touch ground," Jai said. "And let go."

Ace had the idea. He kept his body stiff and dropped, and Jai guided him down, slowing his descent. Ace relaxed his ankles and knees when he got to the ground so he didn't snap anything out of joint, and Jai steadied him just enough for the two of them to turn and run.

Ace followed Jai's guide for where the camera radius was, knowing it would look like a big blond country boy walked into the house on the security cameras and then walked out—and nothing else. Those "home movies" the preacher had been looking at had been shot with a cell phone. Ace had checked twice while the bastard had been bleeding out. No cameras in the rectory—probably a tripod. And there hadn't been a damned thing in the circus room of every kid's nightmares.

The fucker had probably thought he was protecting himself, keeping that sort of evidence confined to his phone, his home computer, and whatever network of pedophiles and scum eaters he engaged with. But no security cameras on the inside of that room, nor on the inside of the office.

Outside, as a warning system.

Not inside, where the feed could incriminate him.

Detectives—good ones—might figure out how the intruder had gotten in and out, but there would be no pictures of Jasper Atchison that could be used as evidence.

No pictures that would identify him at all.

He and Jai climbed into the car in a rush, and Ace was peeling out of the driveway before either of them were properly belted in.

He kept on the hated hat and sweaty gloves, though, because he had an idea.

"What next?" Jai asked, sounding pumped.

Ace opened the phone and handed it over. "Look up his brother's contact number," Ace said. "Track his phone. He's going to be racing down this road, coming toward us, and I've got an idea for how to take him out. We're only halfway done."

"How do we get home?" Jai asked, apparently reading Ace's mind.

"Maybe you want to text Ernie?" Ace told him, and he heard Jai's satisfied grunt.

Yup, they were only halfway done, and the next part? The next part had some fun in it. Maybe some finesse too.

Part III—Flying Cars

"SONNY, CHECK my phone," Ernie said, pointing to the device on the dash, which was charging.

Sonny did, punching in the code like the good friend he was. "Fuck," he muttered and twirled his finger. "One-eighty."

"Fuck," Ernie replied. "What's it say?"

"We'll need a ride outside of Barstow," Sonny read. "If you see a sheriff's vehicle charging with lights and sirens, pull off onto the side of the road and let it pass."

Ernie slow blinked. "Oh Lord," he muttered. "Yeah. Yeah. This is gonna be tricky." He didn't know exactly what Ace had planned, but given what they knew of the preacher's deputy brother, Ernie had a feeling the kittens in the RV were the only creatures with a prayer of staying safe. "Signal our friend and hold on," he muttered, and then, after making sure there wasn't a vehicle near the horizon—or one behind them, other than their friend in the RV—he yanked the emergency brake and then hit the gas while there was still momentum left from the one-eighty. Next to him, Sonny whooped, holding on to the dashboard, pure excitement etched on his peaked face.

"You're just like Ace now!" he crowed.

Ernie gave him a quick grin, pleased with the compliment. Ahead he saw the RV, with a very surprised Mr. Christiansen in the front. Hurriedly, Ernie rolled down his window and slowed down enough to shout, "Change of plan. Gotta go pick someone up."

"I'll follow you!" he said, and Ernie was about to say, "No, meet us later!" when he saw cars approaching ahead *and* behind. He nodded tersely and floored it and let their guest figure out how to do his own one-eighty. There was a sturdy shoulder on either side of the road. With any luck the Winnebago wouldn't bog down and end up stretched across the highway like a big barricade.

The ride toward Barstow continued in a tense silence until suddenly Sonny spoke up.

"Shit," he said.

"What?" Ernie's gift was working—it gave him a general sense of well-being and accomplishment, which meant that whatever was going to happen, his family would probably end up being safe. But it wasn't giving him any specifics, which it tended to do sometimes, particularly when... well, when Ace was involved. Perhaps it was because Ace tended to think on his feet. Sure, he could plan—and his plans could be detailed and specific and successful— but he could also pull a rabbit out of a hat if he needed to, and maybe that combination of intelligence, instinct, and volatility puzzled the forces of the universe on the whole. It was like karma decided "Yes, Aces *are* wild, and this particular Ace is too wild to track, so let's all just cross our fingers and hope, okay?" So far it had worked, mostly, for Ace and Sonny, and in fact it was probably the reason Ace *had* Sonny, because Sonny was volatile enough on his own to negate all the plans in the world. But Ace's ribs had only healed completely in the last month or so, and Ernie and the others were still raw from when Ace's decision to hold on to Sonny and hope for the best had nearly killed them both.

"If we're picking them up, that means your car's toast. And...." Sonny grunted. "Goddammit. Jai and Ace are too damned big to sit in the back seat."

Ernie grunted. "Well, maybe they'll ride with Mr. Christiansen and the cats," he said philosophically. It did seem like a particularly serendipitous placement of a large vehicle and two large men. Then, wistfully, "What do you suppose is going to happen to my car?" On the one hand, Ernie would love to get a big, dependable luxury SUV with the kind of air-conditioning system that would leave frost on his eyebrows in 120-degree heat, but on the other? Being dead was nice. Nobody official knew—or cared—about his skinny psychic ass, and he'd never had so much freedom or so much family in his life. He'd settle for the beater- mobiles (although Ace and Sonny *always* made sure they had at least *some* air-conditioning because they loved Ernie and they lived in the middle of the fucking desert.)

"I'm not sure," Sonny said in response to the question. "But I've got a 2015 Kia Sportage all ready for you. All it needs is a trip to the Maaco guys in Bakersfield. Maybe you can even pick a color this time."

Ernie smiled happily. "Aww—that's sweet. Thanks, Sonny."

"Well, sorry about the Impala," Sonny said soberly. "It was a good friend."

Ernie had never been particularly sentimental about automobiles, but he was always fascinated when Sonny showed his softer side. Everybody in their little group needed reminding that underneath the borderline personality and the potential for explosion, there beat the heart of a kid who was probably younger than Ernie and whom life had left far more damaged. Sonny had *earned* the right to anthropomorphize a beat-up Chevy Impala, because odds were good he'd never had a teddy bear or favorite Matchbox car, and *every* boy should have a teddy bear or favorite toy.

"I'm sure it'll die a good death," Ernie said in comfort, and Sonny nodded happily. Ernie had once had a conversation with George—and then George's friend Amal—in which they'd realized they were the only people in their little group really conversant with pop culture in any capacity. George and Amal knew about *Star Trek* and *Star Wars* and sitcoms and such. It was too bad, Ernie thought now. He felt like Sonny deserved to know about Klingons, and how they lived their life by a code, because sometimes he thought Sonny would be more comfortable as a Klingon than as an auto mechanic making his living in the desert.

At that moment, Ernie saw lights in his rearview. He didn't hear the siren yet, but the cop's SUV had already passed Christiansen, Ernie assumed, because he was *flying*. Ernie waited until the car was a good fifteen lengths behind him before slowing and moving to the road shoulder, allowing the vehicle to soar right by.

"Why'd we do that?" Sonny asked. "He could've passed."

Ernie grunted. "Because if I'm right, I've kept my license plate out of the camera range. I have a feeling that's a good thing. Now text Ace and say we saw his boy."

"*I'm* his boy," Sonny growled. "We just saw an asshole who's gonna get his payback."

"Sure," Ernie told him. "But say it so it can't be held against you in a court of law."

Sonny chuckled. "That I can do."

Ernie kept going—slower than the SUV but still going seventy. He was not surprised when the phone buzzed and Sonny read aloud, "Don't work to catch up with him. Maybe stop and get a soda if you pass a gas station."

Ernie grunted. "Where in the hell does he think we're going to find a gas station?"

Sonny chuckled. "We'll just slow down and leave it at that."

Ernie shook his head and drove on.

"THEY ARE on their way," Jai said decisively, and Ace grunted.

"Did you tell them to hold back?"

"Da."

"Did you tell them to avoid the cop car like the plague?"

"Da."

"Did you tell them to—"

"Neither of these men are stupid," Jai told him gently. "Have faith."

"I am going to do a *very* dangerous thing," Ace told him. "I am not excited about myself as it is, but this—my potential to hurt somebody just standing by is *huge*, and if it's somebody I care about…. Who are you calling?"

"Burton," Jai said.

"*Burton?*" Ace's hands grew clammy on the wheel. "We were supposed to keep him out of this!"

"Ernie thinks he's on a helicopter, headed this way. Oh, hold—"

Ace suppressed the urge to scream, which meant that he was *not* okay with all the things he'd done today, which made what they were doing *now* even more important.

"Lee," Jai said succinctly, which was like code that meant "I am not talking to the military lieutenant, I am talking to our friend."

"What's doing?" Burton said tersely over the speaker. "Jason and I are following Sonny and Ernie in a *helicopter*, mind you, and watching a big RV follow them in turn. I don't know what the deal is, but Ernie had one of his feelings about a cold fish—"

Oh. That. "He said it'd be fine," Ace said. "Cotton's on his way home. Can Jason hear us?"

"Yes, Ace, because otherwise you wouldn't be hearing *me* over a Black Hawk's rotor wash. What's up?"

"Nothing. Go away," Ace said, feeling proud of himself.

"Ace is going to kill a man who needs killing," Jai said, and Ace scowled, but he didn't take his eyes off the road. "He would like to not kill anybody else. We need a clear shot."

"You're fired," Ace said succinctly.

Jai gave him a brilliant, disturbing smile. "I will work for free," he said. "George makes *very* good money, and I am practically a kept man."

"Bad man?" Burton said uncertainly from the phone, and Ace pictured the blood pooling from the brachial artery, the pictures of naked children whimpering on the bed, the atrocities he wished he could scourge from his brain after two seconds of sick comprehension.

The flabby white nakedness of a man who counseled children.

"A *very* bad man," Ace said darkly, hoping he could manage to *not* vomit. "I.... Don't make me tell you what I've seen," he finished at last, his voice bleak.

"What do you need from us?" Jason Constance said, and Ace had a fleeting thought for sound systems and their genius.

"We are just south of Barstow," Ace said, "heading east toward Vegas. I'm not seeing a lot of cars out here. There should be a police vehicle traveling with lights and siren, going about a hundred miles per hour, maybe about twenty miles from us. That's our bad guy. I'm turning Ernie's car into a missile and T-boning him from across the road at a steep angle. Do I have an opening to do that, or do I have to find another way?"

There was a silence while Burton and Jason digested that, and then Ace heard Jason Constance on the radio while Burton barked orders at *him*.

"Step on it, Ace. We're setting up roadblocks five miles north of you and twenty miles south. You've got about two miles before you need to pull off and set up or he'll blow right by you. Jason and I will be your exfil—"

"Ernie's on his way," Ace said. "Make sure you let him and the guy behind him through."

"The guy behind him?" Burton asked in surprise.

"Yeah, we were supposed to meet him about something. I don't know, Lee, I've been a little busy!"

"What's the guy behind him driving?" Burton asked suspiciously.

Ace had been aware of the text streams, even if he'd had his hands on the wheel, so to speak. "A Winnebago with two kittens. I mean, the kittens are on the inside." He paused. "Sonny said they're cute."

There was silence on the other end. "And Ernie *cleared* this Winnebago?" Burton asked, sounding dubious and surprised and a little bit scared all at the same time.

"Da," Jai said. "We are supposed to meet with the man inside. Ernie says he needs sanctuary."

Ace hadn't heard this. "Sanctuary?" he asked.

He could actually feel Jai's shrug rocking the little car. "I suggested he use the hookups for the house that is mostly finished," Jai said.

"Guys," Burton said, sounding shocked. "This guy is bad news. He could be a *professional killer*, do you understand?"

Ace grunted. "Does that mean he'll take jobs us amateurs won't?" he asked. "Because I gotta tell you, I would win a whole lotta races if it meant I could not have to live today all over again."

"Last time I checked," Jai said, "some of us *were* professionals. Did I get that wrong?"

"Did you not get paid?" Ace asked, because he was pretty sure Jai had made good money as an enforcer.

Jai shrugged. "Da, but there was no choice of targets." His next smile showed teeth again. "I like choices. They make life interesting."

"You two can shut up now," Burton grumbled.

"Please," Jason added. "And get ready to pull over. You've got a mile left. We'll spot you and tell you when."

Ace's stomach tightened, and he noted the area Burton and Jason indicated, ahead and off the road. He gunned the motor, pulled a one-eighty on the shoulder, and threw the car into neutral, pausing as the dust settled.

"Think we could put it on a jack, brick the gas pedal, and kick it over?" he asked.

"Da," Jai said. "I will jack the back end, but you need to position it better while I search for a brick."

Ace nodded tersely and set about drawing a perfect vector in his mind that would take the vehicle down the road and into the oncoming SUV's left quarter.

"He's going about a hundred," Ace said. "Think he'll see it coming?"

"Listen," Jai told him, "if this should fail, we have launched Ernie's shitty car into the desert and cleared the way for Burton to shoot a man from a helicopter and fly away. This way is better—no bullet, no Burton—but if we fail, we are not a one-man squad."

"I really wanted to do this by myself," Ace admitted fractiously. "A decision like this—"

"But," Jai said, as though Ace had *meant* to stop there, "a decision like this should *not* be made by one person. It should not be made by a thousand people either," he said, thinking about it. "There is no good way to make a decision like this. These were bad men, hurting children who could not fight back. They had power, and they were using it to continue doing bad things. And anybody who went up against them...." He shrugged. "It is a sign of faith that Burton trusts us to only do this to the very worst of men. This vector looks good. I lied. I shall jack up the vehicle, but *you* find a brick. We should hurry."

They barely made it. First they wiped the thing down with the bleach wipes and gathered the offending disguise and the dead man's phone and the fake registration that Burton had made for Ernie in case he ever got pulled over. The rest of the car was fairly clean. Ace found his "brick"— more like a boulder—to put on the gas pedal just as Jai got the back end of the car jacked. The changing kit came with a wedge for the front wheel, and Ace thanked all the gods for that, because otherwise he would have had to look for *two* boulders, and they would have missed their window.

First, Ace grabbed a bungee cord from the back and fixed the steering wheel to the seat. Unsatisfied, he broke off the windshield wipers and jammed them through the opening in the steering wheel and against the steering column and the windshield. If it wouldn't have left a festival of DNA, he would have used his own belt, because it was *imperative* the damned thing continue in a straight line.

Once Jai had the car jacked up, Ace turned it on again, using his core and touching the floor with his still-gloved fingertips as he leaned in and pressed the ignition button. He had to brace the steering wheel with one hand as he shifted the vehicle from Neutral to Drive, making sure he neither changed the direction nor accidentally put the damned thing in reverse. Then, just as they could barely make out the lights of the SUV over the horizon, Ace dropped the boulder on the gas pedal, watching as the RPMs shot to the red zone from the weight. He stepped back and shut the door carefully, then put one foot on the wedge before pulling out his phone.

"Burton, you nearby?"

"We see your Deputy Scumbag" came the reply. Burton and Jason had obviously been talking to Ernie while Jai and Ace had gotten busy. "He's coming fast, Ace. Get 'er done."

Ace glanced at Jai, who nodded, and then they both stared at the car while Ace's brain was doing the same thing it did when he drove fast. Vectors, acceleration, deceleration, margin for error, the time it would take to dump the car, the time it would take for the wheels to catch, the time—

"*Now!*" he shouted, kicking the wedge out from in front of the tire. Behind him, Jai hit the back end of the vehicle with *all* of his weight, toppling it off the jack even as they both jumped out of the way.

The car took off, peeling out a little as the wheels caught, and kicked gravel back to where Jai had been standing. The car got traction and the fixes on the steering wheel held, and Ace watched its shallow vector as it continued *almost* like it was using the oncoming lane, but shallower, shallower, shallower....

The SUV tried to swerve at the last moment, but by then the car was too close and traveling too fast, the engine whining in protest at the merciless boulder on the gas.

The collision was brutal and spectacular, Ernie's sedan ramming the driver's door at the corner panel and then flipping over the hood of the SUV, spiraling out into the desert while the SUV collapsed on itself and its driver, the airbag cushioning the blow but not nearly enough.

The SUV swerved off the road, rolling again and again on the shoulder, coming to rest on a pile of tumbleweeds as the momentum of the collision finally waned.

Ace and Jai stared at the destruction in absolute awe, listening to the sudden silence as bits and pieces of both vehicles clattered to the ground after sailing as far as a hundred yards away.

"Holleee chit...." Ace breathed, his blood up with exhilaration *watching* a thing like that.

"You are a good friend," Jai said, his face alight with unholy glee. "Only the best of men would give me such a thing. I shall treasure this always."

Ace let out a horrified yelp of laughter, and then to both their surprise, they watched as the SUV caught fire.

"No...," Ace said, transfixed as the flames began to lick from the undercarriage to the door.

"Da!" Jai responded in absolute delight.

"All them shows say this shit never happens."

"Quick," Jai said. "Give me the evidence. The phone, the hat—give me."

Ace did, and Jai dashed as close to the pending inferno as he could reasonably get, weighted the hat down with a rock, and hurled it like a bolo through the shattered passenger window before dropping the well-bleached phone on the shoulder of the highway and hauling ass back to the other side of the road.

The explosion happened just as he arrived and turned around to look, the concussion knocking them both on their asses. They scrambled up, panting, and Ace managed a coherent thought in the middle of the *whoosh* of the holocaust.

"Good thinking," Ace said. "My DNA and shit should be toast, right?"

"Da. And this way they will find the phone and investigate. We shall cross our fingers. Police are slow, but many are not terrible. It would be good if things like this happened less often."

"I am saying," Ace grumbled, and then he swiped his hands through his sweaty hair and turned back the way the deputy's SUV had come. "See anything?" he asked hopefully as they both looked toward the horizon.

"Nyet," Jai said, but neither of them minded much. They continued striding away from the conflagration, and they were about two football-field lengths away when they heard popping noises and other explosions.

"Shit!" Ace muttered, turning toward the vehicle. He saw several more explosions, and he and Jai started to jog. They'd *both* forgotten about the lockbox of weapons that were often carried in the back of a cop shop, and damn if they weren't lucky those things hadn't gone up when they were closer.

They were continuing their jog, both of them grimacing when more munitions went off, when Ace's pocket rang.

"Can we let in rescue vehicles yet?" Burton asked.

"The shit in the back's still going off like the Fourth of July," Ace told him. "Give it another fifteen minutes. No reason to kill anyone besides the scumbag and the car."

Burton grunted. "Ace?"

"Yeah?"

"I would have loved to help more on this one."

"We were *trying* to keep you guys out of trouble," Ace complained. "You're real assassins. We're just vigilante bullshit."

Burton grunted. "They were bad men," he said at last. "You did a public service."

"Kids with chlamydia," Ace said bluntly. "These fuckers died too goddamned fast."

Far behind them now a burst of ammunition went off, distance reducing the sound to popcorn, and Ace brightened.

"But on the plus side, Jai and I did get to see an explosion," he said. "Wait until I tell Sonny that sometimes shit *does* go boom!"

Far off he heard the *whap-whap-whap* of the chopper blades, and Burton said, "Well shit—you're right. Keep walking, guys. As soon as the roadblocks ease up, your ride'll be on its way. Great explosion, though."

"Right? And Jai threw my disguise into the thick of it before it went. As long as Ernie gets through first, I think we might be okay."

Part IV—Bird's Eye View

MY MAN looked tired.

I mean, me and Ernie had seen a semieventful day. We'd had to put the Closed sign up in the shop window with the little clock that said we'd be back by three. I mean, we probably would, but I couldn't remember the last time I'd done that, so that was sort of scary.

And now we had that guy in the Winnebago with the cats. He seemed like an okay guy—Ernie said to be careful, but I say any guy who likes cats and travels with 'em has got to be a good guy. It's like Duke. You know people are okay if they treat your dog right.

But right now we were five miles beyond the roadblock and two miles beyond the smoking hulk of the dead cop's SUV. His body had still been burning as we'd passed, and Ernie had said he hoped the flames were hotter in hell.

Ernie's got a good heart.

In front of us, Jai and Ace were striding down the road. Their backs were straight and their shoulders were high—so were their chins. Anybody else looking at them would see two hard-eyed men who, in spite of Jai's height, seemed suited to have a companionable brisk walk together, like friends. They looked like they could spring into action at a moment's notice, and I could be proud of that.

But I could almost *feel* the weariness wafting off Ace in a slow oily cloud. Jai, I thought, was like me. He was indifferent to what they'd done. Ace wore these things hard, but he wouldn't share unless I asked him.

I was trying harder and harder to be the guy who'd ask him.

Ernie pulled to the side of the road, and I rolled down the window. Ace leaned over, resting his fingertips on the edge, and grinned.

"You here to offer two footsore cowpokes a ride?" he teased, and I glared.

"Kiss," I said, pointing to my cheek.

He raised his eyebrows in surprise but went for it. I turned my head at the last second and took his lips. He sighed, some of his weariness slipping into me, but I was stronger than I looked. I could take it.

When he straightened up, he seemed a little more like my Ace. "Appreciated," he said. He went to rub his knuckle on my cheek, but he caught sight of something—a bit of blood spatter, I think, up on his arm—and drew back.

I captured his finger and kissed it and let it go.

"So," Ace said, like he was trying to pull his brain together, "who's our friend behind you?"

"He wants sanctuary," Ernie said. "I, uhm, think he's an assassin."

Ace's eyebrows went up. "You sure?"

Ernie nodded. "I got Burton vibes," he said frankly, and that was funny because I always forgot Burton was an assassin.

"Military? Pro? What?" Ace asked.

Ernie shrugged. "If I thought he was dangerous, I would have had Sonny crack him over the head and given the kittens to Cotton. But he's still alive, and Cotton thinks he's coming to visit later this weekend. I figure you're the best judge of character. Just remember, that Winnebago's got a long way to go in the desert for us to torch it and not have anybody notice."

Ace nodded and scrubbed his sweaty hair with his hands. "What's for dinner tonight?" he asked me.

"I got enough chicken to fry some for a bunch of us," I told him.

He gave a small smile. "Well, if this guy's not an asshole, we'll ask him by. Be sure to check on George when you get home. He… he shouldn't be alone, and I guess me and Jai might be a little longer."

Ernie nodded. "I'll do that. We should get going to the shop. I know Sonny's got work to do."

"Fair," Ace said. He gave me a soft smile. "You all did real good today. Thanks for the update."

I grinned at him. "See you in a few," I said, and he winked and waved.

As he and Jai were walking away, I heard Jai say, "Thank you for thinking about George."

I didn't even have to see Ace shrug or hear his "He had a rough morning" to know Ace wasn't going to make a big thing out of his kindness.

"Do you really have enough chicken to fry?" Ernie asked.

I grunted. "I may need another flat," I admitted. "And frankly? Some help if I'm gonna finish that one car before the owners come back."

"Tell you what," Ernie said happily. "How about we have George mind the front, and I'll bring my big fryer over after my nap."

Oh Lord—I'd about forgotten Ernie's nap, which happened an hour earlier, usually. "You're doing good!" I said. "You're usually wiped out."

Ernie shrugged. "My gift didn't have much to do today," he said philosophically. "The humans took care of the bad shit."

"That's good," I said. "Not that I don't like your witchy stuff, Ernie, but it's good we don't put too much on your shoulders either."

"And this is why I make chicken for you all," Ernie said happily. "And maybe some pastries."

I glanced behind us as he pulled out and saw Ace and Jai disappearing into the Winnebago. "Think our friend's going to be eating with us?" I asked, and I wasn't consulting the gift, just making some nonwitchy predictions.

"Either that or I'm getting two more kittens," Ernie speculated. Just when I got what that might mean, he flashed a smile at me. "But I'm thinking I'll be putting on some more chicken."

I smiled. It was fine. I used to be freaked out about more people. Alba had about sent me into the stratosphere, but now I missed her. Jai had pissed me off at first, but now he was my best friend. I hadn't understood Ace's need for Burton in his life, but now I got the two of them as buddies. And God, not one of us would be sane without Ernie or George. Even George's friend Amal was welcome, although I think he'd probably be a little shocked at what Ace and Jai just did. Burton's boss was okay, though, and Cotton of course. I didn't find many people I wanted to take care of, but I figured Cotton was like Duke, or Ernie's kittens. You be kind to all of 'em and they'd smile at you, and the world would seem better.

Whoever this Christiansen guy was in the Winnebago, I suspected that if he survived the trip to Victoriana, he might be sticking around a bit.

Part V—Arctic Fish

WHATEVER ERIC Christiansen—not his real name—had been thinking when he'd stopped to help the angelic young man with the flat tire, this moment had not been included.

He thought he'd been prepared for almost anything as he followed the borderline personality and the clairvoyant—for that, surely, must have been what the young man with the dark hair and the deep blue eyes had been. Christiansen had encountered a few psychics in his time. Even killed one whose brain had been crawling with spiders. He recognized the blown pupils, the particular twitch of the shoulders, the absolute global understanding when he touched the flesh of somebody who understood him.

So, he'd thought, the clairvoyant is the leader. This surprised him. They often weren't—so much of their minds were invested… elsewhere.

But then the young psychic had taken his orders from someone else.

So Christiansen had followed him, thinking, *This is it. I'm going to meet the gang. The pit of assassins that has been taking out everybody from drug dealers to mob kingpins to petty criminals in this barren stretch of land.* He was accustomed to snake pits. He figured he'd be fine in this one. All he had to do was reveal his resumé and voila! Everybody would be so impressed by him—or so in need of his services—that he could indulge himself in some much-needed rest.

But he was trying to quit, dammit!

That had been the entire point of taking the contract on Rivers and Cramer. The money… oh, the money had been *choice*. But more than that had been the chaos! He wasn't fond of chaos as a whole. His recreational vehicle was luxuriously appointed and very clean. The cabinets were real wood, the bed had the finest of mattresses, the sheets were 500-count cotton.

Even his cat beds were luxe, and the bathroom was big enough to accommodate a large man—or, well, two. Two large men.

Because while he wasn't fond of chaos, he'd craved the cover that chaos would have given him to get out of this highly lucrative, highly soulless life.

Backing out of the Rivers/Cramer contract had cost him dearly—and not just the money he'd lost. He'd… he'd been so infatuated with Jules. The boy had been pretty, old European aristocracy, and he'd had this swagger. Eric loved a little bit of swagger.

Unfortunately that swagger had translated into cockiness and disrespect, and one little hint of that, and not only was Eric's reputation *destroyed*, but Eric's life was probably not worth much either. Everybody would have been gunning for him. *Everyone*. Eric had made that clear in their last discussion, and Jules? He'd… shrugged.

"Everyone dies. What matters is if we get paid for it," he'd said, with such cavalier certainty that Eric felt in his bones the wrongness of their profession. Eric had always tried to maintain certain standards. No innocent lives. He lived by it. He researched to make sure he wasn't blindly killing random people but performing an important public service. Certainly people were flawed. A cheating spouse deserved *karma*, not a bullet. But a hard-core abuser who would inevitably kill his wife and children? *That* man could have a serious personality revision with a well-timed shot of insulin and no sugar in sight.

"Please don't take this contract," Eric had asked him simply. "It would be a shame if that were true."

He'd known. He'd known the Snowman would venture out into the cold for the lawyer and his fascinating PI friend. So he'd done what he'd needed to do, unmindful of the moments flashing behind his eyes of Jules's supple, muscular body writhing beneath his own, or the gleeful smile gracing those boyish features when Jules had been breathless and dripping come from his mouth, his asshole, his cock, the excitement of sex all the high he seemed to need.

Eric didn't regret that kill so much as he regretted losing the companion. The companion—and the sex—had been fun and intense and invigorating.

But he'd also hated cats, a thing he'd let Eric know when Eric had arrived in his condo with the two kittens currently curled up in the pet bed Eric had been keeping under the table of the RV. He'd made an entire little haven down there, with food and water dispensers (the better not to spill) in a plastic tray. Their litter box was down there too—it had a cover with air freshener, although he cleaned it every time he stopped. He'd thought to put it in the bathroom, but he soon realized the kittens were *not* very active, and when their bodies hurt, it was *hard* to get to the bathroom. So yes. He'd sacrificed his tiny but very classy kitchen to two special-needs kittens that he frequently put on the passenger seat of his vehicle because, while Oliver with the polydactyl feet could gambol, Katie with the hip deformity could mostly roll from one place to the next, and she'd stay put.

Particularly if he put yet another cat bed on the seat.

Yes, he'd spent the last month spoiling these kittens as he'd planned to spoil Jules—his only regret was in not recognizing sooner that kittens were a better return on his emotional investment.

But he tried not to be bitter.

What he was now, as he sat idling behind the vehicle he'd been following as the men by the side of the road had a conference, was intrigued. They'd been allowed past a military roadblock to be here. A *military roadblock.*

Eric had no idea how that came to be, but there'd been a bad ten minutes of sitting behind the idling sedan and feeling his testicles creep up inside his body for warmth as he contemplated how much he did *not* want to confront whatever covert ops division was currently blocking the road. "Military" was a blanket term—if there was no Army, Navy, Air Force, Marine insignia to be seen *anywhere* on the uniforms, well, Eric was in the presence of greatness.

And then that "greatness" simply waved the ancient, battered sedan with its two unusual occupants through. And then they'd waved Eric to follow them.

Who *were* these people?

A couple of miles down the road, Eric had seen what the roadblock had been for, a pretty grisly sight. The vehicle was still burning, and Eric's trained eye was keen enough to note the crispy remains in the driver's seat. In the distance he could see the remnant of a battered sedan—much like the one he was following, he thought, but a different make—lying upside down in front of a boulder.

Given his profession, his first thought was "Where are the bodies?"

There should have been another body—at the *least*—near that sedan. But no. Not even any footsteps leading away. No blood, no battered victim, no *human.*

The more he thought about it, the more it unnerved him.

And still the sedan kept driving, but not quickly. As though the young man behind the wheel was looking for somebody: The driver of the wrecked vehicle, perhaps?

He saw the two figures striding down the road a moment later. Briefly he thought one of them was quite small. Until the sedan came close and Eric had some scale. The dark-haired one—excruciatingly handsome—was tall enough, but the man striding next to him was *at least* six feet, six inches if not bigger.

The dark-haired man leaned forward and talked—intensely—to the passenger, the whippet-thin blond man, Sonny, whom his friend had described as displaying borderline personality tendencies. He gave the Winnebago and Eric a couple of neutral glances before doing the most extraordinary thing.

He leaned forward and kissed the little psychopath on the lips.

Eric stared at them, more stunned than he'd have been if one of them had pulled a gun. The open display of affection hit him so hard he could barely breathe. Then the dark-haired man straightened, gave an affectionate smile to his lover inside, squared his shoulders, and turned toward Eric.

Eric straightened his *own* spine and glanced toward Katie and Oliver, curled up in the passenger seat. "Look sharp," he told them. "Company is coming."

At that moment there was a rap at the door to the Winnebago, and he hit the lock to let them in.

ACE STOOD up straight in the Winnebago, pleased that he could, although he suspected Jai might have to stoop a bit.

"This is real nice," he said, surprised. "I mean—oh! And look! Jai, he's got a little haven for the kittens."

"You may put them down there if you like," said the driver, and Ace got a good gander at him.

He looked like a European prince, Ace thought—his hair was cut just so, his features were clean-cut, his nose a bit Roman, his eyes a crystalline blue. His whole demeanor was like one of those silhouettes that could be drawn with mostly triangles, and his collection of triangles should be holding a gun.

"I'll sit back here," Jai said, and Ace watched the driver's eyebrows rise at the thick accent. "Give me the kittens." His voice dropped. "I do love kittens."

Ace cackled. "Your boyfriend and his roommate have two, and that's enough." He picked the cat bed up carefully and deposited it on the table as Jai backed into the bench, stretching his long legs in front of him so as not to disturb the little shelter underneath.

"Da. But other people's kittens are cute, *and* you do not have to clean up their crap," Jai agreed.

Ace cackled and sat in the swiveling passenger seat before doing his seat belt. "I'm in," he said. "Follow Ernie there. I think we're meeting at the garage." He grimaced. "I hope you don't mind. Our house is a little small. We can put our dog in a crate in our room, but you may have to sit on the floor to eat. We didn't expect to ever know so many people when we bought it."

Jai chuckled warmly behind him. "It was all you could afford," he said. "Do not apologize to this man. Your home is an honor."

Ace grimaced and turned toward… oh. He saw it now. The stone-cold sociopath in the man. Maybe it was kin recognizing kin? Maybe it was just the arctic cold vibrating off him. He could see why Ernie left it up to him and Jai now. This was a *very* dangerous man.

"So," he said. "You're…."

"Eric Christiansen," said the man, and his voice—yeah. His voice sounded uppity East Coast yada yada, but what would Ace know?

"Sure it is," Ace replied dryly.

Those mercilessly cold blue eyes gave him a sideways glance. "You don't believe me?"

Ace gave a humorless laugh. "We… we know some things about names that aren't what we were born with. Me, my name is Jasper Anderson Atchison. People call me Ace. Behind me is Jai. His last name changes. You already met Ernie, Sonny, and Cotton. You get us to where we're going, you'll meet a few more people. Thing is, if you want to get to where we're going, you gotta convince me you got more in common with my friends than a name you weren't born with and an official ID that's worth more than a way to escape."

He heard the intake of breath. "If I… get to where you're going?" the man asked, and Ace knew he'd heard *exactly* what Ace had meant.

"Listen," Ace said. "I got no doubt you're good at what you do. Probably better'n any of us. But if you'd wanted to kill us, you coulda. You coulda attacked Ernie and Sonny, or Cotton. I don't think you're a serial killer—I think you're a professional, and you got standards and criteria and such. So what I want to know is, since that thing in you that says killing is wrong has been fundamentally broke, how do I know you're not gonna hurt someone I care about?"

God, he was tired. This man could have probably pulled off what he and Jai had done and been ready to drive up to NorCal or to Texas for all he knew, but killing was a rough business, and Ace was ready for a sandwich and some TV and a nap.

Which is why, perhaps, the man's next words hit him so hard, vibrating in his absolute core with a chord he knew to his bones.

"I... I want out," said "Eric Christiansen."

Ace glanced back at Jai, who was busy waving his fingers for the adolescent kittens to bat at. Jai caught his eyes and shrugged.

"Why?" Ace asked, fighting off the absurd urge to cry. "You look like you're doin' okay for yourself."

He *heard* Christiansen swallow. "I want to kiss my boyfriend through a car window and wave to him and know I didn't just put a price on his head."

Ace *hmm*ed. "That's a good wish," he admitted. "Why do you think we'd have anything to do with that?"

"Nobody comes here," said Christiansen, almost desperately. "This part of the desert used to be a free passageway. Mobsters whizzed through, meth dealers. But in the last three years, those people have *disappeared*. I don't know why. One of the biggest meth suppliers in Las Vegas blew up a couple months ago, before the storm, and they were located *near here*. This little nothing place called Victoriana. I figured there had to be an outfit here. I'll do what you want. I'll take whatever contract you need." He sighed. "I want to not have to look over my shoulder all the time."

Ace snorted. "Oh please. We can do our own killing. We don't need no cold fish in a Winnebago to do it for us."

Suddenly their friend straightened, some of the desperation easing off his shoulders. "Wait," he said. "*You* did that? The deputy's vehicle? How did you *do* that? There were no footprints away from the other car. How did you manage that?"

"What makes you think we were even in that accident?" Ace asked. "We were a quarter of a mile away when that shit went down."

Christiansen's eyes went wide. "Remote control?" he asked a little wildly.

"Son, we got all our possessions in our pockets. Please, we got no trade secrets you probably can't figure out for yourself, so if that was your plan—"

"No!" said their driver. "I just…." He let out a grunt. "I was curious, that's all. I mean, I *am* a professional, as you said."

Ace snorted. "What we were doing today is not your concern—"

"But it is," said Christiansen. "I need to know why. *Why* did that man have to die?"

"Because he was a fucking pedophile," Ace snapped. "And he used his badge to let his brother rape babies so they could share porn."

There was a shocked silence, and Ace heard Jai's comfort grunt from behind him.

"Sorry," Ace muttered. "I understand you're a professional, but us amateurs have difficulty compartmentalizing."

"I could help with things like that," said Christiansen hopefully. "I'm very good. I could kill the brother—"

"*I* killed the brother," Ace said, shuddering. "Wasn't my finest moment."

"You left DNA?" Christiansen asked, like it was only professional courtesy.

"Probably not," Ace said.

"Somebody heard you?"

"Nope."

"Cameras?"

"Oh my God, do we look stupid?" Ace snapped. "No, no, and no. It's like that… whatyacallit. Hamlet. Hamlet didn't want to kill his uncle in a church 'cause he was afraid his uncle would be all clean and confessed and shit and go to heaven. Well, this guy was a preacher. I don't think he's going to heaven, but I think his bloody death with his wiener out is gonna hurt a lotta people who truly believe, and I am not okay with that. But it had to be done."

There was a shocked gasp. "You… you are *good* people!" Christiansen said. Then with more humility than Ace could imagine in another person, "Please. Please let me come to your home and eat with you. You don't even have to let me stay, just...." He took a breath that Ace could swear broke in his chest. "I had a conversation with somebody who had gotten a convicted felon a deal. The man wanted a prison with a view. That was all. Twenty-five to life, this guy wanted someplace with an ocean view, just so he could smell it and dream. And I asked the guy how much the convict had given up to get that. The guy said not much—they were only treating him like a human being. Now I know that guy. He was a scumbag, but he also had some standards. Didn't hurt kids. Didn't do jobs high. So I know he deserved prison—as do I—but the thought that someone, even his lawyers, would treat him with dignity? That's all I want."

Ace heard a couple of things. He heard the snotty East Coast accent slipping to hard-core working class, much like Ace's broke-assed-central Cali couldn't be curb stomped and forced to disappear. And Ace heard some warmth break through. Some honesty.

He heard the deep breaths that came when safety was only a heartbeat away.

"Keep going on this road," Ace said. "It ain't much. You'll see one of those hanging traffic lights, indicating someone coming crosswise, and you'll see a Subway and a gas station on the right and a garage on the left. Pull your Winnie there into the drive for the garage. It's small. It's dusty. It's probably not nearly as great as you're making it out to be. But you can have dinner there tonight, talk to some people." He glanced back again to where Jai was busy falling in love with the kittens. "There's not much at the garage, but we might have a line on some hookups for your power and water. We'll see."

He heard the indrawn breath next to him and peered at Eric Christiansen's face. It was... eerie, as the man put his composure back on, one facial muscle at a time. But Ace hadn't been mistaken; he was certain of it.

For a moment he'd seen the *real* Eric Christiansen.

And he was very, very lonely.

Part VI—Fried Chicken

THE THING about driving to work with Jason, Burton thought irritably, was that Jason drove the midlife-crisis red convertible sports car. Normally Burton didn't mind—in fact, sometimes Jason let Burton drive, and since Ace *never* let anybody drive the SHO, it was as close to flying as he got outside a helicopter.

So he *liked* the vehicle, but he *disliked* not being able to have this argument with Ace in private.

"Yes, we're coming," he said, knowing Ace would take that as, "We're invading."

"No, you're not," Ace told him, irritatingly patient.

"There is an *assassin* at your garage!" Burton snapped.

"And some days it's Tuesday," Ace snapped back.

Burton gaped, and next to him, Jason snorted.

"But Ace…." Burton was whining, and he knew it. "What's so special about this guy? And I swear to Christ if you say kittens, I'm losing it, because I've already heard about the goddamned kittens. Plenty of sociopaths can keep a cat alive."

"But will they sacrifice their millionaire RVs to give them a home under the table?" Ace asked, and because Burton knew Ace, he knew that was only partially facetious. Choosing substance over style was a point in his favor, and Burton knew it.

"Ernie must love that," Burton grumbled.

"He does," Ace said. "He's already gotten to know Katie and Oliver—special needs kittens, Burton. I mean…."

"It's *so* emotionally manipulative," Burton complained. "Why couldn't it have been an ocelot?"

Ace chuckled, and Burton found himself thawing. "Why?" he said at last. "What was it about this guy that made you want to invite him into our little group?"

"Remember when you paid me cash to make you a spare room so you had a place where somebody knew your real name?" Ace asked, and

Burton swallowed. Before Ernie, before George, before Jason, even, had become a friend instead of just a commander who knew him well. Back when Burton had been so sure his path had excluded any sort of human connection except a garage mechanic and his psycho boyfriend, Ace had simply taken the cash and said sure. He'd changed his own home, literally *added a room* that from the outside didn't make any damned sense to the architecture, so that Lee Burton could come *home* sometimes to sleep.

"Yeah," he said, his throat a little tight. Ace had done that for him.

"You think you're the only one who needed to be called by his real name once in a while?" Ace asked kindly.

"What's his real name?" Burton asked.

"We don't know yet," Ace said. "He's been out in the cold a lot longer than you were."

Burton sighed. "Should I ask Jason to hang back? He could just, you know, remain a name. Cotton's boyfriend. We could keep an ace in the hole." He chuckled, sensing the word play.

"I don't much like holes," Ace replied mildly. "Jason's gotta do what he's gotta. But the man is currently seated out on our patio, petting our ridiculous dog, listening to Sonny talk about my sorry excuse for a lawn. Ernie is serving him chicken, George is…." His voice sank softly. "George is getting a little bit drunk, and I don't blame him a bit. The newscasters didn't prettify things, and George knows what went down. Jai is sitting with George in the living room." Surprise tinged Ace's voice. "I think he is singing. And I think Cotton is in the RV talking to the kittens. And I need you here, to see the man's expression, to confirm my gut feeling, which says he's going to fit just fine."

Oh. There was something about Ace's voice, something plaintive, and it hit Burton that Ace hadn't had an easy day.

Burton's friend didn't need him and Jason parachuting in to save the day—but he *did* need some backup.

"I'll be there in half an hour," Burton said. "Do you need us to bring anything?"

"Ice cream," Ace said. "And beer. Jai and George deserve more beer."

"Then make it forty-five minutes."

"Thanks, Lee," Ace murmured softly.

"Yeah, well, I appreciate those days when it's Tuesday."

Ace chuckled a little and signed off.

"So?" Jason said carefully from the seat next to him.

"Well, as my best friend just pointed out, having a killer eating chicken at his house only means it's a day ending in *Y*."

Jason snorted. "I'd never thought of that," he said. "But yeah. I guess...." He pondered for a moment, probably going through a mental catalogue of their little group, including Ernie, who had taken out two assassins the day he and Burton had officially met because the men's minds were "like bugs, crawling all over him."

"Not Cotton," Burton said brightly, after an uncomfortable minute.

"Sonny?" Jason asked, then shook his head. "I don't want to know."

But Burton knew. "Only in battle," he said. "If there—he worked in the auto bay."

Jason grunted. "But boy, he's got us all scared, doesn't he?"

"Because we know," Burton said with a shrug. "When Sonny goes off about clocking someone with a tire iron or shooting the next person who hits on Ace, we *know* he could do it and not lose sleep over it. Because the rest of us have to plan to kill. Sonny spends all day, every day, planning how *not* to kill, because he knows it would break Ace's heart."

Jason *hmm*ed. "Which is why Ace is the one who does it," he said softly, as though getting it. "Because if Sonny did it, we'd be chipping away at all the things he's built in his head to keep himself human."

"And Ace is the best man I know," Burton said. "Killing hurts him, so he only does it when it absolutely needs to be done."

Jason sighed. "We could have let the justice system—"

"No," Burton murmured. "If Ace did it, it absolutely needed to be done."

"So he's vouching for the new guy?" Jason asked.

"It's okay if you want to come pick Cotton up and drive off all mysterious-like," Burton told him. "But I think Ace is planning to let Christiansen hook his RV up at one of the incomplete housing hookups." Some of the lots in the little unknown cul-de-sac where so many of them lived had power, water, even sewage hookups, but the houses hadn't been finished. Just bare skeletons, waiting for drywall flesh and siding skin.

"Fair," Jason said, nodding. "If he chooses to stay, there's two more finished houses to pick from."

"Let me meet him first," Burton said. "You drive—"

"No," Jason said. "Lee, I know you all are trying to protect me. Hell, that's probably why Ace didn't call you in today, because he knew I'd have to know. But…." He shrugged. "It's dishonest. 'Here, Cotton, these are my friends. You can visit them and play with them on the weekends, but, you know, I'm not really part of the group, so don't mention me that often. We like to pretend I don't know them.' It's bullshit. Living like a monk for ten years was bad enough. Living like a fucking *pariah* is just—I can't do it anymore. I refuse. Sure, you meet him first. Then I'll meet him. If we decide he's too dangerous to stay, that's on you, me, and Ace, not just on Ace. Not just on you. It's on us. I mean, I get we try to shelter Cotton. And Sonny and George and even George's roommate. But I'm too old to play that game. I'm *done*. And Ace *is* a good man. But we just made him go do a terrible thing alone. I'm not saying we make him part of the unit, but I don't want him to feel like he's got to make these terrible decisions alone anymore. It's not fair."

Burton raised his eyebrows. "Jason, I know we're gay, but what? Are we the fairness fairies now?"

Jason's eyes bulged out, even though he kept them on the road. "You're demoted," he said with a straight face. "I'm firing you. I'm shipping you out to Fallujah."

Burton snorted, because none of that was obviously happening. "Cotton would miss Ernie," he said mildly. "I'm just saying—it's a lot of nice talk, but you do realize that Ace is *used* to going it alone."

Jason grunted, still mad about the fairies thing. "And that's our bad. He should never have had to deal with… with *any* of what he's dealing with by himself."

"You like order," Burton told him soothingly. "I get it. I myself don't mind a good order. But, well, both of us have been known to disobey a bad order, and we own that. What do you think Ace has the option of doing?"

Finally Jason's eyes stopped bulging out. "What do you mean?"

"We're officers, Jason. *Officers*. We both went to college, graduated, and were recruited straight into OTS. You remember that?"

"I do know my career trajectory," Colonel Constance said dryly. "What's your point?"

"First time I ever met Ace, we were in a firefight. He was the master sergeant, and he had a squad of new recruits that he was talking patiently into not shitting their pants. About the time he got them into position with their weapons pointed forward, he looked at me and asked me—very polite, because he knew I was a superior officer—if he could possibly go find his friend in the auto bay, because he didn't think his guys had his back."

Constance sucked in a breath. "They didn't *what*?"

"It's what *I* said," Burton told him, remembering the fury all over again. "Do you know what he said?"

"I got nothing."

For a moment they both let the wind from the open windows of the convertible ruffle through their ears, over their faces. They kept the top up in deference to January, but oh, the feeling of speed.

"He said, 'We weren't all born in a fire cradle like you.' Now he meant the Marines, but you know what else he meant?"

"Upper middle, college educated—"

"People with power," Burton told him. "So I let him go. And he shot Sonny's CO in the face."

"I'm *sorry*?" Constance said, and he almost swerved, which at the speed they were going would have killed them both.

"For Christ's sake, either slow down or learn to drive," Burton snapped. God, he missed Ace behind the wheel sometimes. There was more than one reason to shit your pants in a fast car.

"I'm sorry," Jason said humbly, slowing down a little and concentrating on his driving. "But…." Suddenly Burton could see him remember. "Wait," he said softly. "I… I *know* this case. *This* was one of Lacey's first products. *This guy* was—"

"He was one of the first people in the Karl Lacey Academy for Psychos in Training," Burton said. "Only we didn't know about that then, so all Ace had was himself and his gun against a superior officer with a gun to a ten-year-old girl's head. That man would have killed them all: Sonny, the girl, Ace—"

"Aw. Aw fuck," Jason said, recall obviously hitting him hard. "But he only got one shot off before a shell hit. The girl. The girl died. I remember thinking that report looked hinky."

"They called it a friendly-fire incident," Burton conceded. "And Ace spent six weeks in the infirmary nursing some crushed ribs and a concussion, and Sonny got to spend six weeks in the military without worrying that his CO was trying to bully him to death. It was awesome. And I had to vouch for Ace for the first time, and what was I going to say?"

"I remember," Jason said. "You told them that Ace had gone to see if any of his recruits had ended up in auto bay. It... it seemed perfectly reasonable."

"It was a great lie," Burton conceded. "Because we *all* had to lie. Because Ace was a master sergeant, and Sonny's superior officer was a psychopath. So no, Jason. I mean, yes, it's fair if you want to take a bigger role in what Ace and his buddies do when they see something that needs fixing. But no, you don't get to tell Ace he can't do it alone. Arrest him if you have to—although I'd rather you didn't, and so would the rest of us—but... but you're not the colonel of his little army."

"I'm a raw recruit," Jason said.

Burton swallowed, unnerved by the loneliness of his tone, by the bleak look on his face. "But one who's welcome to come share a beer and have some chicken," Burton reminded him. Jason gave a faint smile then.

"Just remind Ace he doesn't have to do it all alone if he doesn't want to," Jason said at last.

"Top of my list," Burton said firmly. "Right after making sure I don't have to shoot Eric Christiansen in the face."

"Also important."

"We need to stop for beer and ice cream," Burton reminded him. "Turn off here. It's the only store for miles."

"Good beer," Jason said stubbornly.

"Also good ice cream," Burton said. "Ice cream is Sonny's favorite thing."

THE PLAN had been for Burton to meet the guy first, but Jason had asked where Cotton was and had been directed to the giant black-and-white Winnebago parked down by the garage, where Cotton, and now Sonny, were apparently getting to know the kittens.

Jason paused for a moment at the steps leading up to the center of the living space, getting a glimpse of both men sitting cross-legged on the floor in what amounted to the kitchen space of the camper. He could see the setup behind Cotton—litter box, beds, food and water bottles, all on their own plastic trays. The carpet in the RV was a lot nicer than these things usually went—having two cats who couldn't consistently get to the bathroom was a big concession, Jason thought.

Then he heard the conversation between Cotton and Sonny.

"Lookie here," Sonny said. "See, Oliver here's got six toes on this foot but only three on this one. I think that's why he limps. 'Cause each one is different. He's got no rhythm."

Jason got a glimpse of Cotton, angel's eyes alight as he leaned forward and stroked the kitten on Sonny's lap between its ears. "Is that your problem, big guy? No rhythm?"

From the couch—which was set toward the front of the RV on the driver's side, Jason heard an educated voice singing softly about having rhythm and music.

Jason chuckled under his breath, thinking this was possibly the wrong crowd. Cotton had been kicked out of the house at seventeen—he hadn't been going to plays in the last five years. And Sonny, well, even Jason knew Sonny's life had been harder than that.

But then Cotton broke in with a Broadway quality tenor and finished the verse. Who *could* ask for anything more?

That educated voice again, chuckling. "Very good. Where did you hear that?"

"High school drama teacher," Cotton said. "She was absolutely nuts about Gene Kelly."

"Who's she?" Sonny asked, and Jason paused midstep.

"He's a famous dancer," said the educated man—Eric Christiansen, Jason had no doubt. "Moved beautifully."

"Have you ever seen *Singing in the Rain*?" Cotton asked. "It's so much fun."

"I could have Ace stream it," Sonny said confidently; then his voice faltered. "It's not… uhm, black and white, is it? 'Cause I have an awful time staying awake."

"No, it's in color." Cotton's voice dropped to the kitten in his arms. "Katie, my love, please don't do that—ouch!"

"Oh, she gotcha!" Sonny laughed a little. "Well, sorry about your wrist, but at least we know she's a fighter."

Jason finally took his step up and found Cotton, still hugging the fighting kitten. He saw immediately that her hips were deformed—poor thing. She probably had to haul her back end around like a trailer. "Let me see," he said gently, picking her up and peering at her with a strategist's eye as she purred in his hands and tried to bat his thumb. "Hello, sweet thing. I think…." He *hmm*ed. "I think we can make her a cart," he said after a moment, and then glanced up at the suave, handsome man with dark blond hair and ice-blue eyes, sprawled on the RV couch with the remains of a fried chicken dinner on a plate on his lap. "Would you mind?" he asked. "I know some guys at work who are bored and know how to weld. We could make her a little aluminum cart with some wheels. She could be racing up and down your hallway here in no time."

"That would be amazing," said Christiansen, sitting up.

Jason made a stay-seated motion and came forward, careful of Cotton, Sonny, and the kittens.

"Eric Christiansen," said the man who, Jason was pretty sure, was *not* named Eric Christiansen.

"Jason," Jason said, glad he'd changed into his civvies before going off base. "Jason Constance."

Christiansen's eyes widened with recognition. "You're Cotton's Jason," he said.

Jason nodded. "I understand we're going to be neighbors."

Christiansen shrugged self-consciously. "I guess this is a meeting of the HOA," he said with an embarrassed little smile. "I hope it's okay."

Jason nodded, thoughtful. "I think it might be," he said. "Although here, let me walk with you as you take your plate back."

"Is it okay if we stay with the kittens?" Sonny asked, turning a face up to them that Jason found heartbreakingly young. He thought of what Burton had said about how Sonny worked every day not to let his demons break free—and how Ace had been the one person who'd always had his back.

"Of course," Christiansen told him with a gentle smile. "They really do seem to love the attention."

Jason backed out of the RV and stepped aside to make way for his new friend.

"Am I going to make it back to the RV alive?" Christiansen asked pleasantly, and Jason knew the man hadn't missed his bearing *or* his seniority. It came to him with a thump that he and Christiansen—and possibly Jai, although it was hard to tell—were the oldest of this little group, all of them in their late thirties.

"That was Ace's call," Jason said frankly. "If he let Sonny in there with you, I think you're safe with us." He paused. "We *are* safe with you, aren't we?"

Christiansen swallowed and nodded. "I am simply looking for… haven," he said.

"For how long?"

Christiansen blew out a breath. "I have no idea. I had a companion for my retirement—"

"Jules Schaefer," Jason said, and Christiansen blanched.

"You know about that," he said.

"Jackson and Ellery are friends of ours," Jason said. "I don't think Ace knows of your involvement in their Christmas celebrations, but Burton and I do."

"I had planned to be out in the wilds somewhere, living in obscurity," Christiansen mused bleakly. "But… but—"

"I know what loneliness is like," Jason said. "And I know what it's like when your job requires you to live above the law. And how that can leave you with a hole in your soul."

Color returned to Christiansen's face, and his eyes grew glossy. "You're very eloquent," he said weakly.

Jason nodded. "You may have noticed that not all of us are as savvy as you."

Christiansen gave a brief glance behind him, probably thinking about the two young men sitting on the floor playing innocently with kittens. "Yes," he said.

"In this place, we protect people who need it."

Christiansen nodded. "I saw some of that," he said.

"At one time or another," Jason continued, "everybody here has needed protection. If that extends to you, we expect the same courtesy."

Those arctic-blue eyes were more than shiny now. They spilled over a little. "I understand," he said gruffly. "I will work to be part of that."

Jason blew out a breath. "There's a lot of history here," he said, nodding with his chin toward the back porch of Ace's house, where people were eating off Ace and Sonny's good Corelle and sitting in fold-up soccer chairs, the good kind with the cup holders for their beers or sodas. Jai and George had moved out of the house, Jason noticed.

Burton and Ace were standing by the door, calling inside to Ernie, who was probably cooking. George's friend Amal had shown up, and he was sitting next to George, matching him beer for beer.

"I don't know how to be a part of that," Christiansen said weakly. "I have so much blood on my hands."

Jason glanced at him. "So do most of us," he said at last. "Protect the innocent here. Have our backs. You're going to be parked in our cul-de-sac. Do us the fucking courtesy of not killing us as we sleep."

Christiansen let out a broken little laugh. "I can promise that," he said, sounding surprised.

"Why does that shock you?" Jason asked.

Christiansen shrugged. "I thought… I don't know. I'd be expected to help with the business, I guess."

"It's not a business," Jason told him bluntly. "Ace and Sonny make money through their garage. They pay Jai and Ernie. Burton and I work elsewhere. George and Amal are nurses, Cotton's going to school. We're not Assassins 'R' Us, Eric. We don't expect you to do any killing here. In fact, we'd prefer you not."

"If I have to, who would I clear it with?" Christiansen asked, shocking him badly.

"Who is it you want to kill?" Jason asked, the fine edge of hysteria in his voice.

"The preacher's wife," Christiansen said, because of course. "She had to be complicit."

Jason swallowed and stared at him. "Do you have proof?" he asked.

Christiansen blinked. "I'm sorry?"

"We had proof. Something that would have stood up in a court of law—in two years, when the case would have come to trial after more lives were ruined. Do you have proof?"

Christiansen studied his fine leather half boots. "I thought it would have been a service," he said with simple dignity.

"God willing, Cotton will never kill," Jason told him, the hope hitting him in the gut. "It's *imperative* that Sonny does not. We don't even *tell* George what happens, although he guesses, and Amal has no idea. You don't have to be a killer to live here, Eric. We don't want you to leave bodies at our doorstep like a cat leaving a gopher. All we ask is that you have our backs."

"But…." And Jason could hear a plaintiveness here. This was a man who at some point had been raised never to show up at a party without a plant or a casserole.

"Bring Ace beer the next time he invites you over. Or soda—that's good too. They also like ice cream." Burton had brought two half-gallons, as well as some chocolate, and Jason thought once again of Sonny. "If you're bored and they're short-staffed, come man the window. When it gets hot, if you haven't decided on a house, feel free to leave the kittens with Ernie so they can stay cool. If Burton or I are deployed, check on Ernie and Cotton. Bring George or Jai food when it looks like George is working a series of graveyards. Neighbor stuff, Eric. Not assassin stuff. Can you manage that?"

Christiansen nodded slowly. "I will be awkward," he said with unsurprising self-perception.

"Of course you will be. *I'm* awkward. You and I are bluebloods here—and not in the good way. We're like a couple of Malinois dropped into a convocation of junkyard dogs. Sure, we're *supposed* to be better/stronger/faster, whatever, but if you don't know the junkyard dogs could rip us apart, you're the dumbest Malinois I've ever met."

He heard a rusty chuckle and figured he'd said enough, which was good because Ace had seen them and was drawing up to shake his hand.

"Jason," he said with a smile. "Gotta thank you for your help today."

Jason shrugged. "It was a roadblock. And the cops, I understand, were having something of a day."

Ace shrugged. "Yeah, well, you never know."

Jason chuckled. "We were watching you through a scope, Ace. The car crash was brilliant. *We* know."

To his delight Ace *blushed*, and Burton drew near. "Fuckin' epic," Burton said, shaking his head. "I mean… *epic*."

And then Eric spoke. "I… how did you do that?" he asked. "I *must* know!"

Jai emerged from the house, Ernie on his heels, and Jason wondered if George hadn't fallen into a boozy sleep from what had to have been a rough day and a rough decision. Jason respected George. He knew that the young nurse wouldn't have told Ace and Ernie about the situation without knowing the consequences. It would have been hard to hear, and one of the things Jason loved most about Burton's friends was that nobody mocked George for his conscience, for wondering if he'd done the right thing.

"You should tell," Jai said. He glanced behind him. "George and Amal will not hear, and everybody standing here will appreciate the story."

Ace's lips curved up. "I gotta tell you," he said after a moment, "it was the best part of a spectacularly shitty day."

Part VII—All the Assassins, All Snug in Their Beds

THE PEOPLE were finally gone. Jai had packed a boozy George into his Crown Vic, and Amal had followed them home. Ernie had driven Burton's truck over, so that's what they took back, and since Ernie had given Cotton a ride, Jason got to take him home in the convertible.

They put the top down and the heater on, Ace suspected, just so they could see the stars.

And bringing up the rear had been a very bemused, very *exhausted* Eric Christiansen in his portable home.

Still not his real name, but Ace rather suspected he'd arrived at his real home.

Ace was beyond caring, as the last of the day settled into his bones.

He'd showered and changed when he'd first returned home, and the time Sonny had spent prepping potatoes and salad for dinner while Ernie had been setting up the fryer, *he'd* spent polishing his beloved boots using a vinegar solution and a toothbrush. The comfort of that moment came back to him now as he leaned against the doorway and watched the last of the cars disappear from his backyard, the smell of fried chicken still hanging in the air.

He remembered being *so grateful* he was finally wearing clothes without blood on them, and particularly pleased with how soft he and Sonny had managed to get his hooded sweatshirt.

Eric Christiansen had sat across from him on one of the soccer chairs, watching what he was doing.

"I would have disposed of them for you," he said as Ace put a little elbow grease into cleaning any blood from the crevices that had not already been worn off by the day.

"We're not made of money," Ace said mildly. "And I *like* these boots. They're perfectly broke in. Do you know how hard it is to break in steel-toed shitkickers—even the kind with the softer soles? Your first month is blisters, calluses, and moleskin."

Christiansen had eyed his own soft leather half boots in surprise. "It hadn't occurred to me," he said humbly.

Ace grunted. "Well, I try not to have to race too much. Money's good, but it makes Sonny twitchy."

"What kind of racing?" Christiansen asked.

"Street racing," Ace said. "Sonny's a miracle worker with cars. He'd probably love to crawl inside your RV and optimize the hoo-ha consumption or whatever would make it go tear-assing across the desert."

"Ace drives like he stole something," Sonny said, bringing them both big plastic cups of iced tea.

"Thanks, Sonny," Ace said, smiling up at him. God, he was tired, but seeing Sonny serving a guest, working hard at being with people, made him feel good.

Sonny didn't kiss his cheek—not in front of a stranger—but Ace did feel the brief brush of their fingers when he handed off the cup. He got a smile that said that had been on purpose, and then Sonny went back inside.

"How long?" Christiansen said. "The two of you?"

Ace shrugged. "Depends. Met five years ago in the service. But we were out for a bit before we got together. Lots of baggage to open. You know how it is."

Christiansen looked surprised. "No," he said. "I don't know about opening baggage."

Ace stared at him. "Well, son," he said, "you got to open your baggage 'cause you got to get rid of some of your own so you can help your person carry his. And vice versa. Didn't you know that?"

Those arctic-blue eyes went somewhat limpid. "You," he said slowly, "are the second person in the span of a month to give me some much-needed advice on dating."

Ace stared at him. "Who was the other guy?"

"A PI named Rivers."

Ace cocked his head. "I know that guy. Listen to what he said. Smart man."

Christiansen laughed softly. "My world," he said after a moment, "is so much smaller than I ever believed."

Ace shrugged. "Don't know what to do about that. You got any questions for me about shit?"

"Was the RV hookup here?"

Ace glanced around and laughed. "We don't hardly got our own water and power. Naw. After everyone gets here and eats, they'll show you the way home."

"How come you don't live there too?" Christiansen asked, cocking his head.

Ace didn't understand this guy at all. "'Cause we live *here*," he said. "We lived here first. Why would we move? It's just me and Sonny." He heard a bark and turned toward Sonny's pride and joy. "And Duke. But he don't take up space none."

Christiansen reached down and allowed the little brown dog to sniff his fingers. "Okay," he said simply. "Okay."

Ace didn't ask okay what. He was so done with talking by then. The next time he said much of anything was when Burton got there and asked him how he and Jai had managed the wreck. Now *that* was a fun story.

But he was glad when it got told, and everybody was ready for ice cream, and to leave.

Now, as he turned into the house that had been mostly cleaned, listening to the last sounds of engines rumbling into the night, he knew there still had to be a little bit of talking. Sonny'd done good that day, and Ace would do anything to have Sonny in his arms.

That's not what happened, though. The talking.

Duke was back in his crate and asleep, and the lights were off, and instead of one more hour watching television, Sonny grabbed Ace's hand and took him to their bedroom, with the moonlight shining down and glowing off their white walls with the dark trim. Gently—when once upon a time, Ace had sworn Sonny didn't have any gentleness in him—he started to undress Ace, making him sit down to get his boots and socks, then stand again for his jeans and briefs. When Ace was nude, staring at his lover in that mystery light, Sonny shucked off his own clothes, his boots already in the entryway from earlier.

And then they were both naked, Ace on the bed, Sonny in front of him, and Sonny stepped between his spread thighs and drew Ace's face against his tight concave stomach. Ace turned his cheek and rubbed up against him, aware that his cock was right there—it was even growing fat—but that didn't seem to be what this was about.

Sonny bent and kissed the top of his head. "I see you," he said softly. "And you're hurting. Can I take some of that away?"

Ace let out a little whimper, feeling the awful weight of the day lifting from his shoulders as Sonny helped him set it down. "You always do," he said and clutched Sonny closer. His shoulders started to heave, and Sonny held him, just held him, as hard sobs rocked him, because he was free here, and Sonny wouldn't hold it against him if he let it go.

When he could breathe again, Sonny bent down and kissed his cheeks, then his mouth, heedless of the mess, and then he kissed Ace some more until Ace drew him down and rolled them, Ace on top, and they made love. The soft, tender kind that Sonny was usually wary of, but tonight he was giving Ace a gift.

Ace knew it. Let it touch his heart. He was gentle too, careful even, as he slid inside Sonny's body and they finished the dance they both knew so well.

When it was over and their breathing had calmed, and Ace was lying with his head on Sonny's shoulder, Sonny spoke.

As usual, it was a surprise.

"That Eric guy," he said. "The one with the kittens. You reckon he's killed a lot of people?"

"Don't know," Ace said on a yawn. "Some, at least. Burton seemed to think he was a big deal."

"Not too big a deal," Sonny said, laughing slightly. "You sure did have him rattled with that car trick."

Ace chuckled. "Jai figured it out immediately," he said.

"That's 'cause Jai's crazy and likes it when you drive like a maniac," Sonny said, voice fond. Then he asked, "Why do you think Jason stayed?"

Ace grunted. "He was tryin' to let me know, I think. That it was okay. That he knew what I'd been doing. That he didn't want us to hide."

Sonny grunted back. "That's not smart," he said. "Smart man would stay far away. Whatsit—plausible deniability." He chuckled. "I liked that music. That was fun."

Ace chuckled sleepily. "Yeah, well, any man who can rhyme 'deniability' has got to have some talent."

"You think Eric's gonna stay here long? He seemed to like us fine."

"I think we'll see," Ace said. "We may need to train him. No pissing on our territory, no killing just to trim the corners. Jason said he wanted to kill the preacher's wife, and he had to tell the guy no."

"Why kill her?" Sonny asked.

"'Cause she knew what her man was doing," Ace said grimly. There was no doubt in his mind.

Sonny grunted too. "That's gross," he said. "But gratuitous." He sounded proud. "That's the word. Like the violence on TV. *Gratuitous.* They'll figure out her part. She'll have a shitty life, I think. We don't need to soil our souls for the likes of her."

Ace relaxed, glad to hear Sonny say it. "Thanks, Sonny," he said softly.

"Love you, Jasper."

"Love you, Sonny Daye," Ace whispered. He wanted to say more—about how proud he was of Sonny, about how he couldn't do the things he did without Sonny there to pick up the pieces. He wanted Sonny to know so badly....

But his body pulled him into sleep.

Epilogue—Fish or Fox

ERIC CHRISTIANSEN could remember his last family cookout before this one, but he didn't like to and wouldn't now. This one, he decided, could stay in his memory, a picture of what such things were supposed to look like.

He'd hold it up often, he suspected, as a template, a paint-by-numbers guide of what he wanted for his life postretirement.

But tonight, with his couch folded out into a bed—because it meant he could see out the windows, which he couldn't from the actual bed in the back—and the kittens curled up on their cushion next to him, he just wanted to live it again and again and again.

It was a family. He hadn't known that when he'd set out from Tahoe. Hearing Rivers confirm its existence was enough to send him tilting after it, like a windmill. When he'd run into Cotton, he'd been clueless. After his discussion with Ernie, he'd thought "mafia."

He'd only been partly right. It was a family, but it was not a criminal enterprise. Jason's frank talk about where everybody got their money, and Ace's solitary dedication to cleaning the blood off his favorite work boots, had been like ice water on his assumption of what kind of family it had been. Nobody eating chicken that night had been there for the money.

They were there, he suspected, for the same reason *he'd* been there, only not as naked. Companionship. Camaraderie. Courtship?

Apparently, Eric thought, blowing a disgruntled sigh, most of them *had courted*—wasn't that always the way?

God, he missed Jules. Not so much as a companion. Jules had been, quite frankly, arrogant and irritating and condescending. Jules had been *born* into the upper classes, he hadn't *made* himself into one. Eric thought about Jason Constance's (and there *had* to be a title or a rank there) analogy between junkyard dogs and Malinois.

Eric Christian had worked hard to be that Malinois, but he knew himself for what he was.

A cringing cur in Malinois clothing.

And for the first time in his life, he was in the company of people who wouldn't *care* what kind of dog he was, as long as he was loyal and didn't bite when he didn't have to.

Again, he thought of Ace cleaning the blood off his boots. After Eric had parked his trailer by the vacant house with the full range of water, sewage, and power hookups, then set about hooking himself up, he'd gone into his RV and changed into sleep pants and a T-shirt, opened the ceiling fan, and turned it on low, letting some of the chill of the desert January into the living space, blowing out any exhaust or sweat or travel into the night.

Then he'd gone surfing, thinking that *one* of the three occupied houses on the block, at the very least, must have a hell of an internet source, because his own tablet had effortlessly piggybacked on the hookup without hardly searching. He'd paused for a moment before joining a provider, looking at the IDs to choose from. *Crullers? Clean Linen? Little George Inc?* There was a story behind every ID, he thought, but all three were stronger than the legit provider he'd been planning to hook up to.

Then his phone had buzzed—Jason Constance had taken his number before leaving him to hook up to the house. *All obvious coms are monitored. Choose one, but be aware.*

Password? he'd texted back.

Clean Linen. Password: Cotton 3701

Eric had stared at the information, thinking that there had to be *layers* of encryption underneath the basic stream. This was what the angel-eyed boy used to research his school subjects, Eric realized. Six hundred passwords on was what the smooth and confident (although equally sloe-eyed) military operator used should he need to contact whomever.

Fair, he thought.

He just wanted to surf the web a little. Scroll up local accidents. Maybe the police blotter….

There.

Grisly Preacher's Death Related to Pedophile Ring. Dead Deputy Involved.

Oh yes, Eric thought, skimming the details with increasing admiration. This was what he'd been looking for.

This man is wanted for questioning in connection with....

And there was... well, Eric *assumed* it was Ace, wearing the OD green T-shirt and jeans he'd been wearing when Eric had picked him and the giant Russian up in the middle of the desert. But under the hat and the laughable blond curls, not even Ace's boyfriend would know who he was. An outside camera had picked up two pairs of boots fleeing the scene—one barely glimpsed by the toe.

Two people. One of them male.

That's all the police had. A possible connection to what even Eric knew would be an untraceable vehicle. He skimmed to the bottom. Ah yes, there it was.

The vehicle, a late model sedan of indeterminate make, had no identifying features.

Eric read between the lines there—the VIN had been filed off, the parts, body, and engine had been used interchangeably, and the license plates were fake and/or from a stolen vehicle that didn't match the sedan. Eric had noticed a number of vehicles on the garage property surrounding the auto bay, most of them under a carport extension from the building to keep off the terrible sun. Some of the vehicles had been customer vehicles, Eric assumed. Nobody at that get-together had seemed the minivan type. Some had been personal—the bright yellow Ford SHO had obviously been built for the racing used to supplement Ace and Sonny's income. But the others?

Well, Ace and Sonny obviously helped their friends out.

And had a nice supply of unmarked, unregistered vehicles to choose from.

Eric had been recruited for Corduroy, an assassin's guild, right out of the military. They'd helped him build himself into a stainless steel Malinois, a sleek killing machine, using all the latest bells and whistles technology had to offer. When Corduroy had been taken over by an unscrupulous military commander—Karl Lacey—Eric had simply left the corporation, no harm no foul, and struck out on his own.

He'd never seen a more invisible operation, with such raw talent, in all that time.

But it wasn't a business. It was... what? A hobby? A calling? A social club?

Eric couldn't label it. Couldn't put his finger on it. In fact, the only thing he *did* know was that everybody took it seriously. And nobody wanted to make a habit of it.

This could be as safe as the man known as Eric Christiansen ever got.

He would not be expected to kill here unless it was to protect himself. Or, perhaps, some of the people in the group who might not be as good at self-defense, if he was in a position to do so. But nobody would come to him with cash or blackmail and say, "We need you to do us a favor."

His eyes burned.

He had not lived this long by getting ahead of himself, by growing complacent, by counting his chickens before they hatched. He knew that he and his new friends had a whole lot of "getting to know you" to come.

But maybe—just maybe—he had found a place where he could make a home.

He'd rigged the RV with all sorts of alarms, cameras, bells, and whistles, which he activated almost without thinking. Still, as he closed his eyes under the sage-scented breeze, he thought he might actually sleep for the first time since he'd left Tahoe… and his lover bleeding in the snow.

Far off, he heard a coyote calling and another one answering, and his kittens purred in his ear.

For the first time in years, he felt hope.

Keep Reading for an Excerpt from
Constantly Cotton,
Book #2 in The Flophouse series!

The Long and Winding Road

"MR. JASON, what was that?"

Lieutenant Colonel Jason Constance, Commander of Covert Operations, self-named Desert Division, wondered if it was possible for his stomach to sink past his balls.

He hadn't been in this much trouble out on the field, looking at a trained assassin through his sniper's scope. And even then he hadn't felt fear.

But then, his ass had been the only one on the line.

"Hang on, Sophie!" Jason called to the back seat of the "borrowed" medical shuttle. He blinked hard to clear the grit of sleep from his eyes. He had managed to pull over to catch a nap for an hour or so, but his internal monitor was pinging danger, and he'd started the bus up when he was certain the kids had all dropped off to sleep.

He couldn't shake the thought that someone was on their tail.

Around lunchtime, his life had seemed so simple.

Stressful—yes. Lonely—hell yes. But… fuck.

Simple was relative.

He was in charge of one of the most complicated, gawdawful tasks on the planet. For years, a powerful man—a commander in the armed forces named Karl Lacey—had utilized his ties to the covert ops community to try to create the perfect assassin. He'd used everything from psychics to behavior modification to outright torture to get men to forget their better angels and to find joy only in the hunt… and the kills.

The results had been predictable. To everyone but Lacey.

He'd set a batch of highly trained serial killers loose on an unsuspecting world.

Jason and one of his best operatives, a man named Lee Burton, had stopped the operation before it went international. They'd had help. Burton's boyfriend, Ernie Caulfield, a psychic Lacey had trained up and then tried to have Burton assassinate, had been their compass, and a batch of civilians who'd seen Lacey's psychological Frankenstein's monsters in action had become weapons.

The fallout had left Jason in charge of Lacey's old hidden military base in the desert outside of Barstow, with Lee Burton. Jason and Lee had spent the better part of the last eight months tracking down Lacey's abominations, and it was grim, dangerous, dirty work.

And painful.

They called it Operation Dead Fish.

Not every man Lacey had turned loose on the world had started out a monster. So many of them were left with tortured bits of soul and heart mangled in the wreckage. But it was hard to bring a patient in when that patient was trained to dismember people with his teeth and a plastic fork. Not a lot of their targets were brought home alive to fix.

The only thing that had kept Jason from hollowing out, becoming the man he and his small contingent of fifty or so operatives, agents, and trackers hunted, had been the other part of that fallout.

Burton's boyfriend, Ernie, was so psychic he really couldn't function in a crowded city or urban area, but he was also sort of a sweet, goofy angel who liked to feed people their favorite pastries and could pull a future out of thin air with a rather spacey look into the clouds. Burton's best friend, Ace Atchison, and Ace's psychotic boyfriend, Sonny Daye, had proved staunch and loyal friends and good soldiers, as had Ace's friend and employee, Jai, no last name, a mobster who had been "given" to Ace because Ace had risked his life to save Jai's boss's granddaughter.

And Ellery Cramer and Jackson Rivers, the lawyer and his PI boyfriend, who had not only stopped one of the first serial killers to escape Lacey's control but had tracked the man to Lacey independently, had proved invaluable, both in a fight and as allies in a dangerous secret war.

And all of them, in one way or another, had become something Jason Constance had never thought to have when he'd signed his name on Uncle Sam's bloody dotted line:

Friends. Family. People who knew who he was and cared about him—not what he could do for the juggernaut corporation that was the US military.

So Jason had started his morning depressingly early, resolving a crisis that had been brewing for a week and then checking with his far-flung agents, who were currently tracking a number of the rogue operatives through various countries, including their own, and then making contact with his field agents, who were keeping tabs on dangerous targets and trying to find a way to take them out without alerting—or hurting—the civilian population, and then finally with his wetwork agents to make sure that killing people for a living hadn't turned them into killers who did it for fun.

By lunchtime, all he'd wanted was a goddamned tuna sandwich. That was all. The limit of his ambitions.

And then Ernie had called him, out of the blue, and complicated his world.

Ace Atchison and Jai were chasing down an RV of trafficked children, he'd said. They would need help. "Jason, you know we can't just let this happen," he said.

And Jason, so desperate to do something good, and do something real, had agreed. He'd had Anton Huntington, his transport guy, fire up the old helicopter and take him out to I-15, that long stretch of nowhere between LA and Vegas, and he'd gotten there just in time to watch the big Russian ex-mob guy and a staff sergeant with a high school education take out the guy ferrying kidnapped children from Sacramento to Vegas.

Literally without trying.

That didn't stop Ace and Jai from being glad to see him. No. But it did feel anticlimactic. Right up until Jason had called his own CO, Brigadier General Stephen Collings, and told him that he'd intercepted some trafficked children and would like permission to use military transportation to take them back up north to Sacramento.

It was a basic request—a courtesy, really. Jason, whose real rank was actually heftier than the silver-leaf Lieutenant Colonel insignia he wore on his uniform, had sort of thrown it out there in the name of keeping to protocols in case he ever had to act civilized.

And Collings, one of the coldest fuckers Jason Constance had ever dealt with, including the assassins in his charge, said, "My division is, at this moment, tracking the group trafficking these minors. We need to see where they're going and follow the money trail. Please put them back on their original transport and designate a soldier to continue to drive them to their original destination."

Jason remembered a feeling of blankness blowing through him, a cold desert wind scouring the duties and the paperwork and the must-dos and the protocols right out of his blood, like the abrasive cleanser used in plumbing.

Every nerve ending was suddenly pristine and alert and awaiting a different set of orders from Jason's tattered, thin soul, as opposed to the ones he usually followed from Washington.

"No, sir," he'd said, his voice sounding tinny, far away, shouted from a mountaintop, even to his own ears. "No, sir. I'm not putting these kids back in that piece-of-shit tin wagon and shipping them back to hell."

The conversation had devolved from there.

And when it was over, Jason turned to Huntington almost as though he was surfacing from a deep pool—or a deep sleep.

"Sergeant Huntington?"

"Yessir?"

"I'm about to do some things my superiors don't approve of. Doing what I ask may get you called in on a court-martial. Let me know if that bothers you."

"You go, I go, sir," Huntington had replied smartly. He was young—late twenties or so—with thick blond hair, Iowa farm-boy blue eyes, and a chest almost too big to fit behind the helicopter controls. Jason had been nursing a crush—a very, very secret crush—on his transport sergeant almost since Anton had joined covert ops, but since he was pretty sure Anton Hungtington was straight (and even if he wasn't, Jason wouldn't hit on someone in his unit, ever), he'd indulged in the crush like other officers indulged in nudie magazines.

He only brought it out at night, when nobody else could see.

But still, it did his heart good to know that he inspired loyalty in somebody.

He'd had Huntington radio for a military transport bus and taken responsibility for the kids, while Jai and Ace had driven off to meet Burton and take out the people on the receiving end of this horror perpetrated against children.

Jason felt like his job was more dangerous.

As soon as the transpo arrived—with cases of water, thank God—Jason had sent the driver back to the base with Anton and hopped behind the wheel.

The trip from the middle of the desert had gone fairly quickly, or as quickly as the old bus could go, given that it overheated if Jason pushed it past fifty miles an hour.

Ernie called him halfway to the I-5 interchange and told him to stop off at a hospital close to the freeway in East Los Angeles. Apparently Jai's boyfriend worked there, and he'd volunteered to take a look at the kids and make sure nobody was suffering from heatstroke or lingering effects from their imprisonment in the back of the sweltering RV.

Jason had pulled into the ambulance bay and been directed toward the side of the big building that was closest to the parking structure. A small, almost hidden, employee entrance sat there, and Jason turned off the laboring engine while he and the kids waited in the shade.

And then the door had opened, and Jason had gotten a good look at another member of Burton and Ernie's hidden family.

He had only the occasional glimpse of Jai, the giant Russian who had been helping Ace Atchison tend to the children as they were moved from the horrible, stench-ridden RV to the slower, air-conditioned military transport bus, but he knew the man existed. When he had dinner with Burton and Ernie, Ernie gossiped to him about all of the denizens of Victoriana, and Jason started listening to their stories like some people paid attention to television shows. Jason Constance, covert ops, living in a hole in the world and tracking down people the US government denied creating, had no family. Or at least in his uniform, he pretended he didn't. His sister was alive and well and living outside of San Diego, teaching, and his parents had retired to Arizona. He texted them from a secure phone reserved for family interactions and exchanged pleasantries because he'd been brought up right and he was loved. But he didn't talk about them to anybody but Ernie and Burton. Ernie was semiofficially dead, and he liked it that way, so Jason felt safe there, but that was the only place. He hadn't had a lover since he'd gone into covert ops ten years ago. Back then, the stigma against being gay was such that any contact, any at all, would have compromised him and the people he worked with beyond forgiveness and redemption.

Things were different now, and even if they weren't, watching Burton and Ernie build their private bastion of tender civilization in the middle of the unforgiving desert would have inspired him to find somebody, anybody, to make the world a warmer, more welcoming place for his stripped-bare, desiccated soul. But his emotional centers felt battered and rusty, like a once-functioning piece of equipment that had been dipped in salt water and left in the sun to rust and gum up with sand.

He wasn't sure he could even touch a lover right now, not with the reverence and joy he seemed to remember that involved.

So seeing George, Jai's boyfriend, jumping into the military bus to smile gently at all of the children and tell them that he had meals prepared and was going to take everybody's temperatures and make sure nobody was sick—that was like watching a movie star walk into his life and invite him to the party.

And to realize that this perfectly average slender blond man with gray eyes and an engaging smile belonged to Jai, the almost terrifying ex-mobster who stayed very intentionally on the periphery of Jason's vision whenever they met? If Jason hadn't just flushed his entire career down the toilet, he would have been almost giddy.

As it was, he'd been up since 4:00 a.m., following an op going down in Europe, and it was nearly eight in the evening by the time George and his boss, Amal, managed to sneak Jason and the children onto a medical transport, practically under Stephen Collings's nose.

He was too tired for giddy. He'd settle for relieved.

Jason pulled out into the thick of Los Angeles weekend traffic, knowing the only way to get the kids away from the military and the mob was to take the 14 through the mountains and then turn back toward I-5 north of Palmdale.

Which would be like a flea taking a tour on a hairless cat. Sure, it could get from nose to tail faster, but it could also get caught and squashed. There wasn't much up in that area—lots of bare stretches of road with housing developments parked in acres of succulents so the wind didn't scour the dirt from the mountaintops.

And not a lot of places to stop.

But the kids had been fed—twice, because he'd stopped for fast food while he'd been clawing his way through traffic to get to the hospital—and they had water, fuel, and AC. If he could tough it out over the mountains, he could find a place to park in Palmdale or Lancaster, before driving the relatively short six hours to Sacramento, where hopefully he could find the authorities to get the kids home.

It was a plan. He liked this plan. There was sleep in this plan; there was another chance to feed the kids. Hell, because it was a medical transport, there was even a bathroom in this plan. This plan was a go!

And it had been a go as he'd made his way through the mountains and found a small town before Palmdale with a gas station.

It wasn't that he needed the fuel—as far as he could see, he had plenty to get him to Sacramento—but having the level place to park the bus was a plus. Once they'd descended from the mountains, and the temperature had leveled out a little from ice fucking cold to warm night breeze, the level place was pretty much his only requirement. There were thin polyester blankets in the compartments above the seats. He, Sophie, and Maxim broke those out and distributed them to the other young people, aged around ten to fourteen as far as he could see, and he had Sophie and Max tell the other kids they were stopping to sleep before he finished the drive. It should be easy, right?

A few hours, that's all. Four hours of sleep, right? He was a soldier; he'd run on less, certainly. But he'd been running on two hours at a time for the last four nights, and it wasn't like he wasn't used to being perpetually tired, but this was stretching it.

He was trying to pilot a land yacht through a traffic tsunami, and the kids in the back were depending on him.

A few hours of sleep.

So he parked the bus and had the kids crack the windows to let in some of the night air, and then he wadded up one of the blankets under his head and leaned against the window and closed his eyes.

He dreamed about the desert.

Not this one here, the one at home, but the one far away, where his job had been to kill people in a war he didn't understand. Half the reason he'd risen up the ranks, really, was so he could understand why he was ordering young soldiers to their death and making them kill people they didn't know.

But back then he'd been barely out of OTS and trying to get the attention of his CO. He remembered all of them in the coms tent, the beginnings of an epic windstorm gathering around the barracks.

"But look," he'd said, pointing to the blips on the screen. "General, these aren't our guys. I know you think they're our guys, but they're not moving in our patterns. We need to get eyes on them because if they get any closer—"

About then the first missile was launched at their fortification, from what they later discovered was the back of a captured Humvee.

He'd seen the trouble, all right—but only when it was right on them.

He woke up in the front of the bus with a strained breath. Fighting his way to consciousness, he knew the one thing he had to do was listen.

He heard the grumble of a big vehicle—a badly tended SUV, he thought—as it exited Highway 14 and rode the hairpin offramp toward their current location.

Where the big medical bus was sitting like a fat bird.

Quietly, so as not to disturb the children, he hit the starter and watched as the warm-up light glowed on the dashboard. These things usually took about two minutes to warm up. Two minutes. That was enough time for the SUV to see them on the way by and to turn around and come back and check on them. Was it enough time to fire? Was it enough time for the men inside to see who was sleeping there and come back to kill them?

"Sophie," he hissed.

The girl—wide gray eyes, a pink stripe in her hair, and a razor-quick mind—had apparently been sleeping as lightly as he had.

"Mr. Jason?"

"Tell everyone to get on the floor. We need to pull out as soon as the engine's ready."

"Yessir," she said. No questions, no whining. God, it was too bad she was twelve years old; he'd like to recruit her.

The SUV passed them, and for a moment he wondered if he wasn't getting on the road too soon. It was an SUV for God's sake. Somebody lived out here, right?

But he got behind the wheel and started up the bus as soon as the light went out.

And as he was pulling away from the gas station, the first bullet zinged by, and the second too. The third didn't zing. Fired from a silencer, he figured, the third bullet ripped through the side of the bus and then tore through the seat where Sophie and Maxim had been sleeping, before it lodged itself solidly in Jason's shoulder.

"Mr. Jason," Sophie said breathlessly from the floor. "What was that?"

And as pain tore through him, every synapse declaring a magnesium fire in his shoulder, and now in his side, all at the same moment, he realized they were fucked.

"Hang on, Sophie!" he called, stomping on the accelerator and going straight. Not toward the freeway, which would take him right by the people shooting at them, but straight, which would take him into some of the least populated places of California and possibly Nevada.

But hopefully, it would not take them to where there would be bullets.

Scan the QR Code
Below to Order!

Writer, knitter, mother, wife, award-winning author AMY LANE shows her love in knitwear, is frequently seen in the company of tiny homicidal dogs, and can't believe all the kids haven't left the house yet. She lives in a crumbling crapmansion in the least romantic area ofCalifornia, has a long-winded explanation for everything, and writes to silence the voices in her head. There are alot of voices—she's written over 120 books.

Website:www.greenshill.com

Blog:www.writerslane.blogspot.com

Email:amylane@greenshill.com

Facebook:www.facebook.com/amy.lane.167

Twitter:@amymaclane

Patreon:https://www.patreon.com/AmyHEALane

Follow me on BookBub

Guess who's swimming in the same pond...

FISH
OUT OF
WATER
Amy Lane

Fish Out of Water: Book One

PI Jackson Rivers grew up on the mean streets of Del Paso Heights—and he doesn't trust cops, even though he was one. When the man he thinks of as his brother is accused of killing a police officer in an obviously doctored crime, Jackson will move heaven and earth to keep Kaden and his family safe.

Defense attorney Ellery Cramer grew up with the proverbial silver spoon in his mouth, but that hasn't stopped him from crushing on street-smart, swaggering Jackson Rivers for the past six years. But when Jackson asks for his help defending Kaden Cameron, Ellery is out of his depth—and not just with guarded, prickly Jackson. Kaden wasn't just framed, he was framed by crooked cops, and the conspiracy goes higher than Ellery dares reach—and deep into Jackson's troubled past.

Both men are soon enmeshed in the mystery of who killed the cop in the minimart, and engaged in a race against time to clear Kaden's name. But when the mystery is solved and the bullets stop flying, they'll have to deal with their personal complications… and an attraction that's spiraled out of control.

SCAN THE QR CODE BELOW TO ORDER!

The Mastermind

AMY LANE

A Long Con Adventure: Book One

Once upon a time in Rome, Felix Salinger got caught picking his first pocket and Danny Mitchell saved his bacon. The two of them were inseparable… until they weren't.

Twenty years after that first meeting, Danny returns to Chicago, the city he shared with Felix and their perfect, secret family, to save him again. Felix's news network—the business that broke them apart—is under fire from an unscrupulous employee pointing the finger at Felix. An official investigation could topple their house of cards. The only way to prove Felix is innocent is to pull off their biggest con yet.

But though Felix still has the gift of grift, his reunion with Danny is bittersweet. Their ten-year separation left holes in their hearts that no amount of stolen property can fill. A green crew of young thieves looks to them for guidance as they negotiate old jewels and new threats to pull off the perfect heist—but the hardest job is proving that love is the only thing of value they've ever had.

SCAN THE QR CODE
BELOW TO ORDER!

SHADES of HENRY

AMY LANE

A Flophouse Story: Book One

One bootstrap act of integrity cost Henry Worrall everything—military career, family, and the secret boyfriend who kept Henry trapped for eleven years. Desperate, Henry shows up on his brother's doorstep and is offered a place to live and a job as a handyman in a flophouse for young porn stars.

Lance Luna's past gave him reasons for being in porn, but as he continues his residency at a local hospital, they now feel more like excuses. He's got the money to move out of the flophouse and live his own life—but who needs privacy when you're taking care of a bunch of young men who think working penises make them adults?

Lance worries Henry won't fit in, but Henry's got a soft spot for lost young men and a way of helping them. Just as Lance and Henry find a rhythm as den mothers, a murder and the ghosts of Henry's abusive past intrude. Lance knows Henry's not capable of murder, but is he capable of caring for Lance's heart?

SCAN THE QR CODE BELOW TO ORDER!

AMY LANE

Sometimes the
best magic is just
a little luck…

THE
RISING TIDE

THE LUCK MECHANICS BOOK ONE

The tidal archipelago of Spinner's Drift is a refuge for misfits.
Can the island's magic help a pie-in-the-sky dreamer and a wounded
soul find a home in each other?

In a flash of light and a clap of thunder, Scout Quintero is banished from his home. Once he's sneaked his sister out too, he's happy, but their power-hungry father is after them, and they need a place to lie low. The thriving resort business on Spinner's Drift provides the perfect way to blend in.

They aren't the only ones who think so.

Six months ago Lucky left his life behind and went on the run from mobsters. Spinner's Drift brings solace to his battered soul, but one look at Scout and he's suddenly terrified of having one more thing to lose.

Lucky tries to keep his distance, but Scout is charming, and the island isn't that big. When they finally connect, all kinds of things come to light, including supernatural mysteries that have been buried for years. But while Scout and Lucky grow closer working on the secret, pissed-off mobsters, supernatural entities, and Scout's father are getting closer to them. Can they hold tight to each other and weather the rising tide together?

SCAN THE QR CODE
BELOW TO ORDER!

AMY
LANE

WEIRDOS

Not all
dogs are
Lassie.

If Taz Oswald has one more gross date, he's resigning himself to a life of celibacy with his irritable Chihuahua, Carl. Carl knows how to bite a banana when he sees one! Then Selby Hirsch invites Taz to walk dogs together, and Taz is suddenly back in the game. Selby is adorkable, awkward, and a little weird—and his dog Ginger is a trip—and Taz is transfixed. Is it really possible this sweet guy with the blurty mouth and a heart as big as the Pacific Ocean wandered into Taz's life by accident? If so, how can Taz convince Selby that he wants to be Selby and Ginger's forever home?

SCAN THE QR CODE BELOW TO ORDER!